P
This Great Wilderness

Seyler's latest novel is a haunting exploration of the long tail of war, depicting griefs that seem to stretch as endlessly as the plains of Patagonia that Raymond, Leni, and Anton traverse. At times brutal, yet always suffused with hope, *This Great Wilderness* is a study of healing and second chances—and a celebration of love that is both patient and kind. A winner for historical fiction readers, hopeless romantics, and those who know both the cost and triumph of survival.

Allison Epstein, author of *A Tip for the Hangman*

Not just another WWII-and-its-aftermath book, *This Great Wilderness* is an exploration of love, grief, and especially resilience, in addition to portraying autistic characters with a sensitivity and depth not often found in fiction. Highly recommended.

Karen Heenan, author of *Lady, in Waiting*

this great wilderness

EVA SEYLER

This is a work of fiction. Any resemblance to actual events or persons, living or dead, is entirely coincidental.

©2021 by Eva Seyler, Holley, Oregon

All rights reserved. No part of this publication may be reproduced in any form without prior written permission from the author, except for use in brief quotations as permitted by United States copyright law.

Edited by Karen Heenan

Cover design and interior layout ©2022 Eva Seyler

All rights reserved

Library of Congress Control Number: 2021922520

Typeset in Buenard and Josefin Sans

E-Book ISBN: 978-1-7360297-5-6
Paperback ISBN: 978-1-7360297-4-9
Audiobook ISBN: 978-1-7360297-6-3

For tamale lovers everywhere

RMS Mauretania

20-21 October 1951

RAYMOND

I WANT TO KEEP some record of this trip as a memento for Anton, but I am not fond of recreational writing the way his mother was. How and where does one begin to tell a story, especially when one is living it in the moment, and does not know ahead of time how it will end?

His mother would tell me to start at the beginning, to write on something I am passionate about, or what prompted our trip—and then she would quickly add, "But *don't* make it sound like one of those articles you're forever sending to that frightful *Journal of the Society of Lepidopterists of Southern England*."

This is all very out of my comfort zone, but I will try.

I am taking this trip because of a butterfly.

When I was five years old I was lying in the park, watching ants in the grass, and a butterfly (*Thymelicus lineola*, Essex Skipper) landed on my thumb. It was so tiny, so perfect and fragile and graceful, and I was instantly, irrevocably in love. My father was still alive then, and he encouraged my interest in butterflies.

When he died in Ypres in 1915, I lost my biggest ally. My sisters and mother humoured me to some extent, but there was a constant refrain of "You are *Just Like Your Father*, Raymond!" accented with sighs of exasperation from my sisters and concern from my mother, who had loved my father, but freely admitted she believed he was a bit touched.

Where could I go, I often wondered, to be accepted for the slightly odd scientist I was born to be—someplace so remote and full of beauty that I could disappear into the wilderness and be surrounded by non-human creatures, accountable to nobody but myself?

That's where Argentina came in. I was already interested in learning Spanish because of my family's ancestry, and Argentina sounded like a veritable fantasyland to my young mind. As soon as I heard about the untouched beauty and remoteness of it, I knew my destiny lay there. Live in Argentina *and* study butterflies? Why not?

Practical considerations stood in my way. Getting a degree in biology and becoming fluent in Spanish was all well and good, but I needed money for the venture. So I joined the police—perhaps the first thing I ever did that truly pleased my mother and sisters. It was safely *ordinary*. They were proud to tell their friends about the family policeman; they had never known quite how to introduce me before.

I didn't intend to stay with the police for more than a few years, but the passing of time brought me a string of feathered and furry dependents I couldn't bear to leave, not the least of which was my beloved cat Mariposa. Then there came the war, and with it my wife and my son.

With one thing and another, it has taken me almost forty years to actually fulfil my dream. Is that boy, so full of wonder and delight at an Essex Skipper, still alive somewhere deep down inside the police inspector I have become?

Finding myself. That sounds so noble, and a bit pompous, even. Maybe I'm not looking to find myself. Maybe I'm just looking for a reason to stay alive.

My son should be a compelling reason to stay alive.

Anton was born a month too early. He was so tiny, so perfect and fragile, weighing barely over four pounds. His mother, frightened of losing him, refused to name him until we were certain he would pull through. Then she died, leaving her not yet two-month-old son unnamed.

The Germans killed Antonia, during their bombing of southern England in late May of 1943. She left the baby with me that day and went to Bournemouth to spend a few hours with her former flatmate Jean. Of all days she might have chosen, *that* was the day the Luftwaffe struck Bournemouth.

Antonia didn't make it into the shelter; she was too busy shooing everyone else in. They found her buried under rubble afterwards. Jean called to tell me as soon as she could get to a phone, and could barely get the news out for her sobs.

Antonia was flighty and maddening and utterly irresistible. Her pursuit of me might have turned off an ordinary man, but I would never have had her otherwise. She saw my attraction to her, and felt no shame in letting me know it was mutual. She drew me out of my shell and made me socialise with people, instead of spending all my spare hours talking to foxes, honeybees, dead butterflies, and my cat. In addition to my son and my grey hair, she gave me the liveliest two years of my life.

When she died, all that ended. I sealed myself off from the social life we'd had together; I stopped caring, redirecting all that love and attention to my son, the only human life left to me that mattered. He has been my anchor since his mother died.

I love him tremendously.

It is for him I have kept going since.

Anton

PAPÁ GAVE ME THIS book last night. I am to write in it every day until we go home, as part of my lessons. Papá has brought along all my schoolbooks and is going to teach me himself so I don't get too behind. I already miss my friends, but this is exciting too. There are other children on board. I saw them when we were waving goodbye to Southampton yesterday. I will have plenty of friends on our voyage.

Things I Will Miss From Home:
1. Pío and Pía, the hens. Mrs Keaton will take good care of them, but they are sweet and I know they will miss us.
2. Papá's fox Dulzura. I don't know that Mrs K will take good care of her, but luckily Dulzura is a wild animal at heart and she does not need Mrs K. She may not even come around for her treats and cuddles at all, if Papá is not there. She is smart.
3. My best friend Bobby Sullivan. He lives three houses down. He has three brothers and two sisters. I like going to their house and pretending they are my brothers and sisters too, and his mum is nice to me and usually sends me home with pots of jam or fresh-baked bread, and mends my clothes, and fusses over me. I wish I had even one brother or sister. I'm lonely sometimes.
4. Both my grans, Carlisle Gran and London Gran. London Gran is Papá's mum, and I see her more often since she is closer, but Carlisle Gran is younger and more adventuresome. Papá says she is rather like my mother. London Gran was a dressmaker, and even though she no longer has a shop, she still makes Papá's suits, and

me a new suit every year. The one she made for this year is light grey. I brought it along (Papá made me), but I don't see how I'll possibly need it once we are off into the wilderness. Papá is terribly proper and he likes me to be terribly proper too. Besides, he was a boy scout and is constantly reminding me to BE PREPARED. We might find ourselves at a funeral or a wedding or invited to the Casa Rosada to dine with the Peróns. I think he is just joking about the Casa Rosada. Anyway, I don't mind dressing up like Papá wants, but I am pleased at his promise that I can run around in my underwear in the wilderness if I want to, because there will be NOBODY THERE TO BE BOTHERED.

Things I Will Not Miss From Home:

1. Mr Phipps, the mean man across the street who lays out poison for rats and drowns squirrels. He is scary. It was him who poisoned Papá's cat Mariposa two years ago. Not on purpose, but poor Mariposa didn't know the poison would hurt her, and if it hadn't been out, she'd not have died. Poor Papá, he loved Mariposa as much as he loves me. He and Mr Phipps do not like each other AT ALL now. Also Mr Phipps smokes like a chimney and I can't breathe when he's anywhere near me.
2. Homework.

Thing I Hope Will Happen On This Trip:

1. I want it to make Papá happy. He always seems so tired and sad, and the last two months or so he has been more angry than usual. Not at me. I know he misses my mum, and he's still angry at Mr Phipps for killing his cat, but suddenly out of nowhere we're going halfway across the world, as if he can't bear to stay at home a single minute longer. I want Papá to be happy again, like he is happy in the wedding photograph of him and my mum.

Things About Mum:

1. She was little. Papá says she couldn't look over his shoulder unless she stood on her toes on a stool. Of course Papá is rather a big man. He used to row at Oxford and he is taller than anyone else I know.
2. She was pale and blonde and Papá says I don't look at all like her except for my eyes. Mostly I look a good deal like Papá. My hair is dark and wavy like his was, before it turned grey.

Both of the Things About Mum have turned into Things About Papá, so I guess I will start a new list.

Things About Papá:

1. Papá is much older than most of my friends' fathers. He'll turn 45 next February. I like to tell him he's only a few years away from being HALF A CENTURY OLD. He's not impressed by this idea.
2. He wears glasses. He says they are to read with, only he forgets to take them off most of the time, so I suspect he needs them more than he lets on. I mean, he IS almost HALF A CENTURY OLD.
3. He talks to animals and they understand him. He is a big man like I already said but he is the most gentle person ever. He knows how to catch butterflies without hurting them, and he is very kind to me.

I suppose since I have talked of my parents I should also talk about me.

Things About Anton (Me):

1. Unlike Papá, I am not strong and I get sick rather easily.
2. I like radios. I've built two. I gave one to Bobby. Mine I take apart and put back together at least once a month. Papá knows a lot about wireless and telegraphy since he

did that during the war, and whatever I can't find in a book, he usually knows.

It is time for breakfast now. I like this ship. Papá says he will walk with me over ALL OF IT. Maybe I will even get to see the radio room! I have been learning Morse code. I want to get a radio operator license soon and I would love to watch them at work in there.
We will be in New York in a few days and there we change to another ship for the rest of the trip. I just made a rhyme!

Buenos Aires

21 October 1951

Leni

THIS IS THE THIRD day since Mauritz locked me into the bathroom. I'm not sure what is going on, but whatever it is, they don't want me knowing about it. It's not the first time they've locked me up, and I'm sure it won't be the last.

They don't trust me, I know, but solitary confinement is ridiculous. I will NEVER manage to escape, and who the hell would I tell anything to, anyway? I don't speak Spanish (they've seen to that), and I don't have a clue how this city is laid out.

Not that that would matter much either, because I can't tell east from west to save my life.

Anyway, here I am, and Mauritz has had the water disconnected, so I can neither get myself drinks of water nor drown myself in the bath. (I can't flush the toilet, either. It smells of bad ham in here.) I'm waiting for Mauritz's thuggish sidekick Erich to appear with my daily prison rations.

Because, no matter what I've tried to tell myself for the last eleven years, I *am* a prisoner. A very well-kept, stylish prisoner, but a prisoner nonetheless, and the fact is, it's so damned impossible to escape Mauritz, to breathe air that isn't full of his hovering exhalations. I'm not sure how much longer I can bear this—only I've been saying the same thing for eleven years already, and I suppose eleven years from now I'll still be saying it.

I'm tired, and my behind is numb from sitting on the hard floor. I tried lying in the bath as a change of position, but it gave me a headache. Jacob's stone was surely a more comfortable pillow than a cast-iron bath.

Mostly I no longer care that I will never not be the prisoner of SS-Sturmbannführer Mauritz von Schlusser. I will never again be anything besides "Mauritz's Leni" or, at best, "Frau von Schlusser". In another life, I was Madeleine Mayer, hapless unofficial member of the resistance, but she is dead, and her replacement, Leni, is here: thousands of miles away from home, in a country she never meant to go to. If she is not careful, Leni von Schlusser will soon find herself dead, too. Her existence has been a drain on Mauritz's credibility for ten years, and sooner or later Leni will find herself Conveniently Dispatched.

I shouldn't mind being dispatched; I mean, it would be *such* a mercy to rest at last, after all I've had to do for the last eleven years. But I should also hate to miss out on a chance to really *live*. I'm thirty-two, and soon I shall be too old to do anything to leave the world a better place than I found it—or even simply have a little fun. It seems so unfair.

It wasn't entirely true when I said earlier I don't know what is going on. I *do* have a reasonably good idea why I'm locked in here. My restlessness of late has made me careless about my behaviour, which is supposed to be unobtrusive, uncurious, and unconditionally submissive.

Erich caught me in the act of looking at the return addresses on the morning post. I wasn't looking for anything in particular. I'm allowed no newspapers or books, and I read any words I can get my eyes on. (I hardly consider the copy of *Mein Kampf* they are forever leaving on my nightstand worth using as toilet paper, let alone actually opening it to read it.) When Mauritz questioned me about the Infraction of the Return Addresses, I told him I was bored out of my mind.

"If you think you are bored," he said, "I will show you what boredom actually is."

So...here I am.

I guess it's better than being burned again.

There was a letter from Chile. I wonder whom Mauritz knows in Chile. Schwammberger is here in Buenos Aires, and Eichmann, and Mengele (I shudder just thinking of *him*, the *schweinekerl*.) They are often here at the house. Eichmann works at the same Mercedes-Benz plant as Mauritz, and he has a wife and some children who have recently joined him here, but she is never brought to visit me. She might be an awful bitch, but it would be a nice change of pace to see another woman. I'm dead tired of men. (I'm all right with not seeing children, though. The sight of children—innocent, lovely children—invariably turns me into a sobbing mess, and Mauritz keeps them far away.)

Mauritz's house is on the outskirts of town and surrounded by a densely wooded park, an ideal location for all these idiots to congregate. During the wintertime, men come and go under cover of darkness and nobody notices. Of course, the local officials are not stupid. It doesn't take a genius to know there are scores of Nazi fugitives in this city and this country. Perón himself sold blank passports by the hundreds to people like Mauritz. We just filled them in with new names and in we came. Too easy.

I am Magdalena Sanchez on my Argentine papers, not that I know where they are kept. I was only allowed the briefest of glances when I signed mine. We don't use our Spanish names in the house, and since I am never allowed out, I do not know what names people like Mengele or Eichmann might also be known by. It is too great a risk for them to trust me with that sort of information.

The fact that the officials turn a blind eye to our presence reduces my faith in them to ashes. Supposing I did escape Mauritz, what then? Even if I knew Spanish, how would I know whom to trust, which policemen were not being paid to wear blinders?

I don't trust policemen. Not since the one from Laa An Der Thaya, the town near the Czech border where I lived when I was captured. He recognised me at Theresienstadt, but he didn't dare acknowledge he knew me.

He might have rescued me, if he'd cared less about his own skin, but by then he'd swapped his ordinary police uniform for that of an SS officer.

And so,
eleven years later,
I am still here.

RMS Mauretania

23 October 1951

Raymond

THIS IS A FINE ship. Even though we are travelling third class—or shall I call it the newfangled term "tourist class"?—everything is most agreeable, and the crew is very solicitous for our comfort and enjoyment. I took Anton to the radio room as promised, and he stayed there (quite contentedly and unobtrusively, I am told) for two hours whilst I went for a swim in the pool. He chattered about what he saw there all through dinner and on the way to bed.

Anton befriends everyone he meets. It is astonishing. He certainly didn't inherit the gift of social ease from me. He has already learnt all the names of the stewards on our deck, made friends with half a dozen boys and girls near his own age, as well as charmed some young American ladies of eighteen or nineteen, whom he tells me have been touring London and Paris for the last month. Somehow I will not be surprised if he ends up on the bridge before we get to New York, fraternising with the captain himself. He does so long to explore this world full of experiences and people he doesn't know yet, and I think I've been holding him back, just by being what I am.

Those young ladies startled me. I didn't talk much to them, but Antonia was only eighteen when I met her. However did I have the audacity to fall in love with a girl, *any* girl, even nine years ago?

The war brought me Antonia. She fluttered in, flamboyant as a Peacock (*Inachis io*), with her love of bright colours and her compulsive flitting from one thing to another, and turned my world upside down, shaking every bit of bachelor stuffiness out of my life.

Antonia came from Carlisle to Bournemouth in late 1940,

right after her eighteenth birthday. Instead of joining the ATS or the WAAF, she found work as a personal driver for a man I will refer to as Colonel X. I do not care to give him the dignity of any other name. Antonia roomed with a girl named Jean, an air raid warden, in a little house on the edge of town. Antonia's job was straightforward: shuttle her colonel around in his fine car and not ask questions.

My own war work was very secret. Still officially a police sergeant; convenient cover for the three days a week I served somewhere else. I can't write about that, except to say that my services were a very odd and usually unglamorous assortment. I didn't have a social life to speak of, so no one had any clue what I was up to. Any time I did get a day or two off, I went up to London to visit my mother and my sisters' families.

One spring evening in 1941, Colonel X arrived at my secret place of service to see the Officer in Charge, and would I please make tea for him and his driver, who was waiting in the sitting room until Colonel X finished his business?

So I fixed the tea (I make a mean pot of tea if I do say so myself) and took it to the Officer in Charge and the colonel first, and then the driver. To my surprise, the driver was a woman, and not in uniform. She wore a trim little dark grey suit, but her perfect flaxen hair and scarlet nail varnish and the matching silk scarf around her neck gave her otherwise officious appearance a rakish touch. She took the tea with a smile of gratitude, and I returned to the kitchen to finish my work so I could go home.

But all I could think of was that lovely girl sitting out there, all alone. I wanted so very, very much to go talk to her, but just taking her tea made me tongue-tied. I'd never manage to initiate a conversation, let alone ask her to go out for a drink or something.

As it happened, she came back with her colonel the next afternoon, and again I took them all tea, and again she beamed at me, and again I was stupidly speechless and left without having made any progress in befriending her.

In the kitchen I mentally rehearsed to myself every objection in the book. She couldn't possibly be interested in some bachelor biologist-policeman who loved his cat more than he'd ever loved any woman.

And then she appeared in the kitchen door, empty teacup in hand. I actually jumped at the sight of her, and (as usual) said nothing.

She laughed at my startlement, not unkindly, set down her cup, folded her arms, and said, "Sergeant Varela, you are the most interesting man in the world."

That was not what I had expected to hear, nor did I expect the pronounced northern English accent out of such a posh-looking girl.

"Do you ever talk?" she asked.

"Yes..." I did chatter Mariposa's ear off on a nightly basis, after all, but I didn't believe it would reflect well on me to reveal this to a goddess-like young lady who would laugh and go tell all her friends about the idiotic man she'd met. So I said, "How do you know my name?"

"I got it out of the cleaning girl, since clearly I'd never get it out of you." Her eyes twinkled and she cocked her head. "I've never met a man who so obviously wanted to talk to me and didn't. I'll bet you want to kiss me."

I *did* want to kiss her. It was as if she read my mind.

She stepped closer. She didn't unfold her arms, but she said, "Maybe you're afraid to, because you think I'm already taken. Well, I'm not, and you are very fetching indeed, and I would like it if you *would* kiss me."

Antonia never, ever wasted time getting to the point. Had the cleaning girl also given her the particulars of my availability? I continued to stare, gaping stupidly no doubt, and she went on, "Don't tell me you've never—!"

I shook my head and finally managed to form a sentence. "I'm thirty-four and I've never had a girl. Draw your own conclusions."

Her eyes lit up, as if I'd presented her a challenge, and she said, "My conclusion is that the sooner you kiss me, the better."

And she walked into my arms, kissed me, got me to kiss her back (twice!) and after that my life was never the same. I felt like the Sleeping Beauty being woken by her true love, only the other way around.

After the (extremely ice-breaking) kisses, she stepped back and glanced towards the door, whispering with a confiding grin, "I feel so daring, like my mum will poke her head in any minute and scold me—but that's silly, she's a million miles away in Carlisle, and anyway she never paid attention to that sort of thing. Tell me about your family."

So I told her of my father, who died in Ypres alongside his beloved carrier pigeons; my mother the dressmaker; my sisters and their husbands and children. She told me of her parents and her brothers, and I realised I was having an ordinary conversation *with a girl*. I could forget myself and my awkwardness and just talk. The novelty of it all pleased me immensely.

"You are very lovely, Antonia. May I call you Antonia?"

"Please do! My brothers call me Tony."

"My name is Raymond."

"A fine name. Fine and strong and good, like you."

Then the colonel was ready to go back to wherever he'd come from, and Antonia had to leave.

But as I walked home, I could still smell her perfume and feel the warmth of her lips on mine. I wished I had asked her for her address, or a telephone number, but of course I had failed to even think of such a thing.

Remembering Antonia is making me melancholy. I miss her so desperately. Time has blurred so much about her already. I find it hard to remember exactly what her voice sounded like, for example. But the emotion she stirred in me, her infectious laughter and mischief that warmed me inside, those I don't believe I can ever forget. Even though I will never find another woman like her, I'm content knowing I had a treasure irreplaceable. I have our son. She lives on in him.

Yes, Anton is enough.

I'm looking at him whilst he sleeps, and although he's not quite nine, he already seems to be crossing the bridge from childhood to manhood. He's begun to lose the curvy baby look in his face. His less-than-perfect health and motherlessness have perhaps matured him too quickly. I do hope this trip will make him stronger.

Anton

I GOT TO GO on the bridge today and the Captain himself shook my hand! And I spent more time in the radio room, but Papá said I needed to do something besides pester the crew, so we went for a swim together in the pool, and two of my new friends joined us. Claire and David Simonson are twins, even though they don't look at all alike. They just turned ten. Their mother is so pretty, with big brown eyes and blonde hair, all wavy. She looks like a film star. Their father died in the war, Claire told me. Right at the very end. She and David made their mother show me the picture of him she still carries with her in her pocketbook. His name was Arthur Simonson, and he was a rear gunner in the RAF.

I told Mrs Simonson about my mum, and I told Papá he should invite her to have dinner with us tonight, but I doubt he will. He is such a stick in the mud whenever I try to find myself a new mother. He'll tell me again about how swans mate for life, and his mate is dead, and he will mourn her FOREVER. I looked it up once and showed him from one of his own books that swans will, in fact, find new mates if their first one dies, but he insisted he's not That Type of Swan.

He's rather shy, I suppose. Not like me. He *likes* to sit by himself, reading for hours, or running circles round the deck, or whatever. I don't know how he stands it. I have to have lots of people around me to talk to and do things with. I guess I will enjoy Claire and David for the few days I'll have them around.

Women I've Tried to Get Papá to Marry:

1. Miss Hannity, the postmistress. She's the same age as Papá and she is a lovely lady. I am sure she likes him, because every time I come in to post letters to my grans or buy stamps for Papá, she asks after him and gives me

a present for him. Homemade biscuits, jam, once even a fruitcake. She says he and I must be so lonely. Papá laughs every time I give him the things and shakes his head.
2. Mrs Veronica Watkins, whose husband died in the war. She is always helping out at school, making costumes for our plays and things. Papá said he'd absolutely never marry someone whose name would change to Veronica Varela. What a silly excuse. *I* think Veronica Varela is a marvellous name.
3. Mrs May, Bobby's cousin's neighbour. Her husband died in the war too. I like her because she is always happy and busy. She has a big garden and grows the most delicious vegetables. When Bobby and I go play with his cousin, she always gives me a sack of carrot tops or other juicy scraps to feed Pío and Pía with. She never says a word about Papá like Miss Hannity does, and Papá has nothing to say about Mrs May, either. Except "Drop it, Anton."

And now he won't even say hello to Mrs Simonson, and I like her more than Miss Hannity OR Mrs Watkins OR Mrs May, because Mrs Simonson comes with CHILDREN.
  I GIVE UP.

Buenos Aires

23 October 1951

Leni

I AM *STILL* IN this blasted bathroom. I spent twenty minutes cursing Erich loudly through the door for overflowing the toilet (on purpose, probably) with the water he brought in to flush it with and leaving me with the mess, until Mauritz's voice said: "SHUT UP OR I WILL TURN THE LIGHTS OUT TOO."
   Damn Mauritz. He knows I am scared of the dark.
   So I shut up.
   Surely he will let me out soon.

   Supposing he did let me out, what would I be doing then?
   Dutifully fulfilling a Long List of Tasks, that's what I'd be doing. I'm not a servant in the technical sense, but I *am* assigned rather a lot of menial jobs which would make actual maids, if there were any, turn up their noses. (There aren't. I am the only woman in the house, ever.)
   Mauritz says women are too curious and talk too much, and therefore he won't risk employing one. (I interpret this as "my ability to keep you Buenos Aires' best-kept secret will be undermined if any women find out you exist and why you are here".)
   The cook is a man. The butler is a man. Mauritz has a personal servant/driver/valet as well. They all look on me with disdain, although when Mauritz is out they are not above having a little fun with me. Not too much fun. Just enough to make me uncomfortable and scared without getting themselves fired.
   And then there is Erich, a level of hell all his own. He is a human sponge, soaking up Mauritz's good life for reasons I'd prefer not to speculate much about.
   So I do many of the tasks a housemaid might do: whatever I can manage without breaking something, as I am notoriously

clumsy. (I *swear* I did not break Mauritz's great-grandmother's Dresden porcelain vase on purpose, but I don't think anyone will ever believe me. It was so silky under my fingers.) I air the bedrooms daily, except for Mauritz's room, which is always locked, and into which I have never set foot. I dust and polish the wooden furniture, except for the mahogany mantelpiece where the still-intact mate of the broken vase resides, and hoover the rugs. Aside from these ordinary things, each morning with my breakfast tray I am brought a list of Other Duties As Required: ranging from counting and polishing the silver, to mending the men's socks and clothes, to shining everyone's shoes. Each evening Mauritz ascertains that these tasks have been completed to his satisfaction.

I am also expected to welcome him at the door each evening when he returns from work, looking perfect. Most days my morning task list includes minute instructions on what he wants to see me wearing that evening.

Mauritz is two men in one, and I never know which one I will greet in the evenings. Will it be the laid-back Mauritz, who expects no more from our evening than a quiet dinner and several hours pretending we are an ordinary couple in the parlour—me with my knitting, him with his newspaper—parting at bedtime with a dutiful kiss on the cheek? Or will it be the jealous Mauritz, who puts me through unspeakable mental torment and rapes me yet again? He switches from one to the other with quicksilver unpredictability. It is unnerving.

I have never, not once, given him permission to sleep with me. I asked for it, he says. I love him and give myself to him, he says. It is good for me, he says. Somewhere deep down I know he is lying, or at least trying to convince himself that what he's doing is all right. Giving in because you're exhausted is not the same as saying yes.

It hurts too much to try to make sense of it all, so I shut off my brain, lie there and take it, do as I am told, anything to keep him from burning me again. (Useless.) I consume the calming pills Mauritz mercifully provides me (even if I do have to get them from the cook, who reports to Mauritz the number I am given in a day and makes me sign a paper each time, like the obsessively organised German that he is). You might suppose facing the cook and having to kiss him or provide other favours in order to get what I need would make me stop wanting the pills, but no. My need for them is stronger than any remaining scraps of self-respect.

I've not had as many as usual whilst stuck here in the bathroom, which is not helping me cope well with my imprisonment, but I have been given enough to get me through. I am quite sure Mauritz obtains them illegally, but I don't care how he gets them, as long as they end up down my throat. It is all that keeps me functioning. It really is.

Mauritz had a wife before me, a woman named Marlene, who looked rather uncannily like me. There is a portrait of her over the mantel in the parlour, which all our guests assume is a portrait of me. He idolised her. He keeps me indoors to maintain my ghostly Marlene-esque complexion, dresses me as she would have dressed, has my hair coloured and styled like hers.

I wonder if she too was punished with cigarette burns. In the portrait her face is a blank, a study in impersonality.

Her sleeves go all the way to her wrists.

New York City

24 October 1951

Anton

TODAY WE LANDED IN New York! I have never SEEN so many people. Papá was very anxious not to lose me. I buttoned my stuffed cat close to me inside my coat, with his head out so he could see too. The wind blew cold as we got off the ship. I waved goodbye to the Simonsons, who are going west on a train to visit Mrs Simonson's father and brother, and we went to make sure Papá's crates got unloaded and sent off to the right place.

We have a day before we board the ship that will take us the rest of the way to Buenos Aires: the SS *Argentina*. How funny, to ride on *Argentina* to Argentina!

Meanwhile Papá and I went to the Statue of Liberty. We walked all the way up. My legs were tired by the time we got to the top, and I had to take lots of rests so I wouldn't start wheezing, and the very last bit was narrow and swirly and made me dizzy. But the view was magnificent and worth all 354 steps. (I counted them.) We could see all the tiny people moving about on the ground below us, and around us so much water, and for a long time we watched the ferries and other boats down there, and beyond all the water there is city, as far as the eye can see. *So much city out there!* I've never seen anything like it. London is big, but it doesn't feel like this. It doesn't look much like it, either. Anyway, after we did that, we found a place to eat dinner, and then we took a cab to our hotel for the night. I want to write more but I am getting sleepy and I can't stop yawning so I am going to bed now.

Buenos Aires

24 October - 4 November 1951

Leni

I AM OUT OF the bathroom.

Mauritz made me clean the mess Erich made, and then he stood in the door with his arms folded and watched me have a bath and comb my hair, lecturing me all the time.

When I was cleansed and combed to his satisfaction, he took me in his arms and whispered against my neck. "It hurts me so much when I am forced to lock you up. You are dangerous to yourself. You might hurt someone through too much curiosity. You wouldn't want to hurt anyone, would you?" His voice is soft and hypnotic, and I closed my eyes. "Remember what you did to that young Jew..."

I didn't argue; I didn't want to remember. He made me lie on the bed and yield to his advances. I did not cry or protest or anything. I hoped I could avoid being burned again, which is always an exercise in futility. The list of infractions punishable by burning is legion, all of them ultimately classifiable as Not Meeting the Impossible Standard of His Dead Wife.

"You do not open yourself completely to me," he said when he had finished. He lit a cigarette and took a drag. How many would he take before he pressed the lit end to my skin? I braced myself and waited, silent, stoic. "You are holding back. If you learn to enjoy yourself, I can stop marking you. Don't you want me to stop marking you?"

Of *course* I want him to stop. He's trained me to not cry or argue, but I cannot manufacture enjoyment for his disgusting acts of intimacy, no matter how often he burns me. He could pop my entire body in a fire and it wouldn't condition me to enjoy sex. I flinched when I felt the cigarette on my skin. Over the last ten years, he has mastered the science of precisely how long to hold it there to be sure it will never fully heal. Mostly the burns are on my arms. It forces me to dress conservatively so nobody else will see the marks, which make me easily identifiable were I to escape, but that is neither here nor there.

Worse than the burns on my arms or the lash-marks on my backside, is the emptiness inside me, an emptiness left behind when the child growing there was stolen from me. That is the scar which haunts me most.

Mauritz says we are leaving Buenos Aires. He has Business, he says. He won't tell me where or what the business is, not that I expected he would. (What *is* it with men and "business"? Can't they just say what they're actually doing?) In the past I wouldn't have dreamt of asking, but as I said before, I am becoming rather careless. My life is cheap. We all know it.

I am so tired. Part of me hopes he will grow weary of bullying me and bump me off. But Nazis like having people to bully and a weakling female who no longer understands the truth about anything is a perfect target for bullying. I will have to become even more aggressive if I want to worry them into getting rid of me.

I wish I could go out sometimes. Anywhere. The flea market on a Sunday, even. Anything to get out of this damn house.

Mauritz has brought more yarn for knitting. He already has *so much*. I could knit socks in my sleep, and he has so many scarves and sweaters—but he refuses to wear storebought knitted goods, claiming that mine are far superior to anything he could buy. (Perhaps one of the few things he says that's actually true.) I guess it does give me something to do, something attractively domestic for me to work at when our friends visit.

I say "our", but they are not *my* friends. They are all men, and I am only allowed to speak German with them, if I speak at all. It has been so long since I have spoken English aloud, I often wonder whether I could still do it, if I needed to.

Today it is a pair of socks I am working on, and they are of wool as black as the void where Mauritz's soul should be.

I am working on them
very
very
slowly.

I have no paper, and would not dare to pen my private thoughts if I did, so I compose imaginary journal entries in my head to keep me sane whilst I knit, or polish silver, or whatever.

I would be happy to never see these blasted needles ever again.

Mauritz is drinking fine wine and sharing biscuits with Ikarus, the spoilt pet cockatoo of the household. He is noisy and obnoxious and curses almost as fluently as I do, and he is Mauritz's pride and joy. Ikarus can do tricks and be entertaining, and when Mauritz tires of him he can go back into his cage.

I can also perform and entertain and be shut away when I become tiresome, so I am almost as good as Ikarus.

Except *I* do not get biscuits and wine.

When I am on display, posing as Mauritz's wife (we are *not* legally married, no matter what he says), he would have his friends believe I am the most stylish woman in South America, carefully schooled to have fine tastes in food and drink and decor. Even when I am not on display, I have clothes, a roof over my head, food to eat. It cannot be said that Mauritz does not meet at least the basic needs of the things he owns, whether bird or mistress.

All the same, I am an exceptionally unsatisfied woman. Mauritz says I am imagining it, that I am actually very happy, much happier than I ever was before I lived with him. He constantly talks over me, telling me what I am feeling when I venture to suggest my dissatisfaction, and what he tells me seems so upside-down from what I think it should be. But if we argue, I am always wrong and he is always right, so I have mostly stopped saying aloud what I feel. I think he is manipulating me, but truth and revision are so tangled now I don't know how or if I shall ever free myself. I'm tired of trying to keep it all straight.

In the darkness of night, when I have been locked into my room (Mauritz says I sleepwalk, and he is afraid I will fall down the stairs) and no one can hear me, I whisper a long string of facts in forbidden English, trying desperately to cling to whatever remains of who I once was.

I am Madeleine Mayer, born 9 January 1919, in Swallownest near Rotherham, England. My father is Dr Tobias Mayer, from Staatz, Austria. My mother was born Klara Fuchs in Laa An Der Thaya, Austria. They emigrated to England in 1903. I am the fourth of five children. There was Maria (1909), Louisa (1911), Hanna (1912), Madeleine (me, 1919), and Frederick (1923). I was the odd one out with that gap in years on either side. I was Daddy's special girl, born purple with my cord wrapped twice around my neck and over my chest like a bandolier...

I was different from my sisters and brother. Fussier. Daddy loved us all equally, but I think I loved him back more than the others did. He never scolded me for being the least intelligent of his children, for being oblivious to things that were plain as day to everyone else. I was as graceful and pretty as an articulated scarecrow. Clothes hung on me, my nose was too big, I tripped on my own shadow, didn't do very well in school, but Daddy loved me anyway. He said my mind was just different from other people's, and it didn't make me bad.

(It is true I have a few skills at which I excel. I pick up languages very fast, which is probably why Mauritz is so paranoid about me being exposed to Spanish. I can knit anything. I'm proficient at wireless. 2E-G2-MM, that was my call sign back at home. Mauritz does not know I was wizard at radio. It's the only real secret I've managed to keep from him. Languages, knitting, radio: all I am good at. I tap Morse code on my blankets at night until I fall asleep. It's comforting.)

Every summer we went to Austria, to Laa An Der Thaya and Staatz and sometimes even Vienna. I moved to L. A. D. T. in early

1939 to care for Tante Madeleine. Daddy didn't want me to go, but I argued I was mature enough and finally, with reservations, he allowed it.

I should have listened to him.

Oh, Daddy.

Anton

WE ARE IN ARGENTINA!

Papá's map of Argentina, on the wall back at home, is as familiar to me as the map of England at school. It's on a cork board with coloured pushpins and threads that he arranged and rearranged until he'd finally worked out the route we'd take for this particular trip, which he marked with red pins and thread. (There's another route he'd like to go on next time, marked in green, going north and west, and a third going along the eastern coast and down to the Falkland Islands in blue. The green route, he says, would have the most butterflies, because it's closer to the jungle, but he's a bit crazy about the glaciers and the remoteness of Patagonia right now, and that's why we're going there this time. There are three or four butterflies he can look out for there, though, and some others along the way south.)

Anyway, coming to Argentina someday is what he's always liked most to talk about. As long back as I can remember, my bedtime stories have been of the places and people here that he so wants to be part of. Of course, not having ever been here, he's had to make a lot of it up, but he gets stuff from magazines and books, too, and letters from his Argentine friends. He has stacks of *National Geographic* dating back to 1922 all over our sitting room, and I enjoy looking at the pictures and keeping them in order for him. Sometimes inside one I'll find a map he missed, and he lets me hang it in my bedroom, or in my little Extra Room. My walls are full of maps, but the one he loves best is the one of Argentina in our sitting room.

Anyway, the real Argentina is nothing like the map or my bedtime stories. It is ALIVE. I liked it at once. And aside from the fact that everyone is speaking Spanish, it doesn't seem so different from London. I mean, it's a proper city, and the people dress like we do, and there are all the usual fancy hotels, and buildings towering upwards, and markets, and cars, and things. Some of the houses we passed are painted funny colours you wouldn't see in England. I guess that's the strangest part. It would be fun to live in a salmon pink house or a mint green house. (Papá disagrees.)

Papá held my hand and I hugged my stuffed cat as we got on the boat that took us to shore. It took time to get our things to the dock, and it began raining, and I was tired, and I stopped liking Argentina for the moment and only wanted to go someplace warm and dry.

Papá brought me to a nice house on the edge of town owned by some friends he has written to for years, and communicated with by radio, too. The lady, who told me to call her Tía Delfina, has me in front of a nice fireplace now. Little Cat, drenched in Papá's cologne, is right under my nose.

I don't know what it is about that lovely spicy smell, but it's hard for me to go to sleep without it. Ever since I was a baby, my cat has had regular doses of the stuff. Papá says it helped me not to cry after Mum died, and I've become so used to it that everywhere I go, Little Cat comes with me. Well, not to school, but I mean anywhere where I'm spending the night. Bobby thinks it's funny, but I don't care. Bobby's mum just shushes him and says, "Bless your heart, Anton."

Mum made Little Cat from one of her old dresses and stuffed him with wool from Carlisle Gran's sheep. Little Cat's grey velveteen is rather worn now, and Papá has had to mend him a good deal, putting his tail back on, or an ear, or sewing a button eye back into place, but I love him, and I will never stop sleeping with him as long as I live.

The rain is pelting against the windows. Papá went to make sure everything we brought from the ship makes it to the station to go on the train tomorrow, but Tía Delfina asked me to stay with her. I am glad I don't have to go out in the wet. I'd hate to start off the trip sick, and I *am* so very tired.

Tía Delfina has brought me some biscuits and tea, and

chocolate she says comes from Bariloche, where we are going tomorrow. The tea is not so good as Papá makes it, but the chocolate is delicious. I will ask him to get us some when we are there.

Things About Argentina:
1. "Argentum" is Latin for silver, but Argentina has no silver! Papá says they called it Argentina when some of the Spaniards who first came here got gifts of silver from the natives, and there was supposedly a king rich with silver, only it ended up he lived in Bolivia actually, not Argentina. The Spanish word for silver is *plata*, and that's why the river by Buenos Aires is the Río de la Plata.
2. Argentina grows a lot of food and ever since the war, Europe has bought a lot of it.

Things About Patagonia:
1. Some people say Patagonia is cursed because the white people were so horrid to the native people and now there are hardly any native people left. I'm sorry for that. I'd have loved to meet some and see what they're like and how they live.
2. Flamingoes live on the coast! We won't see those, but we might see other creatures: pumas, foxes, hares, deer, and a funny thing called a mara that looks like a rabbit and a kangaroo and deer all in one. Of course all Papá *really* cares about are the butterflies, but he's keen on any wild creatures he lays eyes on.
3. Argentines love their beef, but in Patagonia they eat more lamb and fish. Not that we will be eating any of the above. Papá will not eat dead animals and I've never had any either.
4. Patagonia has glaciers, forests of monkey puzzle trees, petrified forests, and cave paintings. I wish we could see ALL the things, but Papá says we won't have time in only six months to do that.

Leni

TONIGHT MAURITZ HOSTED A dinner party. I *hate* dinner parties. I have to look Absolutely Flawless, and because I'm not allowed a maid, I have to prepare all by myself. Mauritz does have a hairdresser friend who comes in to do my hair each week to his exacting specifications, so at least I'm not saddled with that. Anyway, I wore a slinky black dress Mauritz brought in for me— as slinky as a dress can be with full-length sleeves, I mean. It's skin-tight to compensate for any other deficiencies. He likes me in black in the evenings. Tonight he told me to wear the diamond set. I expect the men were blinded by the glare when I walked in with all that ice weighing me down.

I'd like to say I sailed in, but I'm honestly lucky if I can get through the evening without tripping on my own feet and falling on my face. I *walked* in. Very sedately.

The men who come to these dinner parties come not only for Mauritz's fine wines and delicious food. They talk Mercedes-Benz business during dinner, since it is where many of them work, or of how much they hate the Jews in Buenos Aires, or they make jokes at my expense, and I am expected to be invested, witty, and entertaining, even though I want to scream.

To his (dubious) credit, Mauritz hasn't sold me to any of his friends since we've lived here, but there's no reason for me to believe that might not change at any moment. He hired me out freely enough during the war, when there were profits to make from sexually frustrated SS guards who wanted to fuck someone who wasn't a Jew. I helped him amass quite a tidy sum, probably. Whenever I protested, he would shrug and say I needed to earn my keep, and then lock me in the room with the highest bidder for anywhere from fifteen minutes to two hours, depending on how much money they forked over. But that's me going off on irrelevant personal history. I was talking about the dinner party tonight.

It doesn't help that I know what most of these men did for Hitler. Eichmann, for example, was largely responsible for those mass roundings-up of Jews. Seeing him at Mauritz's table and hearing him tell again of all his Noble Exploits for the Reich, I wanted to scream at him for cheating the man I had once loved out of a future, with or without me. That one dear man and who knew how many others.

It is *so hard* for me not to eat like an absolute pig with all that delightful food before me. I'm always kept on the edge of hunger (the former, real Frau von Schlusser was rather waif-like) and tonight an amazing German sausage featured in the menu, and I could have eaten the entire rich, greasy platter of it all by myself. Mama used to make fine sausage, and the smell of the spices is the best scent my nose ever could run into.

After dinner, they retire to Mauritz's Room of Secrets (it is actually called the smoking room, but I like my name for it better) and discuss the Fourth Reich amid expensive blue smoke. I'm not supposed to know that, but it doesn't take a nuclear scientist to figure out their ambitions. Besides, there is a flue between the Room of Secrets and one of the unused bedrooms upstairs which carries conversations remarkably well. I don't eavesdrop often, not so much because I fear getting caught as because it is all just so *incredibly boring*.

Erich escorted me to my room after Mauritz dismissed me. This is, eight times out of ten, a regular feature of dinner party evenings. Erich likes to remind me how I am a Gigantic Liability for the Nazis here and that he does not trust me. Mauritz doesn't trust me, either (why else would he keep me so secluded?), but his obsession outweighs his common sense, and it's not like Erich's open hostility.

He didn't leave me when we got to my room. He usually doesn't. I know better than to make a fuss. I grew tired of fighting him years ago; it only makes him more of a brute. So I made no protest when he followed me in. I stood there like a statue, my back to him, tensed and waiting for his serpent strike.

Erich took several leisurely steps towards me, around me, and when he stood in front of me he grabbed a handful of my hair in his fist and pulled. Not enough to hurt, but enough to force my head back to look at him. Mauritz is scarcely taller than me, but Erich is six feet. Then he closed his mouth over mine, without anything in the kiss but ferocity and anger and too much tongue. "Why were you looking at Bohne so hard tonight?" he asked me when he finally pulled away. He didn't let go of my hair.

"No reason," I stammered. "Really, no reason at all."

He gave my hair a hard jerk and I gasped. The fingers of his other hand encircled my throat, lightly, menacingly. "What are you after, bitch?"

"I am after nothing," I said wearily. "Have I ever betrayed any of you? In all these years, have I?" I wanted his hands off me.

"Not that we can prove. Yet." He did not move. "You think you know something about Bohne. What is it?"

I sighed. Of course I knew what Bohne had done. That wasn't why I'd looked at him tonight. I'd been watching the way his tie caught the light. It was burgundy, like Daddy's best tie, and I'd looked at it because I was as hungry for my father's embrace as I was for Mama's sausage. I wanted Daddy's voice in my ear telling me he still loved me; I wanted to weep for not knowing if he was even still alive, and if so whether he would condescend to speak to his traitorous, collaborative offspring.

But I would not admit these vulnerable longings to beastly Erich. So I said, mechanically, "'Aktion T4: an initiative to cleanse the Aryan race through the euthanising of those who are sick, infirm, insane, old, or defective.' He's a bastard."

Erich laughed. "You think you're smart," he said, tightening his hand around my throat. "You aren't. You're such a stupid cow. Insane and defective both."

He has very strong hands. I saw him strangle a stray dog to death once, just for the hell of it. It is safer for me to do whatever he says. He will rape me in the end no matter what, and I do prefer not to be battered or bleeding for days afterwards.

Mauritz's clinically sadistic advances are gentle in comparison with Erich's cruelty. Mauritz toys with me: experimenting, pushing buttons, analysing the effects of this or that type of treatment on my morale. Sometimes, more recently, he can't get it up, so mentally torturing me has to stand in for the unrealised urges of the flesh. Erich, though, is rough with me for roughness' sake. He is the quintessential bully, the epitome of all that is terrible about the entire Nazi party.

I don't know if Mauritz knows Erich does this on a regular basis. Probably Mauritz is scared of Erich's hands too, and simply doesn't care to challenge him. Life is cheap among these men. Just a hint that one of them is a traitor, and the rest dispose of him. Since we arrived here in 1947, roughly fourteen men who used to regularly visit the house have disappeared. I wish the remaining ones would all hurry and dispose of each other so the world would be rid of them for good.

Anyway, I did what I always do in bed with a man: I closed my eyes and let my mind go somewhere else, somewhere sunny and safe, where my family is all together again. When he finally finished and went away, I staggered to the bathroom and scrubbed away all traces of his presence, tried to scrub away my guilt and sin, and then I hid inside my wardrobe for a while, its closeness and the softness of the furs and silks within as comforting as a womb, until I had calmed enough to climb into bed.

In the dim light I saw the hideous bruises encircling my wrists. I supposed I should be thankful he didn't actually break any bones.

I am foul.

I shouldn't kid myself. Daddy would be ashamed of me, just like everyone else.

I am so alone.

Raymond

THE RAIN ON THE cab windows made our initial view of Buenos Aires less than impressive yesterday. Anton and I will leave for San Carlos de Bariloche by rail this afternoon. We won't arrive until tomorrow evening. It is astonishing how enormous this country is.

In Bariloche I have made arrangements to borrow a truck to carry us and our supplies south to Tres Lagos, where we can acquire mules and a cart and set off for our six months in Patagonia.

We will wander around the lakes and glaciers, and there will be El Calafate or Tres Lagos we could go to in emergencies. I can hardly believe I am *in Argentina*. Incredibly, my heart feels dead. How can I have wanted to come here for more than thirty years and yet feel no anticipation or pleasure or *anything*?

I do hope I will acquire some enthusiasm soon, or our venture will be pointless. Deep in my heart I am afraid I have lost my ability to care, that my love for Patagonia is only a thing I have clung to because it has provided a constant in my life: going back farther than Antonia, farther than Mariposa, almost all the way back to the day I lost my own father.

Now it is evening. We are on our way. The coach is crowded, but not completely uncomfortable. Anton has laid his head in my lap and fallen asleep, and I've the newspaper to read. Perhaps I'll doze a bit myself.

San Carlos de Bariloche

5 November 1951

LENI

EVEN MAURITZ SHOULD HAVE known he could not keep me contained forever.

I am the fugitive now, and I still can't breathe easily, not until I find a way to Disappear.

It started because of that damned cockatoo.

Along with the very glamorous job of cleaning out his cage, I'm supposed to keep his wings clipped, but I haven't done either recently (see: Leni Trapped in the Bathroom for Inhumane Amounts of Time). Today we took a train to a town somewhere outside of Buenos Aires. I don't have any idea what direction the train was going or how long it took (they gave me something to make me sleep), but since we left in the afternoon and now it is evening, I suppose it must have been several hours. I knew we must be going away for an extended period of time since Mauritz had Ikarus' cage in hand, and he told me to pack my trunk, not my suitcase. All out of the blue. Last night would apparently have been an ideal night to eavesdrop on the Room of Secrets, but Erich saw to it I couldn't.

Maybe they know I listen. Maybe Erich is an orchestrated distraction on nights when particularly incriminating topics are discussed.

That gives me the shivers.

We stood on the platform, waiting for something or somebody, when I heard Erich say the word "plane" in undertones to Mauritz, and instantly I was on my guard. Probably it was only meant as a quick and easy way to get across a border without being traced, but it would also have been a quick and easy way to dispose of unwanted baggage.

Me?

I glanced around quickly. There were still a good many people on the platform, enough that I could lose myself in the crowd if I was quick about it. Covertly I undid the latch on Ikarus' cage and tripped myself (on purpose for once), grabbing Mauritz for balance. The cage jarred, and Ikarus flew out. Mauritz ran after the bird, cursing and hollering. In the two seconds he and Erich were preoccupied, I vanished.

Those first few minutes were the worst. I dove into the bed of a nearby truck loaded with crates and paraphernalia and held my breath, panic constricting my throat like Erich's hands. I had thrown myself under a heap of canvas, so I couldn't see, but I could hear clearly enough. I heard the click as they latched the bird back in. I heard Mauritz and Erich call for me a few times. A man asked something, probably to the effect of "have you lost someone", because Mauritz's reply sounded like "do not worry, we are fine." Then I heard a hushed conference between my keepers, disturbingly close to my hiding place, as to whether it was worthwhile to make a fuss about my being missing. Erich cursed Mauritz for putting his stupid bird ahead of keeping tabs on me. Mauritz cursed Erich for not watching me whilst he went after the bird. Erich argued that if I got away, exactly how did Mauritz plan to explain my absence to someone-or-other? Mauritz said he didn't know what would happen if he showed up without me safely in tow, and Erich retorted that he had a pretty solid idea.

I am dangerous to Mauritz, too. I have power? What an odd sensation that idea gives me! I wish I'd thought of it sooner. They can't make too big a fuss without making themselves conspicuous. Despite the general favour the Argentine government bestows on Nazi fugitives, they never know who might recognise them. They are never truly safe. So they are their own law, and they settle scores in their own way.

Erich agreed to loiter around the station a while and make discreet enquiries, and meet Mauritz later. I am far more frightened of Erich than Mauritz. Mauritz's obsession ensures I stay alive; Erich would kill me with no regret or ceremony, and he would do it cleverly enough that he would never be caught.

Despite knowing Erich was prowling nearby, I fell asleep under the canvas. Imagine that! I was that tired. Or perhaps the sleeping draught still affected me. Whatever the case, even fear for my life couldn't keep me awake, and the lurching of the truck as it set off didn't do more than slightly rouse me. I hadn't planned to stay hidden there—after all, I didn't know who the driver was or where he was going and whether it would take me far enough out of the path of Erich and the reinforcements he would surely call in.

I really did panic when I came fully awake and realised three things.

it was dark
a man nearby was speaking Spanish
where the hell had I got myself to

I sat up (not easy, with every joint stiff and achy from being surrounded by heavy Things) and poked my head cautiously over the edge of the truck. I saw a small figure with a bandana over nose and mouth stirring a pot over some sort of stove thing, and a positive giant of a man speaking to him. His voice belied his size, strong but gentle, tenor rather than baritone—and the lilting sound of the Spanish was soothing. The small one at the fire saw me first and pointed. The big one whipped around and greeted me with a volley of not-very-welcoming-sounding Spanish.

I backed away, brain still fuzzy from sleep and instinctively shielding my face with my arm, fearing he would hit me. It's what Erich would have done. I shook my head violently and held my hands in a non-combative gesture.

"*Ich verstehe nicht,*" I said, because German was automatic to me. The sound of the words seemed to shock him and he fell silent, gesturing to me sharply to get out of his truck. The firelight glinted off his glasses so I could not see his eyes, but all I *could* see about his face was taut and hostile. I stumbled as I descended to the ground and tried again in English. "I don't understand," I repeated, hoping I looked meek and doelike. I felt like death.

"You're German?" He spoke English now, too. British English, with an Oxford accent.

"Yes—no—well—" I stammered. The words tasted odd and unfamiliar on my tongue. I leant my back against the truck for support. "My parents were Austrian. I was born in Swallownest near Rotherham. I was captured by Nazis in 1940, but I *am* a British subject."

He looked at me coldly. "I've heard of Nazis escaping to Argentina, but I hadn't expected the pleasure of meeting one."

"I'm not a Nazi," I protested, my voice thin and shaky. "I've been a *prisoner* of Nazis. Didn't you hear anything I just said to you?"

The small one came to stand by the big one and drew his bandana down, revealing a delicate little face. "Nazis killed my mum," he said solemnly. He wasn't accusing me; it was simply a fact of his life. Perhaps he meant to diffuse the severity of the man's reaction to my speaking German.

I looked at the boy. He couldn't possibly be old enough to remember his mother, if she'd died during the war. He met my gaze steadily. His eyes, unlike the man's, were warm and curious—cautious, but not unfriendly. I looked at him and without thinking I said, "Nazis killed me, too."

"Are you a ghost?" His face brightened with interest.

"Not a ghost." I sighed. I felt wobbly. "Could I trouble you for some water? I'll explain whatever you want to know, but I've lain under that canvas for a very long time, and—"

Anton

I RAN AND DIPPED my own cup into our bucket and handed it to the lady. She drank it quickly, and I saw her eyes flick towards the simmering pot of beans, but she looked away again immediately, stiffening as if she didn't want us to think she was hungry. But she was. I could see in her eyes that she was.

Papá kept staring at her, and she leant back against the truck as if she'd fall over without it holding her up. I couldn't really see her face well in the dark but I could see she was a fancy lady, with ropes of pearls and a dress that looked straight off one of London Gran's fashion sketches. And a fur wrap. Bet Papá wanted to throw *that* in the fire. But at least it didn't have heads still on it like that creepy little one Carlisle Gran wears. "Rats on a string," he calls it. "Don't you know how many innocent animals got slaughtered so you can flaunt their carcasses?" he says. He's said it to both my grans. He doesn't care that they're soft and warm. He says that unless you're native to Siberia or the Arctic or something, there's no reason to wear furs, that it's just to show people you have money to spend. Carlisle Gran was sorry for offending him and hasn't worn it since when we're around, but London Gran just waves off the comments and says, *"You're Just Like Your Father*, Raymond!" She's not very nice to him, sometimes, even though I sort of understand why. He can be awfully immoveable about things.

Anyway, my cup dangled from her white-gloved fingers as she stared at the ground, avoiding Papá's gaze. She didn't belong here, I thought. She belonged in the city. She glanced at me again and I smiled at her. She didn't smile back, only looked hungry and scared.

Leni

THE MAN TOOK ME by the elbow with the casual ease of one who is used to moving truants from one place to another and sat me on a rock near the fire. He remained standing, his arms folded across his chest.

"What's your name?"

"My real name? Or the one they gave me after I was supposedly killed? Or the one on my Argentine passport?"

"All would be useful."

I struggled to form words, and they came out stilted and slurred. "My Argentine passport, which I have not got on me, says Magdalena Sanchez. The papers my keeper provided me in Europe said Marlene von Schlusser. He makes me pose as his wife. I was born Madeleine Mayer."

"How did a British citizen end up with Nazis in Argentina?"

"My mother's invalid sister, in Austria—Madeleine Albrecht was her married name—she lived in Laa An Der Thaya. I was living with her when Hitler invaded Poland. I could have gone home, but I chose to stay. They caught me out after curfew one night. I had Czech friends—we were right by the border. I got entangled in the resistance—"

"Why didn't they shoot you?"

I had no energy to explain that they didn't arrest me for my resistance activities; they arrested me on Mauritz's orders because I looked like his dead wife. "I don't know. They put my clothes on someone else's body and made it look like I'd been in a smashup on my bike. So they did kill me, in a way."

"What did you *do* for them? They can't have kept you for the fun of it."

I didn't want to answer that question, either: too complicated, too convoluted and unbelievably ridiculous. The man's cold stare was beginning to make me angry. I jumped to my feet, swaying a little from light-headedness, and jabbed my finger in his direction. "Listen," I said, "I've just risked my life running away from those bastards and I would sooner shoot myself than have them find me, see?"

My bravado toppled, and so did I. My vision sparkled. Maybe I did need to eat. I dropped back towards my rock seat, missed, and landed on the ground. The man was speaking, but I couldn't make out his words through the daze of pain which shot through my tailbone, and I stared at him blankly until he repeated himself.

"Who is your keeper?"

Didn't he notice I'd hit the ground hard, that I was barely able to answer his questions? I forced the words out somehow. "SS-Sturmbannführer Mauritz von Schlusser, with some... *help*... from his underling Erich Linzer. They, and their fellow escaped Nazis, are planning the Fourth Reich."

Again a twitch. Now he did sit down, on the rock off which I had slid, and bored into my soul with those eyes of his. Irrelevantly I observed that his face, under its accumulation of several days' beard, was a very nice face to look at. But I did not have time to appreciate this further, because at that moment I passed out.

The next thing I knew, the man and the boy were working over me.

"When did you last eat?" the man asked.

"Before we left Buenos Aires," I breathed. "I think I—"

"The train left Buenos Aires TWO DAYS AGO," the man exploded. "How have you not eaten in two DAYS?"

I stared at him. "I don't know," I said, summoning a weak shrug. "They gave me something and I slept. I thought we were only on the train for a few hours. Weren't we, only a few hours?"

"Get her some beans," the man said, jerking his head towards the pot, and the boy scurried off to fetch me some. I proved too weak even to hold the spoon, so the boy fed me whilst his father propped me up. I managed only a few bites before I fell into a hard sleep right there by the fire, and I did not wake again until late in the night.

The disreputable-looking man still sat alert and watchful, staring at me from his perch on the rock, a lantern glowing at his feet. I felt slightly strengthened from the food, and I needed to make him understand. I picked up the conversation where we had left off earlier.

"I just want to go home," I said.

His reply was immediate. "Well, if you want to go home, you've come to the wrong place. We're here to spend six months in deep wilderness. If you're a British subject as you claim, you should have gone to the embassy and let them sort you out."

At that I sat up straight and shouted in rage. "How could I have gone to the embassy? I've never gone out of Mauritz's house except under his supervision. I don't know my way around Buenos Aires, and I have no Spanish to help me find what I need. If I *could* get to the British Embassy, I would tell them anything they wanted to know. Anything. I hate the Nazis. All my information is probably useless now the war is over, but whatever it takes to convince them, I'll do it."

He sighed. "I'm not taking you to Buenos Aires. If you want to go back there, you're on your own."

"I can't go anywhere on my own! I don't even know where we are now," I said, crossly.

He removed his glasses and covered his eyes as if he couldn't believe he was having to deal with this level of stupidity. "Between Río Mayo and Perito Moreno."

As if *that* meant anything to me. I hoped he recognised that I intended my glare to incinerate him.

Finally he elaborated, "We are currently sixteen hundred miles from Buenos Aires. Roughly the distance between Paris and Moscow."

My mouth dropped open.

"Listen," he said, with the begrudging condescension of a put-out parent. "You can come with us as far as Tres Lagos—that's south of here," he added, before I could protest ignorance again. "After that you're on your own. My son and I did not come here for anything but a wilderness wander."

"I can't speak Spanish," I reminded him.

"You'll find a way to get what you need." He looked me up and down, and his thoughts were crystal clear. He believed I hadn't been given my expensive clothes and jewels for nothing.

"You snobby English bastard," I snapped, bristling.

"Filthy Nazi whore," he countered. "I'll not have prostitutes hanging about my son."

I slapped him in the face. He barely flinched, and I suddenly hated him tremendously. *Fine*, I thought. *Drop me in Trace Lagers or whatever it was. Leave me to die of ignorance and misery. Enjoy having that on your conscience whilst you burn in hell.*

Tres Lagos

6-10 November 1951

Anton

PAPÁ AND THE LADY from the truck got very angry with each other last night and called each other names. He called her a filthy Nazi horror and she called him a snobby English bastard, and he said he wouldn't let any prosecutors around his son, and she slapped him in the face and said he had no idea *what* she was, and that he was a beast to be so mean, and then she started crying. I've never heard Papá sound so angry. I suppose sometimes he must have to get tough with people at work, but I never thought about it before. He's not like that at home with me.

This morning I woke before Papá did, and I saw the lady curled up close to the firepit, her fur wrap over herself for warmth. She's got loads of pearls on. I can see better now it's light. Not just the necklace and the bracelet, but earrings and a pin too. And she's got two rings. I couldn't see those until she took off her gloves. One looks like a wedding ring, and one is pearls to match the rest. I've never seen so many pearls. Mum had a pearl necklace. Papa keeps it in the drawer where she kept all her jewellery, but it's hardly anything at all compared to the one this lady is wearing.

I thought her legs must still be freezing, so I took my blanket and laid it over her whilst I whispered in her ear, "Don't be too cross with Papá. He misses Mummy so much. He's nice really."

She stirred, clutching the blanket and asking me sleepily, "What's your name, kid?"

"Anton Varela. I'm eight. Papá is Inspector Raymond Varela. Your English sounds a bit like Carlisle Gran's."

She didn't answer for a minute, but I saw the tiniest smile on her face. Then she said, "Yours is southern. Southampton?"

"How'd you ever guess that?" I asked, impressed. "Tangmere. Pretty close."

"And your father went to Oxford."

She spoke in barely more than a whisper, and she still hadn't opened her eyes. She looked tired and kind of old in the daylight, but maybe it was just because her face was dirty. When she did finally open her eyes, they looked hungry, and I left her long enough to go fetch a handful of raisins from the truck. She looked at me when I held them out, as if she didn't believe I was offering them to *her*.

"Take them," I said. "They'll help you until breakfast is ready." And I opened her hand and poured them in. She never took her eyes off me, wide and a bit crazy-looking.

"I'll get you some water to wash your face while you eat those," I said, and I went away.

As soon as she thought I wasn't watching, she stuffed the entire handful into her mouth, as if afraid someone would snatch them away again.

I think perhaps she is really starving.

LENI

SO HE'S A POLICEMAN, and not just any old policeman, but an *inspector*. No wonder he's so implacably obnoxious. He probably thinks he knows everything. Can I trust him? It doesn't appear I have much choice. Even if he does assume I'm a whore, does it matter? So would any other man with two eyes and half a brain.

The pearl set was a bit of overkill on Mauritz's part. Usually he is more restrained. I just now had the thought that he would not have thrown me out of a plane with so many valuables on my person. What was he up to, then?

All the same, Inspector Varela has a point. I could sell the pearls for money, if not myself. Selling myself is what I do, after all.

Except that circles back to the fact that I cannot speak Spanish, and would therefore get nowhere negotiating.

I am sitting in the back of the truck by unspoken agreement that my tainted self should stay as far away from Old Varela's precious son as possible. I should be grateful to him for not abandoning me by the side of the road, I suppose, but instead I'm just angry.

I haven't felt this angry in a long time. Angry and jittery. I need a fix badly, but I only had one dose left in my handbag, the last of my emergency stash, and I took that last night, trying to calm myself after our shouting match.

I've no cigarettes either. I wonder if there's any alcohol on this venture I could pilfer. Maybe I'll ask Little Varela tonight. He's a nice kid. Sharp, too. He could tell my English accent was northern. But for now, there is nothing for it but to sit here in the back of a bumping truck, wishing I could tear my hair out or scream. There's not even any nice scenery to look at. Why in the world has this man travelled so far from home to see a barren brown wasteland?

The kid brought me raisins this morning, and water to wash my face, and he tried to share his own breakfast with me, but I couldn't swallow a single bite as long as his big scary father remained anywhere in sight. I kept hearing *Nazi whore* in my head, and I just couldn't. It's not so much that I'm offended (facts are facts) as that I'm simply wishing I could spool the thread of time backwards and make a fresh start. How far back would I have to go? Sometime when I still lived in England and hadn't yet gotten it into my head to move to Austria. Seventeen, perhaps eighteen?

I *am* very hungry, and the sun is very hot, so I shall lie down among the canvas again and allow myself to faint.

The sun sets late here at this time of year, and over the hours since we set off I've gone from the angry, drug-addicted jitterer of the morning to a passed-out, starving, impassive brick. This sleepy little village is called Tres Lagos (says Young V) and I doubt more than a hundred people live in it, but somehow Old Inspector V knows some of them.

I am sitting at a small table in the home of one of these Someones He Knows, who has graciously fed us and has beds for us to rest in tonight. Inspector Varela (whom I would *like* to call Old V to his face) and Young V are in front of the cold fireplace, petting the house's cat and talking to one another in Spanish. I suspect Old V is doing it on purpose to exclude me. Young V glances at me occasionally and smiles, displaying his funny snaggly collection of half-adult, half-child teeth (with a couple missing). I want to smile back but I am frozen. Despite the warmth of the evening, I am shivering inside my fur wrap.

What am I *doing?* I can't do anything but sit and stare. I think maybe I'm in shock. I can't remember what you're supposed to do for shock. Girl Guides was a long, long time ago.

I'm realising I am ON MY OWN. I wanted to get away, but now that I am away, I am terrified of all the empty open space and of—of *everything*.

For ten years I've never made any choices for myself. From the first night when I was captured until now, Mauritz has done all my thinking for me. He decided when I should sleep and eat, where I could go and to whom I could speak, what I should wear, how I should fix my hair.

I need someone to tell me what I ought to do now. *I don't know.*

Mauritz would tell me what to do, if he was here. Old Varela is doubtless disinclined to waste his time fussing over me.

As afraid of Mauritz as I have always been, he *is* comfortingly familiar, and I need something familiar in this surreal world I find myself in now. I no longer fool myself into believing I love Mauritz. I fear and hate him. But I have been completely dependent upon the man. He held my life in his hands.

He still does.

He *is* my life.

I'm not fooling Old Varela when I say I really wouldn't know what to do if he abandons me here. I know as much about the geography of Argentina as I do the dark side of the moon.

My flight from Mauritz was purely impulse and instinct. How long has it been? Not twenty-four hours, surely.

I spoke the truth when I said the Nazis killed Madeleine Mayer. Maybe Young Varela is right and I *am* only a ghost now.

Anton

THE RUNAWAY LADY IS sitting at the table by herself wrapped in her fur thing, staring. Like an animal in a car's path. Frozen, like.
    I'll go to her.

    I am back now. She had trouble talking to me, as if her tongue didn't work. I asked her if I could get her anything, and she stuttered out something about a drink. I got her water and then had to hold the cup because her hands went clumsy.
    "Papá," I called, "something's very wrong with her!"
    Papá came over, and he spoke more nicely to her than before. He asked if she was all right and looked into her eyes, made her lie down with her feet up. She can't stop shivering, so he's bringing her another blanket.

    She is asleep now. Papá is sitting beside me and he looks... worried or annoyed or maybe both. He turns to Señora Ríos, the lady who owns this house, and he says quietly that the runaway lady is *dejando la adicción*.
    "What's that?" I ask, but he gives me the Look that means it's not something he thinks I need to know about. He goes on to discuss leaving the lady here whilst he and I go on, and he says he will leave some money behind to pay for her care until she's well enough to go back to Buenos Aires.
    I don't like this idea. What I overheard last night when they were arguing sounds like Buenos Aires would be a bad place for her to go back to, especially all alone. I may be only eight, but even I know she can't leave the country without a passport, and she doesn't have anything with her real name on it.
    Madeleine Mayer, she said her real name was. I like that. It's

pretty, the way Veronica Varela would be.

I'm not sure what to make of her. Miss Mayer, I mean. She scares me a little, but mostly I think she is scared herself. She reminds me of a dog or a horse who's been mistreated. They are scared of being bitten, so they bite first to save time.

But all the same, I don't like that Papá wants to leave her behind. We should take care of her, keep her safe from those bad men who want to hurt her. If it was Mum, I know he would stop at nothing to keep *her* safe. The runaway lady *needs* us. I don't think it was an accident that she jumped into our truck.

Now that she is asleep we'll go out to choose the three mules we will hire for our journey. Señora Ríos has twelve, all named after the apostles!

Raymond

WELL, I WANTED TO get out of my slump, didn't I? Be careful what you wish for, Varela. You didn't want *this* sort of excitement.

Anton is worried about that woman. She acted very peculiarly tonight, after we ate our supper. She went dead silent, and her speech when Anton tried to talk to her was slurred, so I went to investigate. I think she has been taking drugs and is having withdrawal symptoms, on top of being in shock. Her eyes were unfocused and frightening. She might believe she can hide such things from me, but there isn't much I haven't seen in the last twenty years. I've seen enough addicts and tramps and "kept women" to instantly know them for what they are.

Why did she have to dive into my truck? I can't conceive of a woman I would less like around my son. What am I to do with her?

I kept a close eye on her last night after we had our heated disagreement. Señora Ríos says the woman may stay here. Can I possibly make her understand it would be in her best interests to do so? I cannot get away from her soon enough to suit me.

Leni

OLD VARELA CAME TO speak to me before the kid woke up this morning. He asked if I've been taking drugs and I admitted I'd been on them a long time. Small doses at first, once in a while. More, lately. Opiates numbed my pain and made me think I was happy-ish. Coming off them cold is not so wonderful. I couldn't eat any breakfast; my stomach hurt.

They set off right after breakfast, and I rose to leave with them, but Old V said absolutely no, I would never make it anywhere with my ridiculous high-heeled shoes and haute couture clothes, and he'd arranged for me to stay here until I could get a ride back to civilisation.

I shouted all the curses I could come up with at his retreating figure (in German, of course, as I don't know the English equivalents of most of these words, and besides German name-calling is *far* more creative than English). As much as I hated Old V, I hated even more the idea of staying with some strange woman in the middle of nowhere. Men were beasts, but I was used to them. Women, though?

No, I'd sooner stick with a creature I understood than one I did not. But Old V was charging on down the road as if he couldn't get away from me fast enough, and with every step he took, all my hopes of getting home cracked just a little more.

As if he sensed my distress, the kid stopped his mule not far outside the gate where I stood. He glanced at his father, then at me, and made a tiny motion with his hand, beckoning me to follow him.

It was all I needed. I kicked off my shoes into the shrubs by the gate and walked after the Varelas in my stockings. We followed a main road all morning, with little traffic.

Old V's attitude made me livid. The nerve of him, trying to get rid of me like that, when I was literally helpless. Did he think I was proud of the fact that I had to trail after him begging for crumbs? Because I most definitely wasn't.

My legs, unused to any exertion beyond moving from one room to another a few times a day, soon screamed at me in their weariness. The gravel along the road scalded my tender feet in the summer sun. I trailed along painfully behind, cursing to myself. I managed to stay far enough back that Old V didn't notice me until they stopped for lunch. Then he flew into a state of crimson rage.

"What are you doing here, woman? I told you where you were supposed to go!"

"I'm not staying behind with people I don't know!"

"You don't know *us*," he shouted.

"But *you* speak English," I shouted back. "And you *are* English. I've stumbled along for the last twenty miles or whatever. I'm not going back."

He snorted. "Twenty miles. More like five."

"That's still further than I've walked at once in the last eleven years," I countered. In spite of myself, tears burst out and flooded my face. I was exhausted and so, so angry.

We faced each other, his arms crossed, mine hanging limply at my sides, silently defying each other. Young V, on the sidelines, watched, his eyes wide, until this pause, and then he said, "Papá, her feet are bleeding."

In my rage, I hadn't even noticed, but they were bleeding, right through my now-tattered silk stockings: filthy and oozing and very, very painful. Old V let out a huge sigh and said, unkindly, "You are without doubt the biggest nuisance in the history of any travel anywhere, and I'm not sure what I did to deserve this." He stalked off to tend to the mules and get lunch ready, leaving me alone with the kid and my miserable feet.

Young V, meantime, had gone for the water in the cart, and in a moment he was at my side, urging me to sit whilst he tended my hot, revolting feet. He peeled away the silk scraps, washed my feet gently with water, sun-warmed from the bottle, and dried them with a towel. He found a pair of his father's socks for me to put on. They were too large, but they would do.

"Why did you motion for me to follow?" I asked, my voice barely over a whisper. It wouldn't do to have his father hear *that*.

He had his bandana on again, but his eyes crinkled in a smile. "Because you need friends."

"Thank you," I breathed, wincing at the pain in my feet.

"Papá is acting like a Giant Hedgehog, but he's nice under the prickles, really."

I would have rolled my eyes, but I was too tired. So I changed the subject. "Why the bandana?"

"Asthma," he answered simply. "I can't be near smoke or dust without it on. Especially smoke. And I have to ride my mule more than I walk. I start wheezing if I get too winded."

He's so delicate, I thought, but not out of derision—he had a strength of character that seemed greater than his eight years. A beautiful child, and my heart wrenched inside me to think, for the fifty thousandth time, how I would never have any beautiful little boys or girls of my own.

Young V's mother must have been tiny. I can't imagine him ever becoming a big strapping man like his father. "You'll ride my mule the rest of today," he said. "It's level. I'll be all right walking, and you need to keep off those feet."

I was grateful to the kid, although I felt a distinct pang of guilt for being so much trouble to these people who shouldn't have had to look after me in the first place.

Old Varela supposes I am the worst kind of garbage. He can't wait to be rid of me. He's right.

I shouldn't have left Mauritz.

I'm sure Mauritz is dead now because of my running away. Another death on my conscience, bringing the total to—oh, I don't want to think about it.

The guilt is eating me alive.

Raymond

ANTON WAS DEAD TIRED from the afternoon's slog. He gave that woman his mule and fell asleep without a bite of supper. It's a mercy he hasn't had an asthma attack from the exertion, or the woman would not be hearing the end of it anytime soon. Why did she follow us after I explicitly told her to stay behind?

She has gone through several extremes over the course of the afternoon: brash and bold, raging, withdrawn, cursing again, daft, frightened. Tonight as I prepared our supper, I avoided looking at her, yet I sensed she was watching me. She disappeared for a time into the darkness—relieving herself, I assumed—and when she came limping back three-quarters of an hour later, she took a tiny piece of flatbread from the plate and nibbled at it somewhat distastefully. She's not eaten anything of substance today.

I know I should apologise for calling her a whore, but I'm not going to do so until the sentiment is genuine. I'm still annoyed at her for intruding. But I made up my mind to at the very least be civil.

"You should get some sleep," I advised her. "Long slog tomorrow."

"Don't you eat any normal food?" she asked, making a face at the bread in her hand.

"Define normal."

She went quiet, but her unimpressed grimace did not alter. Eventually she answered me.

"Sausage and sauerkraut and fresh caraway buns and roasted potatoes." She beamed, her eyes staring off glassily, as if entranced by the idea of fermented cabbage and casings full of animal bits nobody in their right mind would eat. "Have you any sausage?"

"I don't eat dead animals."

"What do you eat?"

"*Normal* food," I replied, with perhaps greater sternness than the situation called for. "Normal is purely subjective."

She shrugged and changed the subject, dropping the flatbread into her lap. "Where do I sleep? In the firepit again?"

"I don't care where you sleep." *Just as far away from me as possible*, I added mentally. "We've got six blankets. You can have two of them. One for underneath you and one for on top."

"So I do still have to sleep on the ground?"

"What does for us will do for you," I answered shortly. "You're the one who wanted to come, remember. You would have had a bed, back in Tres Lagos."

She let out a dry, humourless laugh. "Given the choice," she asked, after a long silence, "would you lie down and sleep, and risk dreaming of your owners coming to slit your throat, or would you sit up watching for them in case they really do come along and slit your throat?"

"Nobody owns me," I retorted. "I haven't had to make any such choices."

I turned towards her and caught a flash of something in her hand in the firelight, something she was trying to keep out of my sight. I realised she hadn't gone to the bathroom earlier; she'd been raiding the wagon for alcohol. I snatched the bottle out of her hand and shook it in horror. Completely empty. "That was for emergencies," I spluttered furiously. "Now look what you've done."

"My entire life is an emergency," she countered, a touch melodramatically. She snatched at my arm and held on, her nails digging claw-like into my skin as she got to her feet. I could have shaken her off easily, but I didn't. If she meant to hurt me, to get a reaction of pain or surprise or anger, I wasn't about to give her the satisfaction.

But then she hooked her other arm around my neck and drew my face towards hers. She had a stronger grip than I'd have given her credit for. "My current emergency," she whispered, her brandy-scented breath hot against my mouth, "is that I have no more dope to finish knocking me into oblivion, but you're here, and you're quite a dish, and you could distract me by fucking me."

I swallowed and took a step backward, peeling her hands off me and holding her at arm's length, beyond furious at her having the audacity to proposition me.

"Get your filthy whore hands off me," I hissed, all civility forgotten. "I don't sleep with Nazis."

"I'm not a Nazi," she said, slurring a little. She looked unsteady. I suspected it was as much exhaustion as booze.

"That's what you said before," I snapped. "Nazi pet, then. I don't sleep with those either." And I stalked off to fetch the blankets, tossed them at her feet from several yards away, and left her alone with her demons and the decision to watch or dream.

LENI

I WOKE WITH A splitting headache. It has been a good while since I've had alcohol in quantity (opiates were always so much easier, and anyway Mauritz only ever let me have the cheap booze he'd never dream of serving his cronies) and my body was unhappy with my impulsive overindulgence. The sunshine hurt my eyes, the birds belting their morning arias pierced my eardrums, and Young V dancing around, singing spontaneous made-up songs, made my head spin. Every muscle in my body blazed in resentment.

Young V stopped dancing eventually and took the wrappings off my feet, which were a frightful mess of blisters and blood, gave them another wash, and put fresh socks on me. Thank goodness *he* didn't mind touching filthy whore feet.

And he gave me his mule again, because even if my feet had been all healed, I was too hungover to walk. I draped myself slothlike over the back of the longsuffering creature and closed my eyes, wishing with panicky, single-minded obsession that I could have just one of my pills. Just *one*. It would make everything all better again. Wouldn't it?

Young V walked beside me, watching that I didn't slip off, and occasionally chattered at me, anytime I appeared semi-conscious. I am not sure what all he said: too deep in my personal hell to pay any attention. I cringed and went hot with shame every time I remembered how I'd asked Old V to screw me. What had I been thinking, anyway? Since when do I want that from anyone? I couldn't have borne to look at him. Just as well I was mostly passed out on the mule.

We went fifteen miles that day. Young V's fortitude impressed me. He did ride in the wagon a good bit of the time, but before supper finished cooking, he tossed his blankets to the ground, curled himself around his stuffed cat, and passed out like a light.

Another evening alone in the company of Inspector Raymond Bundle-of-Joy Varela was hardly what I could call a marvellous time, but as he'd said the night before, it was me who'd insisted on coming. Not to mention I'd made an utter idiot of myself last night, so I bit my tongue when tempted to insult him for his insolence towards me.

He made some more of that odd flatbread, and tonight I was hungry enough it actually tasted all right. He also tossed me an apple, as if I were a bear in a zoo. It slipped through my hands to the ground, but I dusted it off on my skirt and ate it anyway.

"About last night—" I began, but he cut me off.

"Don't mention it," he said crisply. "I didn't come to Patagonia for women."

"You don't understand. I wanted to apologise," I said, barely audible. I shook all over, and his chilliness deflated me.

"Accepted," he said, but without any warmth.

"I'll pay you back for all of this somehow." A promise I didn't have any clue how I would keep, short of selling my body to him, which was obviously not a payment method he found appealing.

I stalled. I have been taught to make pointless small talk, charming Mauritz's guests, usually with assistance from his illicit pharmaceutical cupboard. But trying to sound brilliant and chirpy without such help falls terribly flat.

"I guess you must have loved your kid's mother a lot." The words tripped gracelessly over themselves on their way out of my mouth, the way my feet trip over themselves if I don't watch where I'm putting them. I wanted to hit my tactless, idiot self. I was not witty or charming or *anything*. What was I doing here? I took a mental vow of silence.

He surprised me by answering the question, if brusquely. "I did love her. She's been dead nearly nine years."

Forgetting my vow of silence, I burst out, "You've never slept with anyone else in all that time?" I don't know why I said it, why I assumed it, only somehow I divined that this idea lurked in between the lines of what he'd deigned to share with me. He wanted me to perceive his moral superiority, no doubt.

The men in my life had barely been able to go nine hours, let alone nine years. If it wasn't Mauritz, it was Erich, and if not Erich—well, it doesn't matter now. Let's just say I was never left to myself for long.

"It isn't that difficult to be reasonably self-controlled," he answered stiffly.

I stared at him, still disbelieving. "And before her?"

"She was the only one. Not that it's any of your business."

He was right, it wasn't my business. But the idea that some men had other things to do with their time than to spend it destroying women's lives and bodies baffled me. "Are there many men like you?"

He shrugged. "How should I know? I'm not in the habit of prying into other men's personal affairs unless I'm questioning them officially."

I stared at him, mouth open, and for a long time sat digesting this idea. I allowed myself to think about the men I'd known before Mauritz.

Daddy, who had loved my mother, and my brother and sisters and me, wouldn't sleep around as long as my mother lived, and probably if anything happened to my mother still wouldn't. Not casually.

Tante Madeleine's husband Klaus had never been anything but nice to Tante Madeleine and me.

The baker's boy Josef, whom I'd hoped to marry someday, had been the sweetest, loveliest young man.

I supposed it was my bad luck that I'd been in the wrong place at the wrong time and gotten captured by the wrong type of men.

I came and knelt before Old V, laying one hand on his arm. His muscles tensed under my touch, and he twitched, as if to make me remove my hand. Probably he was remembering last night.

"Look at me," I pleaded. "It's demeaning, the way you won't even *look* at me." I hoped he wouldn't notice I wasn't meeting *his* eyes, either.

He gave me a quick furtive glance and turned away again. "Get your hand off my arm."

I backed away, afraid. This kind of man, I didn't know anything about. He frightened me simply by being so different.

I didn't know if he was listening to me, but I sat back on my heels, hands safely folded on my own knees, and said softly, "It's true I've been a whore, but I didn't have any say. I didn't want to die, and they would have killed me, if I didn't do whatever they said."

"I'd sooner have died."

"I would say the same thing now. I was younger then. I had my whole life before me. I thought I would get away when the war ended. Be able to go home."

"Why didn't you?"

I inhaled a shaky breath. "They didn't let me access the wireless or have friends, not even a maid who might tell me the news. I didn't know how the war was going or who was winning. One night, they woke me and told me to get dressed and come. We got on a plane, landed somewhere in Spain, and lived in someone's basement for what seemed like years, and the next thing I knew we were on a ship coming here. I didn't even know the Germans had lost the war until long after it happened." I twisted my hands together, trying to not tap my fingers on my knee in that way that Mauritz found so annoying. "I've gotten used to being a... a Thing. I feel empty since I left Mauritz. I've no purpose, nothing to offer you in return for tolerating my presence here." I glanced up again. "So if you change your mind, I—well, I'll—do whatever you require of me."

I could tell the mere idea of intimacy with me was, to his mind, akin to sleeping in a fresh dunghill. "I want no favours from you," his voice said. His eyes said more. They said, *I don't want you here at all.*

I bowed my head submissively, walked to the wagon, and made my bed underneath it, smoothing it out over the grass. I felt safer there, with the illusion of confinement, than in the open, even though it would have been warmer by the fire.

Of course it didn't surprise me that he'd refused my advances. If I were him—upright, respectable, whatever else he is or people think he is—I would likely do the same.

The difference is, *he* has self-respect. He feels himself worth something, worth treating with dignity.

And I do not.

The way Old V speaks of his wife—he *reverences* her. It makes me ache inside. Mauritz never reverenced me. I wonder where he is now, what he is doing. Plotting my demise? Dead himself for having let me escape? That would leave Erich to come find me and drag me back again.

I suppose I'm putting both Varelas in peril simply by being here. I should go away, for their sake. There's a creek nearby. I'll follow it. Doesn't water lead eventually to civilisation or the sea?

I did not get far. Old Varela noticed my absence only five minutes later, and he called out for me. Probably he assumed I was looking for more brandy. I did not answer, of course. I started to run, but he is bigger and faster, and he had an electric torch. I tripped on a rock and sprawled on the gravel. My hands stung from the abrasion.

"Get up, you little idiot," he said sharply. I obeyed, meek and unprotesting, until I stumbled and stifled a gasp of pain. I'd twisted my ankle.

He sighed, but he picked me up and slung me over his shoulder as unceremoniously as a sack of potatoes and stalked back to the camp, where he set me down near my blanket under the wagon.

"Don't do that again," he said.

Anton

MISS MAYER THOUGHT SHE could walk today, so we took turns on my mule Santiago, swapping every hour or so. She limped quite a bit, but she managed all right. I don't think Papá knows she's with us because of me. I should probably fess up, but I'll wait until we've reached camp, because by then we'll surely be too far away from Señora Ríos for Papá to send her back.

We are following a road which goes around the southern edge of Lago Viedma, heading west towards the mountains and Glaciar Viedma. Tonight was the first time in a couple of days I've stayed awake to have supper with Papá and Miss Mayer! She didn't want to talk, though. Actually all day she seemed like something bothered her, but she's always a little strange, so I didn't think much about it until she took her food to her bed with her and sat with her back to us to eat it, and I realised she was crying. I wonder if she and Papá quarrelled again last night. I didn't hear anything.

But I didn't want her to be sad. So I went to my bag and I took out Little Cat, and held him out to her. I told her Little Cat would make her feel better and to please cuddle with him.

She looked at me with her eyes all wet and her cheeks stripey from tears running through all the dirt, and for a moment she didn't move. But she took Little Cat and whispered, "Thank you."

She had already fallen asleep when Papá put me to bed, but she had Little Cat tucked under her chin, hugging him close. I do so hope she is better tomorrow.

She is strange, but I want to be her friend. I think she is very lonely.

Like me.

Lago Viedma

15 November -2 December 1951

Raymond

AFTER A WALK OF about thirty miles, we have reached the first site I intended to stay a while, a little peninsula jutting into Lago Viedma. So today we did more than merely roll out blankets at the end of our journey. I stretched canvas over the bows on the wagon, for shade from the sun or protection from the rain, should we get any (not likely), and took greater technical care crafting our fireplace. The woman is quite sunburnt, and she retreated with her blankets into a thicket of notro bushes as soon as we arrived, presumably to sulk. That silly fussy frock she's wearing is so unsuitable for this venture, and she has nothing to change into.

Anton and I worked hard, and after three hours we had a pleasant, homey campsite. He fetched some water for cooking, and I set a pot of beans to soak for tomorrow. For tonight I made another batch of the flatbread, but I fried it for a treat, and we ate it with melted cheese.

Having a collaborator within spitting distance of my son—*my son*, whose mother was murdered by Nazis—is more than I can gracefully bear. It is hardly fair that I had to wait thirty-four years for the love of my life, only to have her snatched from me a mere two years later. And then I lost my cat, the best friend any man could hope to have, no thanks to my idiot neighbour and his rat poison. If anything happens to my son, I will go on a rampage that will probably end with me dead too.

Superintendent Perkins was doubtless right when he told me I was going crackers and had better take some time off. The smallest things seem to set me off lately. And yet here I am, stuck with a drug-addicted madwoman in the middle of nowhere, and the worst of it is, Anton seems to like her.

Not to mention that, assuming her story is true, I have reason to be more than a little concerned that whatever Nazis are tracking her, are tracking us as well.

Anton

I LOVE OUR CAMPSITE!

    We have a wonderful view of the mountains, and lots of notro bushes (Papá says they would have been blooming last month! It's a pity we missed that.) The lake is so beautiful and it whispers to the shore all day long and all night long, telling it secrets. I will like listening to it as I go to sleep.
    Papá and Miss Mayer have the two mattresses that we brought along, and I get the hammock. We weren't sure there would be trees to hang it in, but there are, so I can use it after all!
    In the morning, Papá says we will find some nice place to do my schoolwork together and then go look for some butterflies. He is extremely pleased. He told me to make sure all my books are in my school satchel and then spent forty-five minutes lovingly packing his own satchel of Explorer Things. I could pack it for him, if he asked. He's very specific. He always carries a notebook and pencil in his shirt pocket to make notes, but his satchel has all he needs to capture and kill butterflies (even though he almost never kills them) and Nettie (what he calls his butterfly net) and some reference books and binoculars and a magnifying glass. But he's nothing if not fussy when it comes to people touching his BUTTERFLY THINGS, so I don't bother to ask if I can pack them for him.
    I think he's still mad at Miss Mayer. He won't talk English around her, but I answer him in English. I'm not mad at her. I like her to know what we're talking about.
    Poor Miss Mayer, her clothes are so terribly dusty. Well, so are Papá's and mine, but she has nothing to change into! I have an idea, though. Tomorrow morning I will ask her about it, since when I peeked at her a minute ago she looked asleep.

Leni

HE'S LEFT ME WITH his kid this morning.

I'm not sure to what I owe such an unexpected privilege, but I feel like I can breathe again now that Old Varela is not here glowering.

"Papá's gone to the lake to bathe. Would you like me to bring you some water so you can wash too?" Young V asked me. "You could go in the wagon and draw the canvas closed, and nobody could see you."

He was so bright-eyed and enthusiastic about his suggestion. It did sound lovely, but I had one problem: nothing to change into once I peeled off my sweat-soaked, filthy clothes.

"We'll wash them later," he said, confidently, when I voiced this dilemma. "You can borrow one of Papá's shirts in the meantime."

I wavered. I did so want to be clean again.

I gave in.

He grinned and brought me the bucket of water and a bar of soap and left me inside the wagon to get on with it.

The ice-cold water was not exactly pleasant, but I gritted my teeth and made the best of it. I washed my hair first, leaning over the back of the wagon to let the soap suds run to the ground below, and then I retreated inside, pulled the canvas closed, took off my clothes, and scrubbed myself, wincing at the sensitive sunburnt skin on my neck and face. I wrapped myself in a big colourful towel (presumably Young V's own) and poked my head through the opening in the back of the canvas. I didn't want to emerge so close to naked in the open, especially since my arms are such a disaster. I needn't have worried; Anton waited close at hand with the promised pilfered shirt, pale blue like the dress

I'd been wearing. I reached to take it from his outstretched hand. It smelled fresh and cottony, and I was suddenly transported to Tante Madeleine's linen cupboard, the way her sheets always smelled like sunshine as I opened the door and took out fresh bedding. For a moment I closed my eyes and inhaled, allowing myself to relive a pleasant memory of life before it became hell. Then I put on the shirt, which hung on me like a tent.

I tied the towel around my waist as a skirt and emerged from the wagon. I sat near the fireplace to roll up the sleeves a bit and comb out my hair, and I realised I hadn't even looked at myself in a mirror since leaving Buenos Aires. I searched for my handbag and found my compact and my mouth dropped open in horror at what I saw reflected there.

My skin was red and flaky from sunburn and liberally covered with freckles. I used to get freckled in the summertime, I remembered now, but I've been inside for so long my skin had grown almost translucently white. And my hair? Total disaster. I snapped the mirror shut and made a face. I have never considered myself beautiful, but I had always been able to compensate for it by being well turned out.

Old V came back not long after, and he didn't seem to even see me. I had been certain he would kick up a fuss over my wearing his shirt. He had shaved and trimmed his moustache for the first time since I'd joined them, and he looked scholarly and civilised, hardly my mental image of a policeman. More like a university professor or something. He really *was* terribly dishy, and I hated myself for thinking so. It occurred to me that I still didn't know why he was here. Wandering Patagonia, for the sake of wandering, didn't seem to add up to any logical end in my mind.

I asked him after supper, once Anton had gone to bed, and he told me, "Butterflies."

I started a little, smacked with a memory, and squeezed my eyes shut. He didn't seem to notice, his own eyes fixed on the journal in his lap, his pen scrawling across the page. I forced calm into my voice when I replied. "Your kid told me you're a police inspector. What have butterflies to do with that?"

He paused in his writing and shrugged. "They haven't. I just like butterflies."

Well, Old Varela was the last person in the world I might have suspected would be interested in *butterflies.*

"I've a degree in biology," he went on, tapping the pen lightly against the pages. "The only reason I didn't come here sooner is my police work and the war and then my wife and son—well, it all added up to me being stuck in England."

"Why didn't you move here, if you went to all the trouble to come here for six months?"

"Bit old for that, don't you think?" he said. "I've a good job at home. Ten, fifteen years ago, I might have made a successful life for myself here. I doubt I could now."

"Getting old is shit," I agreed. My leg twitched, agitation and jitters setting in. I wanted a fix.

"What would you know about it?" he asked. "You can't be so old."

"Nearly thirty-three. That's old for a woman who's been held hostage since she was twenty-one, and sheltered by doting parents and aunties before that."

He seemed to turn this over in his mind for a long time, and then he said, in quite a different tone than I'd heard him use towards me so far, "Are you prone to—harming yourself?"

"What do you mean?" I asked.

"I mean, should I lock up the knives? Your arms—Anton was a bit worried about them. He told me they were..." he trailed off.

"Oh." It surprised me that he even cared whether I slit my wrists, although I suppose the only thing he wants less on his venture than my presence would be my dead presence. "No. I'm not interested in cutting myself or anyone else. Except maybe Mauritz or Erich. It's the opiates that call to me."

"Haven't any of those here," he said.

Bully for you, I thought, but I didn't say it. Why did he have to be so damned good-looking? I leant hard on my knee to force my leg to stop jittering, fixed my eyes on the ground instead of his face.

"What *did* happen to your arms?" he asked at last.

I wanted to casually shrug off his question, but instead I shuddered. The burns always blistered and rubbed against my clothes, and the latest ones had only just stopped their oozing. I could never leave them alone. They'd start itching and I'd claw them open, over and over again. Perhaps it was my own fault they never healed better than they did.

"Cigarette ends," I said finally. "Not my cigarette ends," I added. I looked away from his inscrutable dark eyes, away across the twilit valley spread below us, and came out in chills all over. "They wanted me marked, to make identifying me easy if I ever got away. And for punishment. And because causing pain gets them off." I forced out a laugh. "They might have lavishly tattooed me instead and made a pretty freak show of me instead of a scary one."

He opened his mouth as though he would speak, then shook his head almost imperceptibly and turned back to his journal, hunching as if battling some demon of his own.

Since we set up camp here, Old and Young V have gone out most of the day, every day, from right after breakfast until time to make supper. I've no idea what they're doing or where they go, and I don't actually care much. The quiet is both wonderful and unsettling and vast: full of sounds you wouldn't even notice unless you held very, very still. The world is a big place, and for me, hemmed in by walls for most of the last eleven years, it is *overwhelming.*

The first few days, I lay down on my blankets under the wagon and held still, occasionally tracing with an idle finger the grain patterns in the wood of the wagon overhead. Sleeping outside always sounds exotic and romantic in books, but in fact it is terrible, and I am not sure I will ever become used to it. I was so cold and it got so dark at night. I do miss the little light I used to have burning all the time in my room at Mauritz's, and the silk eiderdown. These blankets the Varelas have are stiff heavy wool things, not one bit cuddly. I feel actual pangs of distress and grief over this. I want my soft, cosy bed.

At least I still have my fur wrap.

Much as Old V might dislike me, I do not really believe he'd let anyone harm me. When he is gone and I have no idea where, I imagine unspeakable scenarios where Erich or Mauritz find me, and I am alone and defenceless in this great wilderness. I had hysterics the first day over this; the second day, exhausted from the hysterics, I slept most of the day.

Last night I slept with my too-big shirt pulled up over my head in a desperate attempt to keep my head warm, and I woke this morning with a dew-dampened blanket underneath me, and inexplicably a line from the Bible came to mind, about being *wet with the dew of heaven*. A jarring thing to remember.

Daddy was very devout, and each night as we were gathered at the dinner table, he would read the Bible aloud. I believed in God because he did, and I memorised large portions of Scripture because it made him proud of me, but I haven't given it much thought for years—I don't know what to think about God now, and, if he exists, whether he would care for a filthy Nazi whore like me.

I remember. It was Nebuchadnezzar. *He was driven from men, and did eat grass as oxen, and his body was wet with the dew of heaven, till his hairs were grown like eagles' feathers, and his nails like birds' claws.*

Well, I haven't descended quite that far into madness, but I have certainly been driven out into solitude.

I have stopped feeling sick now from not having my pills. I still crave them, but at least I seem to have gotten over the worst of the physical effects of going off them. There is no more alcohol for me to swill, and even if cigarettes were available, I wouldn't use them, for the sake of Young V's lungs.

There *is* a strapping, achingly beautiful man here, though. I've never felt attracted to any of the men in whose arms I have lain in the last ten years, not a single one, not since Josef the baker's son, and my attraction to him was less physical than sentimental.

I didn't think it possible for me to be attracted to men ever again, and here I find myself inexplicably longing for the one man I know doesn't want me anywhere near him.

I find his remote attitude almost as magnetic as his beauty, but I am afraid of him too. There is an anger inside him which has nothing to do with me. But he *believes* it is to do with me.

And, honestly, even with a man so pleasing to look at, even if he did not have that latent anger, I am terrified of the idea of intimacy. But I think about it all the same.

Yesterday and today I have come out from under the wagon a bit and walked around the Varelas' little camp, not venturing further than to the creek for water. My feet are toughening, which is good, as I am unlikely to have any sensible shoes in the near future. I feel stronger than I have in years, as though the air is cleansing me with every breath: cleansing out the years of hurt and replacing it with something pure and unadulterated. Still, I fear each unfamiliar rustle and splash and fleeting shadow. Will I ever truly relax again? This place is remote, but is it remote enough? Is anywhere?

I sat with my toes in the water for a while in the afternoon. The breeze lifted my hair with invisible fingers, letting the cool air in close to my scalp. The glassy lake mirrored the snow-capped, jagged teeth of the Andes in the distance. They were fierce, but stunning too. I was a very small organism in a giant world: insignificant, really.

Insignificant, but also the bullseye of a Nazi target—if only they knew where to begin looking. And surely they *would* track me down. They could hardly afford not to. I kept remembering those shoes I kicked off back in Tres Lagos, and my insides curled up in terror. Mauritz had only recently bought me this outfit and those shoes, and he and Erich would both recognise them as mine. I should have stuffed them in my purse and brought them along.

I should have let Old V know the extent of the danger he could be in by having me here, but not telling him meant *I* could avoid thinking about it too much myself.

I kept sifting through the contents of my purse. So odd, that these few paltry bits and pieces were all I had left to my name: the half-finished pair of black socks, my toothbrush and lipstick and hairpins. Nothing *useful*.

What to do with myself? I wanted to help around camp, but at the same time I didn't want to touch anything. Mauritz had intensified my already healthy fear of spoiling something important. Old V might not punish me with burns, but there was that anger. I did not want him to raise his voice at me again.

In the end I went back to my bed under the wagon. As long as I was on my bed, I could not possibly get into any trouble, and I felt safer there than I did out in the open.

Anton

WE CAME BACK FROM our tramp this evening and Miss Mayer was on her bed under the wagon. She's always on her bed, it seems. Does she ever move while we're gone?

I went over to her and sat beside her and asked her.

She looked surprised, and she said, "Not much."

"Why?"

She crawled out and sat beside me, her back against the wheel of the wagon. When she finally answered she seemed to be talking to herself. "I'm not used to freedom."

"Were you kidnapped and held hostage?" I asked, impressed with the idea that here was a person who'd had something *really exciting happen to her.*

"You might call it that, only they weren't holding me for ransom or anything. Don't look so starry-eyed, kid, capture is horrible." Her voice went hard all of a sudden. "It was me speaking Czech they wanted to exploit. And also other things they made me do that I don't want to talk about." She shuddered, and I scooted up next to her and laid my head against her shoulder. She felt stiff as a board to lean on, but I hoped she might put her arm around me, so I left my head right there and waited.

"They put me in Theresienstadt for six months. That was a ghetto, a prison place where they put Jews for a while before sending them off to another camp to kill them. I was there so they could punish me for..." Her lips quivered. "For trying to defend a Jew. After that, I went to live with Mauritz, and ever since, I've almost never been allowed to leave the house. Sometimes not even my room. For longer than you've been alive, kid, that's how I've had to live. Don't you ever get the idea it's exciting." She sounded like she might cry. "So you see I don't know what to do with myself. It scares me, not having someone telling me exactly what to do and not do all the time. I'm afraid of hurting someone. People were killed when the Nazis got me, and I—"

She didn't finish her sentence for a long time. "It's my fault," she whispered. "I killed them."

Raymond

I OVERHEARD WHAT SHE said, and decided to move in and make sure she wasn't giving my son an education in things I'd rather not have him know at this age. At the sight of me, the light in her eyes winked out into shadow and she crumpled. She is terrified of me.

As I approached, she stood, backing away a little, trembling, avoiding eye contact.

"What are you telling my son?" I asked, trying to maintain calm in my voice.

"I asked her why she sits on her blanket all the time," Anton answered before she could open her mouth.

"And why does she?" I asked, my eyes fixed on her.

"She says she's afraid of being free."

The woman nodded in agreement.

"You said you killed someone," I said. "Give me one reason why I should trust you around my son."

She wavered. Her expression filled with unspeakable pain, and her eyes with tears, as she whispered, "I can't."

"What did you do for the Nazis?" I asked again, stepping closer. She looked away.

"I translated for interrogations," she said. I could scarcely make out her words. "I speak Czech and German and English. I tried to save my own skin by cooperating with them, until—until someone I loved was brought in, and I couldn't do it. So they made me watch as they killed him, and they sent me to prison. They broke me there."

I stepped even closer, spluttering. She seemed frozen in place, and my noises made her hug herself as if she might disintegrate from my anger. She closed her eyes and began speaking again, an odd monotonous sing-song.

"I'm a murderer, a collaborator, a traitor to my country and my family. I think perhaps you should shoot me right here and dump me in the lake and let the blot on Britain's honour be erased."

"No!" Anton's voice piped up, high and anxious. He wrapped his arms around the woman's legs and hung on. "No, Papá, please!"

His obvious terror that I might actually do what the woman suggested tore at my heart. She was muttering again.

"Or I should go find where you keep those knives and end it myself. But I am afraid. *I am so broken.*"

After asking me to shoot her, the woman neither spoke to Anton or me, nor did she get off her bed except to go to the bathroom. When she did, she staggered as though weighed down by some unutterable burden. She cried almost constantly: sometimes softly, sometimes not. Anton faithfully took her meals and cups of water. She drank the water, very slowly, but she barely touched the food.

Initially, I assumed it was a hunger strike, some form of revenge or manipulation, but after ten days, I began to think there was something really wrong. I had behaved abominably, I knew. Anton's accusing eyes when I shouted at the woman, when she asked me to shoot her, haunted me. There was a barrier between him and me that had never existed before, and I was displeased with myself for having wounded him, as well as ashamed at the way I'd treated her.

I did not sleep well, remembering the days immediately following Antonia's death, when I started drinking too much and sealed myself off from people. My mother came from London to care for Anton. I just couldn't do it. I was so miserable and bereft, I didn't want to eat either. I made myself, but it was one of the hardest things I'd ever had to do, forcing that food past the strangling knot of my guilt.

It flooded back into me unbidden, the guilt and regret I had buried and denied for so long under the guise of bereavement.

The Germans killed Antonia: technically it was true, but there had been more to it than that. I hid my face in my hands and tried to stuff all of it back down, but this time it wouldn't go. It wanted me to not make the same mistake twice. I didn't want to make the same mistake twice. I breathed deeply, thinking hard.

This woman is dangerously close to giving up; perhaps she has already given up. If she dies, it will be my fault, because my anger and bitterness set her off when what she needed was kindness and compassion.

I'll go to her. I don't know what I'll say, but I need to say something.

Leni

WHEN I WAS A little girl we had a very old cat. One day, she wandered off and never came back. Daddy said animals know when their time is up, that she had gone away to find some place to die alone and undisturbed.

I didn't know how many days had gone by since the altercation with Old V. I could hardly move, I was so weak from hunger, and my heart hurt so intensely I felt certain I could not live much longer. I had never known such pain. Mauritz was not there to burn me for crying, so I surely let out a decade's worth of suppressed tears. Escaping Mauritz should have been an automatic improvement to my life; instead it was turning out to be a disaster.

If I could have moved, I would have done like our cat and gone somewhere solitary to let myself die. My time was up. I was sure of it.

Something rustled nearby, and my heart turned to ice.

"Miss Mayer?"

It was Old V's voice. I couldn't see him in the darkness, but I sensed his presence. He had never addressed me by any name at all before, and tears stung my eyes.

I wanted to turn over and hide my face, but I hadn't the strength for movement.

He cleared his throat and proceeded hesitantly. "Miss Mayer, I wanted to speak with you. Are you awake?"

"Yes." I didn't know if he could hear me. I couldn't hear myself.

"May I turn on the torch?"

I didn't answer. I couldn't.

He switched it on and set it on the ground between us. I closed my eyes so I did not have to look at him.

"Miss Mayer, I am concerned about you not eating."

It took me ages to summon the ability to rasp out, "Why do you care?"

He sat silent a moment. "I may be an ungracious and inhospitable man, but—" he hesitated. "After my wife died, I felt much like you do now, see. Only—I had the ability to force myself to eat, and I don't think you do. I don't want you to die out here."

That would *be an inconvenience, wouldn't it,* I thought, but aloud I whispered, "I don't want to live. I want oblivion." A sob escaped my throat. "I want my daddy."

The next thing I knew, Old Varela had gathered me into his arms, held me close. The dam of my emotion burst open afresh and I wept bitterly. He rocked me. "Shh—shh," he whispered into my hair, stroking it with his big hand. "Let it all go."

I don't know how long I sobbed in his arms, but it seemed forever. I didn't understand how my body could produce any more tears, since I'd cried for days. But at last, with a little shudder, I gave out. I think perhaps I dozed; I dreamed briefly of my father, something vague and shadowy that slipped through my fingers when I tried to grasp it later.

Old Varela lay me back on my blanket and stood. "I'll be back," he said, and took the torch and disappeared into the darkness.

When he returned a few minutes later he sat beside me and spread out a small cloth. In spite of myself, curiosity rose and I looked. He'd brought an apple and some other things. He sliced a piece of the apple and held it to my lips.

"Open up," he said. It was a command. I opened my mouth and he dropped it in. I held it there on my tongue, tasting the sweetness for a few seconds before I chewed it and swallowed it. He had another piece waiting, and then a bit of cheese.

"Do you have any skills?" he asked me, after I'd downed the third bite of cheese. "Anything you can do to earn a living for yourself once you're back in the real world?"

I let out a hollow hard laugh, but he pressed on, giving me another slice of apple. "What did you want to grow up to do when you were little? Surely you had some idea. Attend university? Have a family?"

I'll never have a family. "I wanted to be a doctor, like Daddy," I confessed after a while.

"You still could be," he said, quietly. More apple.

"Who would want me caring for them?" I spat out bitterly, then spent minutes coughing on the apple when it went down the wrong way. "I can't even take care of myself."

"Right now you can't," he agreed. "But that will change in time."

Was he exhibiting faith in my potential or reminding me of my inferiority? I couldn't decide. I accepted more apple. Speech came more easily now.

"My skills are few," I said. "I'm not sure I should tell you what they are. If Mauritz found out, that would be the end of me."

"He won't find out from me," he said.

I considered. "Languages," I said. "I spoke English and German always, and I picked up Czech from our summers in Austria. Daddy taught me a good bit of Latin. I could have been fluent in Spanish in two weeks, if they'd ever allowed me to hear it spoken. I used to speak French; we learnt it in school, but I had nobody to speak it to after I wasn't around my teacher, so I lost it. I think Mauritz knows I'm a language sponge."

"What are the skills he doesn't know of?"

"Wireless." Automatically I launched into my old familiar protocol. *2E-G2-MM calling...* I laughed again. "A lot of good that can do me. They thought at first I would be a *wunderkind*, Mama and Daddy did. I was reading at four, and sending Morse code by the time I was seven, and assembling and disassembling my own radios by the time I was nine. And then I stalled out. There was nothing about radios I didn't know and no problem with them I couldn't fix, but ask me to do practical maths or defend an opinion or have a normal conversation with a classmate, and I stuttered into a hopeless muddle." I took a deep breath. "All I have of value now is my pearl set, and once I've pawned those off, well." I shrugged. "As you kindly pointed out the other day, I shouldn't have too much trouble finding a way to earn money."

"I shouldn't have said that," he said quietly. "It was very rude of me. I'm sorry."

I stared at him, and he went on hastily, "I shouldn't make assumptions, I mean. I don't know you. Not really. The sound of the German when you first spoke triggered something nasty in me. It's... quite impossible for me to forget what they... what happened to my wife."

"Your son told me she was killed in a bombing."

"Yes," he answered simply.

"That would have been hard for you, with him still so tiny."

He ignored my remark. "You won't have to sell your pearls. Or yourself. You're a woman. Not a thing."

I could not believe this was the same man who had called me a Nazi whore.

Or perchance all this was only a dream, as I hallucinated my way into the slumbers of death.

Raymond

SHE FADED QUICKLY AFTER she'd had half an apple and the bits of cheese last night, but as she drifted off, she whispered something that gave me chills. It sounded like, "It wasn't the ghetto that broke me. It was my baby. They killed it."

I doubt it would be prudent to mention it again, much as I would like her to clarify. I'm not sure she meant to tell me that. I'm not sure she meant to tell me any of what she said last night.

Today, instead of sending her breakfast with Anton, I took it myself. I had made up my mind I would not let her continue like this. If I had to bully her into eating to keep from having a dead woman on my hands, then I *would* bully her, and Anton is no good at bullying anyone.

In the thin morning light the woman looked positively deathly. She had felt like nothing at all in my arms last night, nothing but bones, light and fragile as a bird. It was a miracle she hadn't died already, I thought. I sat beside her and watched her drawn, slumbering face for a minute, then I shook her and said, as amiably as I could manage, "Sit up. You're going to eat breakfast if I have to force it down your throat."

Her eyes fluttered open. She has pale eyes, a sort of colourless grey, and for a minute she didn't seem to know who I was. She made a moaning noise and turned her head away, so I set down the plate, lifted her up, propped her against me, and held out a piece of buttered bread with jam.

"I'm not hungry," she said petulantly.

"Not so," I contradicted. "You're *so* hungry by now you don't know it anymore, that's all. Now open up."

It was akin to dragging an unwilling cat out from under a bed, getting her to eat that piece of bread and bowl of porridge, swallow that mug of tea, finish the apple I'd cut open for her in the night. It took the better part of two hours and every ounce of my patience before she finally finished, and then I made her come out of her cave under the wagon. Anton brought her blankets over for her, and I said I'd let her lie down again *if* she would come into the sunshine. She didn't argue. I think breakfast had exhausted her almost as much as it had me.

Anton and I didn't leave camp that day. At lunchtime we went through the same routine, only that time I let Anton help. She resisted less when he offered her food.

Leni

FOR THE LAST SEVERAL meals Old V has force-fed me, and if I'd had the energy to be angry at him, I would have been. I half wish he'd slap me, or shout at me again. Did I dream he held me the other night? Or was that a dream of Daddy? It's all fuzzy. I feel like we spoke to each other, Old V and me, but I can't seem to remember now what either of us said.

At ten or eleven years old, I used to have nightmares—horrible things about giant spiders, usually. Daddy, a light sleeper, would hear me crying, come hold me in his arms and sing to me, even though I was probably too old to cry over bad dreams. He knew dozens of hymns by heart, and like a good Lutheran, his favourite was *A Mighty Fortress*. Usually he sang that to me, and he would make me sing it with him, using the German words as often as the English version. By the end of the song, I wouldn't be afraid anymore.

For the first year or so after Mauritz captured me, through the time at Theresienstadt at least, I would still whisper the words to myself in the lonely darkness. But after the Disastrous Event following my release from Theresienstadt, I stopped singing it, and until this moment I've not given it another thought. How did it go? *A mighty fortress is our God, a bulwark never failing?*

I stumbled through it in my head, silently mouthing the words, searching the recesses of my brain for lines gone missing. I can't remember it all.

> *The Prince of darkness grim—*
> *We tremble not for him;*
> *His rage we can endure,*
> *For lo! his doom is sure,—*
> *One little word shall fell him.*

That part I remember. It was my favourite part of the hymn, because Daddy's words would banish all the evil creatures of my dreams, just like that.

Words are such beautiful things. And also such terrible things.

Lago Viedma

20 December 1951 - 1 January 1952

RAYMOND

MY MOTHER AND SISTERS tried countless times to set me up with girls, *the way Anton continues to do*, only to have one girl after another huff away out of annoyance or sheer boredom. I was dull and all I cared for was butterflies, they said.

Antonia didn't particularly care for butterflies, either, but she saw deeper into me and pursued the man she said lurked under my shy, scholarly exterior. Perhaps it was her transient quality, her quicksilver beauty like my beloved butterflies, that made me fall so hard for her. Whatever it was, she seemed content to put up with me. Fortunately Anton is willing to put up with me, too.

He and I have gone out every day since Miss Mayer has gotten on her feet again. I feel conflicted between the sheer relief of escaping her—pretending she isn't here at all, and it is just Anton and me as originally planned—and the fear that she will die or go absolutely bonkers out here.

She seems stable enough for the moment. We don't talk much. I make sure she does not forget to eat. I try not to say anything that will set her off, which is difficult. She's stopped trying to look civilised. I don't think she's brushed her hair in two weeks. She still doesn't look well, but she's no longer on the verge of death, so perhaps she can safely stay alone.

As a precaution, however, I have locked up the knives.

We have found some of the places where the butterflies are, and each day Anton and I visit them. Today we sat on the bank of the lake eating our lunch and looking across to the glacier, which I would have visited sooner had it just been the two of us.

"Papá," Anton said. "Miss Mayer needs shoes. Couldn't you go into town and get her some?"

I didn't answer immediately. The nearest town, El Calafate, is a day and a half's walk away from here, and I hadn't any idea if they'd have suitable footwear in the right size. As if sensing my hesitation, he said, "I measured her foot the other day whilst she was sleeping. We could call into town on the wireless and ask if they have boots in her size."

"We could ask," I agreed tentatively.

"But if they have some, you *will* go get them, won't you?"

I sighed. My son's unconditional love for all humanity is so like his mother, and even I knew it would be unacceptable for the woman to spend the next five months barefoot.

"Anton, I'm not sure it would be wise to leave you alone with her," I said, since that was truly the weight on my heart.

"She's been fine for a while now," he pointed out.

"I'll think about it," I said.

"And you could find out if anyone's looking for her, too!"

"I'll think about it."

Anton had a point. And boots could be a peace offering, I suppose. She is terrified of me, and I've done little to lessen her fear. I'm not smooth with women. I never have been. There are reasons why I was thirty-four before I ever had a girl, and reasons why I've never found another. I discovered at a very early age that dead butterflies and tree bark and empty wasp nests are not the kinds of gifts young ladies find endearing, nor is having a funeral for a dead badger picked up off the road considered a hot date.

Antonia was one of a kind. I keep telling Anton nobody will ever replace her. He doesn't believe me, but it is true. How could I ever marry again? Besides, I can't talk to women. Even at work, I am at my worst when I have to interview women. Without talking, a friendship would be doomed, let alone a love affair.

ANTON

LAST NIGHT AFTER WE got back to camp, I helped Papá with the radio, and Miss Mayer was immediately interested. She even sat up! She didn't say a word, but her eyes got bright, like she wanted to get her hands on the machine. She looked suddenly much younger.

"Do you like radios too?" I asked.

She nodded, and came a few steps closer and laid her hand lightly on the box. "I haven't been near one of these in years." She looked at me, grabbed my hand impulsively, and tapped my name in Morse code onto my palm. I grinned and tapped back. *I like you.* She looked very pink and pleased by that. Well, pinker than she already was from sunburn.

"Run along, you two," Papá told us, waving his hand at Miss M and me. "I don't need everyone breathing down my neck."

I took Miss M's hand and walked with her into the trees, Little Cat dangling by his tail from my free hand.

Raymond

I WATCHED ANTON AND the woman walk away together, saw the trusting and casual way he took her hand and skipped along beside her. Then I looked at the radio, and back at them again, and thought to myself: *The Nazis* will *be looking for her. They aren't likely to find her here, if I don't leave any trace of our whereabouts.*

The radio was definitely a trace of our whereabouts.

I didn't call El Calafate. I contacted Señora Ríos instead, and fortunately for me, she replied within a few minutes.

> **Me:** Señora Ríos, this is Raymond Varela.
> **Señora Ríos:** Are you safe and well?
> **Me:** Yes.
> **Señora Ríos:** The woman with you. Doing better?
> **Me:** A little.
> **Señora Ríos:** She left her shoes here.
> **Me:** Burn them. If anyone comes along asking for her, say nothing.
> **Señora Ríos:** Someone came two days ago asking. Did not know where you were. Had nothing to tell them. They went south.
> **Me:** Did they question anyone else?
> **Señora Ríos:** They went to every house.
> **Me:** They are escaped Nazi criminals. She has been their hostage. Am trying to decide what to do with her.
> **Señora Ríos:** Will say nothing to anyone.
> **Me:** Have to go to El Calafate. Woman staying here with Anton. Leaving instructions for A to call if needed. If I am not back in five days, can you come collect A and woman,

keep them at your house? Have coordinates, will leave with A.
Señora Ríos: Will check in on them. But Helsingfors is closer. I'll tell you how to contact them...

After we signed off, I sat there for a long time brooding. I didn't want to worry the woman with the news that she was, in fact, being looked for. I crumpled my transcription of the conversation and tossed it into the fire. If I ran into any Nazis in El Calafate, and they recognised me from Bariloche, I would in all likelihood not be coming back. But if I took the woman and Anton along, I would be putting *them* at great risk. No, better and safer for them to stay behind. I doubted they'd have noticed me at the station in Bariloche, let alone connected me with their missing hostage, but one never knew.

Leni

YOUNG V AND I scaled a rock to its flat top, from which we had a most splendid view of the countryside around us. I have noticed, since going shoeless, how much more surefooted I feel. It's as if having my toes out in the open helps me have a better sense of things. My toes could grip easily to the warm rock. I was very pleased with myself about this.

The scenery is stark and incredible. There is the brown, desert-like landscape going one direction, like what the American West always looked like in the cowboy pictures we sometimes sneaked out to see when I was little.

But face the other direction, and it is saw-toothed mountains, and snow, and ice, and vast lake.

Two worlds. The desert is my life with Mauritz. The mountains are my life now. Both of them are terrifying to me, and the solitude is immense.

Anton flopped onto his stomach and made his cat walk to the edge of our rock. "Don't go too far, Little Cat," he dictated. "It's a long ways down. You might break your leg!"

"What's its name?" I asked. He rolled onto his back and lifted the cat into the air.

"He's never had a proper name. I called him Little Cat when I was a baby because Papá's cat Mariposa was 'Big Cat'. That's all the name he's ever had."

"Where'd he come from?"

"My mum made him before I was born. He was supposed to look like Mariposa, except her tail was fluffy like a fox and Mum didn't know how to make a fluffy tail out of velveteen, so she gave him an ordinary tail instead." He put the cat into my outstretched hand and I took it, stroking its worn little nose and thread whiskers.

"You miss your mother, don't you?"

"I guess so." He gave a shrug. "I don't remember her. I was only seven weeks old."

We sat in companionable silence for a while, and I thought of the shadowy wife and mother who had crafted this little toy for a son she barely had time to know. What had she been like? What type of woman would go for a person like Inspector Raymond Varela?

I reached for a handful of gravel and leant forward, arranging my bits of rock in a tidy line. One for a dot, three for a dash. *I'm better at Morse code than at talking.*

He grinned and took his own handful of gravel. *It's okay,* he spelled back.

Do you have pictures of your mother?

I do back at camp. I'll show you sometime.

I'd like that.

Then, after a few minutes, he spelled out: *Can I teach you Spanish?*

Yes, I replied immediately. I'd listened intently to every word the boy and his father exchanged, and I had the rhythms and the accent very solidly in my head. I just needed the key to unlock my understanding, and I'd been afraid to ask for it.

I listened intently as he said, "*Yo me llamo Anton. Mucho gusto.*" I repeated back his words, and he stared at me in surprise. "Wow," he said. "That was perfect."

"What does it mean?" I asked him.

Still staring at me, he said, "I said my name is Anton, nice to meet you. And you say *Igualmente.*"

Again I parroted the word easily. Anton took Little Cat back, stuffed him down his shirtfront, took my hand, and led me back the way we had come, all the while handing phrases and sentences to me that I repeated back—flawlessly, according to my small teacher. It quite entertained him. *¿Cómo vas?* How are you? *Todo bien, vos?* Good, and you?

When we got back to camp, Anton was still playing this game, and I was still mimicking. Old V looked up, startled at the sound of me saying words in Spanish, rudimentary as they might be.

"Papá!" Anton exclaimed gleefully. "She repeats anything I say to her even though she doesn't know what it means!"

"So I hear," he said, passively. I avoided meeting his eyes; I felt self-conscious.

After what seemed like an eternal pause, he spoke. "I'm going to El Calafate at first light tomorrow," he said. "Do you suppose you can manage here?"

Me, manage anything? What a joke.

"We'll manage!" Anton said brightly, slipping his arm through the curve of mine. "Won't we?"

"I suppose we will," I said quietly.

Old V didn't seem to hear. His eyes looked into the far distance, towards the peak I later learnt was named Cerro Norte, whilst his finger drummed absently on his Morse key. Over and over again, one word.

Anton.

Anton.

Anton.

He got up abruptly, found some paper and a pencil, and scribbled furiously for a few minutes before turning his attention back to his son.

"Anton, about ten miles east of here is an *estancia* called Helsingfors. Señora Ríos told me about it, and I'm going to leave you this map. They're closer than she is, if you have any trouble. They have a radio, and I've already contacted them to let them know you are to check in with them morning and evening. These are our coordinates for where we are standing right now—" he went on and I stopped listening, because...

The nearest humans lived *ten miles away*. That was further than Laa An Der Thaya from Staatz (about six miles), or Swallownest from Rotherham (four miles), and both those places had been full of other people all the way. Ten miles of space could accommodate hundreds of thousands at home in England.

Yet here we were, three lone souls, with nobody closer than ten miles.

I was startled out of my concentrated thoughts by Anton poking my arm.

"Sorry," he said, a little sheepish. "I was asking you if you want to try the radio."

Anton

PAPÁ WANTED MISS MAYER to have a go at calling this Helsingfors place. I'm not sure he believed she really could do it. She sat down and touched the Morse key, almost reverently, the way Bobby's mother touches her prayer beads. And she asked, "What call sign should I use?"

Papá told her his, and she put on the headset and we both watched her. She *did* know what she was doing. Her hands shook, but she didn't have to ask any more questions once she got started.

Raymond

THIS COUNTRY IS SO beautiful.

I hope I am not making a mistake, leaving my son alone in the care of that woman, but I have no alternative if I am to surprise her with the boots, as Anton is so determined to do. Taking him along would slow me down too much, and I would then have to fret over whether she was alive or not.

She has settled down since the initial difficulties of her opiate withdrawals wore off. Still, I shall worry constantly that I have done the wrong thing in leaving Anton with her.

In one respect I am glad to be alone. Today would have been Antonia's and my ninth anniversary, and I appreciate the solitude in which to reflect on the simple ceremony at her parents' home and how very, very happy we were. I want her back so much.

Antonia would have welcomed this woman with open arms and no questions or conditions, the way I welcome animals into my domain.

Animals I trust. Animals are, with a few exceptions, predictable. They are intelligent but simple creatures who will trade services with you if you know how to go about it. A carrier pigeon, like my father had in his war, will carry messages of import. A chicken will provide you with eggs: the better food and more love one provides them, the better the eggs. A cat will stop mice invading your home and bless you with warm cuddles and purrs on a cold winter's night. (Oh, Mariposa, I miss you still.)

Humans are different. Humans, with their calculating minds, their capabilities to intentionally hurt and destroy, are far worse than a tiger who kills because it is merely following its instinct. Humans alone on earth have as much power to hurt and destroy as to love and build up.

I've met all kinds of people in my work. I've encountered the depths of depravity as well as true nobility, but out of the thousands of humans with whom I have interacted, only Antonia made me dare to bind my life with that of another person. The love we shared was the purest thing I have ever experienced. She's not at fault for dying, but the Nazis who killed her are. A mindless collective, whose entire reason to exist was for the purpose of destruction, and whose pernicious ideology did not end with the war.

How can we ever hope to stamp it out, when it retreats to remote corners of the globe to grow and strengthen?

Señora Ríos said the men who questioned her went south. Aside from scattered estancias, El Calafate is the next reasonable destination for them. There *are* towns further south, but how dedicated are they to their search? How much do they know?

I suppose I will look for them when I arrive. I will find out what they know and, perhaps, confirm whether the woman's story is true.

Leni

IN THE MORNING, I woke to find Old V already gone. Young V was sitting cross-legged on the ground beside my head, hugging Little Cat. He looked a bit sleepy himself. I felt at an utter loss what to do. Was I expected to feed this boy? I experienced a few minutes of sheer terror at the idea of *responsibility*.

I needn't have worried. Anton, bless him, knew more about cooking at eight than I did at eighteen. He fixed us porridge quite capably and afterwards, as he washed up and I attempted to dry the dishes without dropping them in the dirt, I asked him, somewhat shyly, how he could speak Spanish so well.

"Papá taught me," he said. "Ever since I was a baby. He learnt it at Oxford and made friends with people from the university in Buenos Aires too. Some of them even visited him in England, before I was born. He has photo albums of all the things they found out exploring together."

More biologists, perhaps? "Your name is Spanish," I said. "Varela... it's unusual for England, isn't it?"

"Papá says his great-grandfather or someone came to England from Spain a long time ago with his wife, and they settled in England and their children married English people. Papá is the first one to take an interest in our Spanish ancestors in a long time. Tía Matilda and Tía Lucinda think Papá is cute because of it. He's the youngest. They have children too, but they're all at least ten years older than me, and most have families of their own."

I hadn't considered Old V having any other family. He has sisters? Nieces and nephews? I had difficulty wrapping my head around the idea of him as a doting uncle. "Have you grandparents?"

"Papá's father died at Ypres in 1915, from a gas attack. Papá hardly remembers him, but he liked animals. He was in charge of carrier pigeons, and he helped take care of horses too. Papá's mum is in London now because that is where my tías live. My other gran and granddad live in the north, in Carlisle, and Mum had lots of brothers. I see those cousins sometimes too." Anton prattled on happily about each cousin in detail, and I half-listened as I hugged my knees to myself and looked at the fearsome mountains. Today they were capped in cloud.

"How has your father managed without your mother?" I asked, after he had run out of stories to tell about his cousins.

Another little shrug. "I had a nanny as a baby, but she got married when I was four. Then Carlisle Gran came to stay until I started school. Now Mrs Keaton next door takes in our laundry, and I go to her house or to Bobby's house anytime Papá isn't home from work. Sometimes one of my grans still comes to stay with me, or one of my tías."

He looked at me, and for the first time I noticed his eyes, the rich golden-brown of a hazelnut, a bit incongruous with his tanned face and dark hair. "I wish Papá would marry again. There was a nice lady on the *Mauretania*, a widow with children near my age, but he refused to ask her to dinner or *anything*. He's so stubborn." Anton sighed melodramatically. "Every time I find someone I'd like to have for a mother, he tells me again how nobody can ever take Mum's place, and that's all there is to it."

"You want sisters and brothers too, don't you?" I asked.

He nodded. "That would be nice."

I felt a pang, but before I could respond, he'd gone on talking again. "But what I'd really like would be to come home from school every day and have a mother waiting for me with tea and biscuits. Somebody to talk to. Papá is swell, but he's not much of a mother."

He wasn't looking at me anymore. He lay on his back, shading his eyes as he watched the birds wheeling overhead.

"When is he coming back?" I asked Anton.

"I don't know. Probably not 'til tomorrow."

I asked him if he would show me his mother now, and he brightened right up. He scrambled away to his father's things, rifling around for a few minutes, and came back with two photographs in a cardboard folder. "These are my mum," he said, opening it with obvious pride.

I studied them. One was a gorgeous, hand-tinted studio portrait of a blonde beauty with mischief in her eyes—eyes like Anton's—magnificent in a strand of pearls and red silk. The other showed a much younger-looking Old V with his arms tightly around Anton's mother, both of them beaming in front of a sparkling Christmas tree. My insides wrenched at their obvious joy and delight in each other.

"Their wedding picture," he said.

"She's lovely," I said. *Much, much more beautiful than I.* I turned over the photograph. *Antonia and Raymond—22 December 1942.* He was named for his mother.

December. I looked at the boy and a theory formed in my mind, and I tried coming up with a roundabout way to ask my question.

"That's today," I said.

"It is!" he exclaimed. "I hadn't thought of that!"

"When was her birthday? How old was she in these?"

"In September. She was twenty when she married Papá. He was almost thirty-six. His birthday's in February."

"When's yours?"

"March. I should have been born in April but I came early."

And there I had my answer: simple, electrifying math. Raymond Paragon-of-Virtue Varela had some explaining to do. I handed the photographs back to Little V to put away, and thought to myself with great satisfaction that now Old V would have to stop playing his Moral Superiority Game and be nicer to me.

When Anton came back I cleared my throat. "I'm not much of a cook, I'm afraid."

"That's all right. I know how to make flatbread and we'll put some beans in water to soak."

"I don't know how to build a fire either," I confessed. I felt myself reddening in embarrassment at my ineptitude, but he didn't seem to notice.

"I do," he said easily. "We'll be all right."

His cheery confidence waned as it began to get dusk, though. He brought his bedding near to mine, and we lay down to sleep.

"*Buenas noches*, Señorita Mayer," he said with a shy little smile.

"It's all right if you call me Madeleine," I said, also a little shyly. "Or Leni, if you like."

"Papá would insist I at least call you Tía," he said. "Tía Leni?"

"What does that mean?" I asked, although I suspected I knew.

"It means aunt."

I'd been right. *Tía*, like *Tante* in French and German, or *Teta* in Czech. I thought of my sister Hanna's children, the ones I'd met and the ones I knew nothing about, and whether I was fit for such a lofty role in this lad's life.

I decided I liked it. "All right," I agreed. "*Buenas noches*, little Varela."

I thought he'd gone to sleep, but a few minutes later I heard his voice. "Tía Leni?"

"Yes?"

"What's 'leaving behind an addiction'?"

I hesitated. "Where did you hear that?"

"Papá told Señora Ríos that you were *dejando la adicción*. Addiction to what?"

I'd have thought Anton would ask his father for an answer to that question, and I said as much.

"He wouldn't tell me," Anton said.

I was quiet a moment. Was it wrong to overstep his father's choice to withhold the information? I decided it didn't matter what his father thought. "It means I'd been given a lot of drugs, and my body was dependent on them, and when you suddenly don't have the drugs any more, you feel very sick."

"But drugs are bad," Anton said. "Why would you get sick from not having them?"

"Drugs aren't all bad," I said. "They can do a lot of good, if you use them the proper way. My daddy was a doctor and he taught me about it. My—um, Mauritz—wanted me to be utterly dependent on him, so he gave me too many drugs. Stopping having them all of a sudden is very, very hard. You get to where you have to have them, or you go crazy."

This time Anton was quiet for a long time. Then he said, "But are you feeling better now? Are you all right without them?"

"I guess so," I said. "It will be a long time before I don't want them at all, I guess."

"What would happen if you got some more of the drugs and took them?"

"Then I would feel very, very good for a little while. And then I would feel like sh—very terrible again."

"Oh."

And then he didn't ask any more questions, because he had fallen asleep.

Sometime in the night I became aware of Anton climbing under my blanket with me. "What's the matter?" I asked sleepily.

"I miss Papá," he said, and he buried his face in my neck and I felt the dampness of tears on his cheeks. I laid one of my hands on his thick hair and stroked it lightly. *So soft.*

"I'm here," I whispered back, and in moments we were both asleep again.

Raymond

EL CALAFATE WAS MANY miles from our camp, and the fact was, I would not be getting to the village in one day. I was a fast walker, and I was travelling light and running occasionally to speed up the journey. But I was not as young as I used to be.

Despite the fact that Anton believed I could conquer the world, and it was true that I had always worked hard to be very fit and intended to stay that way as long as I could, I *was* almost fifty, and I was beginning to feel it. This sleeping on the ground thing was something that I would have been considerably better at twenty years earlier, but being here was worth a little morning stiffness.

It gave me time enough to form a battle plan for facing down any Nazis I met; the trouble was I never could decide what that plan should be. When I arrived in the village, I pocketed my glasses, which I knew I had been wearing at the station in San Carlos, put the Nazis out of my head, and sought out someone who could sell me shoes.

"I need a pair of boots for this size," I told the man in the shop. I handed him the tracing my sneaky son had done of the woman's foot, declining to add that the boots were intended for a woman. No point in giving people any information they didn't absolutely need.

The shoe man rummaged around his stock, measuring and muttering to himself. "I don't know you," he said, as he held one boot after another to my sheet of paper. "I know everyone in town, but not you. Are you a tourist?"

"Hardly," I said.

"Your accent says you're from up north." He kept eyeing me, and I knew he was bursting with more questions.

He set three pairs of boots on the counter. "I have two new pairs and one pair that has been used. By a tourist. He paid to use them while he was here and then returned them."

"I'll take the used pair," I said, and handed him the money. He reached for some paper to wrap them and I said, "You needn't bother. I'll carry them in my pack."

"In a hurry, are you?" The shopkeeper's eyes narrowed suspiciously.

"And if I am, what is that to you?"

He counted the money and wrote me a receipt as I stuffed the boots into my pack before speaking again. "Are you with those other strangers that are running about asking questions?" he asked.

"What strangers?"

"It's a long story and you are in a hurry," he said, his eyes glinting.

I shrugged and slung my pack over my back and walked out. I'd act like I didn't care and go on my way.

As I was heading north along the street, I saw a man walking along the opposite side of the road in a swanky black suit, tailored and out of place in this outpost of civilisation, and instantly my guard went up. I knew that even aside from my Spanish, I blended in well here. I didn't have to look at my sweat-stained clothes and unshaven face to know that I was just rough and dark enough to pass as a local. I didn't look out of place one bit.

The black-suited man was definitely out of place.

When he turned into a shop, I turned in after him. It was a shop selling clothes, and I flipped casually through a display of hats, one ear remaining wide open, one eye flicking glances at the man in the black suit. He was silver-blond and spoke Spanish in a clipped, formal way. Although his voice was soft, his accent was the verbal equivalent of clicking heels...or heiling the Führer.

"I am looking for this lady," he told the shop owner, with an embarrassed half-smile and shrug. "Have you seen her?" He opened his wallet and displayed a photo. The shop owner studied it, and I set a hat and two pairs of socks down on the counter and craned my neck to see too. Any nosy local would do the same.

The woman in the photograph was exactly who I expected to see. "Have you seen her?" the man asked again. His pale blue eyes met mine and the shopkeeper's in turn. He looked calm, but I saw the raw terror lurking deep in them, and I almost felt sorry for him.

But only for an instant.

I didn't answer him. I paid for the hat and socks I hadn't planned to buy and walked out without giving the man another sliver of interest.

I kept an eye on him, though. I bought a newspaper and went into a little restaurant with it, eating several fried cheese sandwiches slowly (it is hard to find anything in Argentina to eat that does not have dead animals involved somehow). There were a few other men sitting about talking with one another. I sat alone, absorbed in my sandwiches and newspaper. The man in the black suit came in and ordered coffee, and shortly afterwards another black-suited man joined him at his table. He was bigger, not as tall as me, but bulkier. The two men put their heads together and I listened carefully as they hissed to one another over their coffees.

I couldn't make out all that they were saying, but I got the gist of it. They were looking for a missing woman. A missing woman they called Leni. But the part that interested me more was that the man I'd seen in the shop earlier was clearly panicked.

"I will lose everything," he said.

The younger man grinned maliciously. "I'll say you will," he said. "Idiot."

"I *have* to have Leni," the older man said. "Show her off. Have her on hand to sign things. You know that, Erich. What am I going to tell *him* when we come back without her? Her absence lessens our power."

Erich still smirked. *Unsympathetic, power-hungry ass.* I supposed he stood to benefit somehow if the older man came to a sticky end.

"Your power, not mine. If we don't find her by tonight," Erich said, "we're going back to *him*. And I'll be telling him you're the king of fakes."

"I'm not a fake," the older man snapped. "She's the fake."

"*Your* fake," Erich drawled. "I've been waiting for this moment for so many years, Mauritz. Sooner or later it was bound to come out that she's an imposter."

"If she tells on us," Mauritz said pointedly, "it's not just me who's on the line."

"She won't tell on us," Erich said, arrogant confidence in his voice. "With any luck she's starved to death or gotten mauled by a lion by now. I can't believe she'd have come south, anyway. Maybe a white slaver got a hold of her on the station platform." He guffawed, far too loudly. "She's gone. Gone forever. Dead, or silenced, or whoring to stay alive."

"She can't speak Spanish," Mauritz said. "And nobody's seen the pearls. She hasn't pawned them or sold them to anyone we've talked to."

"Must have had fun with whoever nabbed her," Erich said. His eyes glittered; I could see it even minus my specs. "Why you ever fancied her beats me. She's such a stupid bitch."

"They will kill me," Mauritz said, his face a blank.

"You could still kill yourself first," he pointed out cheerfully. "Honour."

"Honour," Mauritz echoed absently. He took out his wallet and caressed the photo inside it with his thumb. "Those pearls were worth a fortune…"

The other man snorted. "Serves you right, trying to impress *him*."

"I only wanted to bring about the Fourth Reich," said Mauritz, softly.

"So? We will find another way. Or I will, at any rate."

I had finished my sandwiches by this time, and I'd heard enough, so I got up and left the place, stuffing the newspaper into my pack. I hung about a bit, carefully out of sight, until the men exited the cafe and I had assured myself that they were not following or searching for me. Then I walked away from El

Calafate as fast as I could go without actually running, until it had disappeared over the horizon.

All the time I was thinking: *this woman represents power to Mauritz.* She may be just a pawn, but she was—is?—a very powerful pawn. Did she know that? From what she'd told me, she considered herself merely his sex slave and the object of fanatical obsession.

By the time I'd rolled up in my blanket for the night, I still hadn't decided whether to tell the woman I'd seen her mortal enemies, just as she was beginning to be more stable. Now that I had their faces in my memory, I could be on the lookout, and I would shoot either of them without remorse, if they ever got close to our camp.

Butterflies' lives run on reliable cycles of birth and metamorphosis and reproduction and death. They don't respond much to human love, at least not visibly, but the sun shining upon newly emerged wings gives their weak flutterings strength.

I will try to think of Madeleine Mayer as a butterfly, trapped and fighting to be released from her chrysalis. I will think of my son as the warmth that might give her the strength to fly. And when I get back to camp, I will attempt to make peace.

Leni

WHEN I WOKE THIS morning, Anton was still nestled up to me, his cat tucked into one arm, lips slightly parted. I felt surprised at the warmth he'd brought to my sleeping hours.

Since I left England to go to Austria, I've always slept alone. Of all the men in and out of my bed, only Mauritz had any lasting claim on me, and even he never *slept* with me, always leaving me once he'd finished with me for the night. I'm used to having to heap blankets about me to keep myself warm, and the past few weeks of sleeping with only one blanket over me have been rather miserable. But I don't think I woke at all last night from the cold, not with Anton sharing his warmth with me, his weight soothingly pressed to my side.

It occurred to me with a sudden wrenching pang that, had I been allowed to keep my own child, it would be only a little older than Anton was now. Would my child have been like Anton, loving and sweet? Or a cold, calculating monster like whichever Nazi bastard had sired it, the kind of kid who tortures small animals for fun? Tears spilled out of my eyes, and I leant forward and kissed Anton's cheek lightly.

He stirred and put his arm around my neck and snuggled in even closer. I had an irrational urge to tell him about my own baby, but he was only eight. I had already explained my drug addiction; I ought not burden him with anything further. What would I say, anyway?

It is odd, but I think the reason I feel so much more at ease with Anton than with his father is that I never had a chance to really grow up. I was so sheltered and clueless compared to my peers, I was still quite a child when the Nazis caught me. Just a child.

Even though I had been twenty-one.

Twenty-one?

In December, twenty-one means the first day of winter (or summer, if you're in Argentina). Twenty-two means the anniversary of Raymond and Antonia. Twenty-three means...

My heart sank.

It's the twenty-third, I thought. It came into my head abruptly and unbidden, as it did on the twenty-third of almost every month, but with extra cold and pain, because on the twenty-third of December, eleven years ago, Mauritz banished me into Theresienstadt.

Imprisonment itself was less traumatic than the event that landed me there, or the horrors that happened inside the walls less than two weeks later, but the date had been seared into my brain, and I felt myself choking up, unable to stop the memories from pouring through the sluice-gates of my mind.

Mauritz didn't put me there because I was a Jew; it was because I'd been in love with a Jew.

Josef, the son of Laa An Der Thaya's baker, whom I'd known as far back as I could remember, had been the one who awoke in me the first flushes of attraction, the one who gave me shy little smiles, nosegays of wildflowers, and buns with my name iced on in pink frosting. The one who met me at the steps of church to walk me home every Sunday, even though he was Jewish. He was five years older than I was, but he, like Daddy, accepted me with all my imperfections, inviting me to dance with him at village gatherings knowing full well I'd step on his feet or trip over my own.

Nothing serious had passed between us, but the real reason I hadn't gone back to England when war broke out was that he obviously liked me, and I wanted to be close at hand when he got around to asking me to marry him. I knew the day would eventually come. Of course, by the time I arrived in Austria, Jews were being proscribed and excluded, and Josef's family was, I believe, attempting to seek asylum elsewhere—but they were far from wealthy, and it was a difficult process. I suppose I assumed that as soon as they got out, I'd go with them. I don't know what I thought. My mind had a single track: acquire Josef as a husband. The logistics of how I was going to get to that point, when he was more or less a criminal for simply existing, were not something it ever occurred to me that I should try to work out.

When Mauritz captured me, I'd given up any hope of seeing Josef again, let alone building a future with him. But I hadn't seen the last of him.

It would have been better for all of us if I had.

One morning, perhaps a month after I'd been captured, Erich drove me through a wrought-iron gate in a sandstone wall, not far from Mauritz's house. Taking my arm a bit more tightly than necessary, he guided me into a brightly lit office where Mauritz sat behind a gleaming desk, perfectly turned out as usual. In front of the desk sat two comparatively shabby people, and Mauritz explained to me in German that he required my services as translator for these Czech speakers.

I stared him down in silence for a moment, and he asked me calmly if I wished to be given to Erich for convincing. I glanced over my shoulder, where Erich still lounged against the doorframe, handsome in his sulky, bad boy sort of way, grinning insolently at me. He'd been trying to corner me ever since I'd been captured, and I perceived that he would delight in causing me pain.

I couldn't bear the idea of being handed over to that brute, and I gave in to Mauritz's request without further argument. I closed my eyes against the faces of the people I was probably betraying to their deaths, and I translated.

I also translated documents and went around the ghetto, interpreting for people, giving instructions. I knew what it was like there, and it horrified me. But I was so obsessed with living, so I could make it back to England somehow, someday, and so afraid of being handed over to Erich, that I blindly obeyed orders and pretended not to see what was before my eyes.

But conscience stirred back to life when I came to the office as usual on 23 December 1940. I stopped just inside the door, rendered speechless by the sight of Josef, Josef himself and his parents and sister, coats emblazoned with yellow stars that had never before seemed so ominous. My mouth dropped open. The rest of his family did not recognise me, with my perfect hair and elegant clothes and hints of makeup, but Josef took half a step forward and whispered, "Madeleine?"

He knew me.

He didn't need a translator, but he damned us both by voicing his recognition. Damned us all, really, me and him and his whole family.

Mauritz stiffened visibly, and instantly ordered the door locked. From that minute, I was no longer the fashionable, dutiful translator-wife of the Sturmbannführer. I was in trouble. Mauritz got in my face, demanding how I knew these people, while Josef's mother burst into tears, and Josef and his father tried to interpose on my behalf, despite not having a clue what was going on. I turned to Josef and started to tell him what had happened, but Mauritz gave me a hard slap across the face with the back of his hand, something he had never done before, and I shut up, pleading with my eyes to Josef for him to do likewise.

They would have died anyway, Josef's family. Theresienstadt was only a holding camp, and they would have been sent to Auschwitz or somewhere else like it and gassed. Or so I have kept telling myself.

As if anything could make less painful the fact that, within ten minutes of Josef's fatal mistake of saying my name, all of us were outside in the cold, without our coats, while Josef and his family were lined up against a wall. Erich held my head in place, forcing me to watch as Mauritz dispatched them one at a time with perfectly-aimed shots between the eyes. His face was expressionless except for the firm set of his mouth, his eyes ice, his hand completely steady. If I had doubted he had a soul before, I was sure he had none now.

He saved Josef for last, and I tried to reach out and touch him, but Erich held me back. I couldn't make any sound. I wanted to beg for forgiveness, to try to make him understand, tell him I

loved him and would die in his place if I could.
I couldn't make any sound.
Mauritz seemed to take *so long* about that shot. Josef stood straight and unashamed and brave. I did not hear the shot, but I stood so close I saw the explosion of blood, felt it spatter my face.

And then Mauritz holstered his pistol, took me by the arm, and marched me back to the office. For the next two hours, he battered me (mentally and emotionally more than physically) for having loved a Jew. His rage and fury turned me into a snivelling, pitiable puddle. When he saw I harboured no remorse for my illicit attachment, he said, "If you love Jews so much, you can go to prison with them." And he strong-armed me to some of the Theresienstadt guards in the place they called *die Schleuse*, and the next thing I knew I was no longer me, but one more body in a crowd of miserable wretches being processed into the ghetto: stripped of my nice clothes and my beautiful hair, and thrown into a mad world of prison life.

The tears streamed silently down my cheeks. I hadn't noticed Anton was awake until he bent over me. "What's wrong?" he asked. "Did you have a bad dream, Tía Leni?"

Oh, if only it *had* been a bad dream.

Anton being awake forced me to pull myself together more quickly than I might otherwise have done. He taught me a number of things that day. He showed me how to feed the fire at breakfast, and by supper I was able to do it all myself. We lived on beans and flatbread, porridge and raisins, because it was all he knew how to make. As the day came to an end, and Anton leant yawning against my shoulder, he murmured, "I wonder where Papá is right now."

"Perhaps he'll be back when you wake in the morning," I said.

"Can I sleep by you again tonight?" he asked.

"Sure, if you like," I said.

The fire was dying and the stars were coming out as we lay there, with two blankets beneath us (such luxury!) and two on top and the stuffed cat between us. Anton reached for my hand and tapped onto it. He was slow and his spelling was wobbly, but I understood him.

I like you, Tía Leni. I'm glad I'm not alone.

I took his hand and answered, taking care to slow myself to his pace. *I'm glad you're here too.*

He smiled, turned onto his side, and fell asleep in moments.

My thoughts and my heart raced. I had never had a chance to interact with a child in this way, and I was becoming terribly fond of him. *Don't get too attached*, I told myself. *You'll soon have to leave him behind.*

But oh, how powerful maternal instinct is. I *needed* to protect and care for this boy with an intensity I had not known I possessed.

I know little about parenting aside from having watched my own parents; caring for babies had never been something I'd done growing up. Everyone had worried I'd drop their children, and they'd had a point. Yet here was Anton, and I found myself desperate to win his trust and affection. The idea of having to leave him someday cut like a knife to my heart.

The tears for Josef which I'd dammed up in the morning broke through, and I cried myself to sleep.

In the morning, still no Old Varela tramped into view, and as we ate last night's leftover beans for breakfast (kept cold overnight in a container submerged in lake water), Anton seemed unusually morose.

"Tomorrow is Christmas," I said, trying to cheer the boy, who clearly worried for his father's safety. "What do you usually do for Christmas?"

"Nothing at home," he said. "We take turns going to see my different grans. This year it would have been Carlisle Gran's turn to have us. London Gran's Christmases are very fancy and pretty, but also kind of fussy. Carlisle Gran's Christmases are more exciting. She always has something unusual to stir things up a bit."

When Anton had exhausted his tales of Unconventional Actions of Carlisle Gran at Christmastime, the sadness returned to his eyes and his lips trembled. I knew he was trying hard to keep back the tears. He missed that father of his in the way I had missed mine in the early days of my captivity, desperate for reassurance that someone still loved me. Anton needed distracting badly.

I glanced around the camp and said, "Do you know how to make paper snowflakes?"

Anton

TODAY IS CHRISTMAS EVE, and Papá is still not back. I am trying not to worry. Tía Leni is doing all she can to distract me. I've been teaching her Spanish words and she's been testing my Morse code, and we've been so busy doing things together, I haven't taken the time to write for a couple of days.

It is odd to have Christmas in the summertime. Tía Leni took my scissors and some paper, which she cut into squares and folded a certain way to make paper snowflakes. She showed me how to do it, but mine are not so pretty as hers. She made me one that had the letter A in the pattern, and one for Papá with butterflies on, but she said she didn't want to give it to him herself. I do wish he'd be nicer to her. She's so scared of him, and he's so nice *really*. I wonder why he has to be so grouchy to her. Anyway, we made a lot of snowflakes, and she and I hung them from the notro bush near camp. It's a pity it's not blooming. The red flowers would make it look so festive. Oh well.

In the evening, as Tía Leni and I took a walk to the big rock where we could see far into the distance, we saw someone walking. I was sure it was Papá, and I wanted to run to him, but she reminded me I'd probably start wheezing. So I just bounced right there until he got closer, and we hurried back to camp to wait for him. Well, I hurried; she kind of hung back. Anyway, as soon as he came close, I did run, and he dropped his pack and swung me around in circles and kissed me.

Then he put me down and I took his hand and ran to camp, dragging him along behind. "Tía Leni, Tía Leni! Papá, come look at the tree!"

Leni

I HUNG BACK WITH my hands clasped behind me, not daring to make eye contact with Old V, especially after the look of surprise on his face when he heard Anton calling me *Tía Leni*. He looked even bigger than I remembered, and considering how much closer I felt to Anton now, the sensation of distance between his father and me seemed proportionately magnified. I had felt free to move about when it had been only me and Anton. A kid posed no threat.

But his father was another thing entirely. I feared Old V's obvious ability to overpower me and pulled back into my shell, quaking as I seated myself out of the way, hugging my knees to my chest, trying to stay as small and inconspicuous as possible.

"What took you so long, Papá?" Anton demanded, and his father laughed.

"Did you expect me to run all the way there and back?"

"Didn't you?"

"Well, I did run a good deal of the way," admitted Old V. Anton dragged him over to the notro bush full of snowflakes, and Old V admired them. "Did you make all of these?" he asked.

"Tía Leni made most of them," Anton said. "She didn't draw on the paper first, either, like I had to, she just took her scissors and snip snip and she did it *so fast*. This one is mine with the letter A in, and this one has kitties in, and the butterfly one she made for you, only she won't give it to you herself because you're scary."

I felt myself blushing deeply as Old V turned to look at me, only I wasn't where I had been the last time he'd looked at me. "Where'd she go?" he asked, his eyes scanning the camp until they landed on me. I wondered if the raw terror coursing through me was palpable. I flinched away, but when he spoke, his tone held no threat. "Thank you," he said quietly. "It's lovely." Then he reached into his pack and took out a parcel and held it out. "This is for you."

I couldn't move. He closed the distance between us in a few steps and I took it from him, hesitant, tentative.

"Open it!" Anton begged, bouncing up and down.

"Do you know what's in it?" I asked him, my voice quavering, my fingers trembling on the twine that bound it.

"Of course I do," he said, his grin wide and bright. His father rested one hand on the boy's shoulder and they both watched as I fumbled with the twine until I'd undone it, and I pulled aside the newspaper, clapped my hand over my mouth, and burst into tears.

He'd brought me a pair of boots.

I raised my face, opening my mouth to make words but unable to produce them. Anton came and hugged me, and Old V said, "His idea," gesturing to the boy.

"But *you* walked all those miles to fetch them," I managed to choke out.

"Only about two marathons," Anton said dismissively, lifting the boots out and pushing them at me. "Try them on!" he said, as excited as if he'd just been given a million pounds.

"Wait," his father said, and he pulled something else out of his pack. "Here, have some socks that will fit you better than mine, and a hat to keep the sun off your face."

I was overwhelmed. I had expected moodiness and anger to return with Old V, and instead he bestowed only kindness. I felt rooted to the spot.

Anton took over. He washed and dried my feet again, slipped them into the socks, and then the boots. They fit perfectly, and I sobbed shamelessly at the simple joy of having my feet properly shod. When he'd finished lacing them for me, his father held out a hand to help me up. His hand was warm and his grip firm, but unexpectedly gentle. I stood and took a few tentative steps. They weren't new boots, but in very good keep, and already broken in.

Anton's face clouded with concern. "What's the matter, Tía

Leni?" He turned to his father. "She was fine all the time you were gone."

Old V's face twitched at the unintended accusation of his son's words.

I stuffed my fist to my mouth and plucked up my courage. "Thank you," I whispered in the general direction of Old V, and then asked, haltingly, "Does this mean you don't intend to send me away after all?"

"If you're determined to stay, I guess you stay," he said. There was neither pleasure nor displeasure in his tone. I dared at last to peek at those eyes that had previously avoided meeting mine, and their expression made me oddly hungry for something I couldn't define. For a long time we stood there, not moving. But I didn't have time to dwell on what that something might be just now, as he had a gift for Anton too: a book called *The Wool-Pack* which he'd brought from England, and for an hour Anton read to us from it before time for bed. He kissed his father good night, then he came and gave me a hug and kiss too. I was so surprised that again I teared up.

"*Buenas noches*, Tía Leni," he whispered.

"*Buenas noches*, Anton," I whispered back.

And then I lay awake, alone again, huddled into my blanket, staring at the stars, hugging my boots the way Anton hugged Little Cat.

I'd nothing to give either of them. It felt so dreadfully unfair.

I'm not used to people giving me gifts with no strings attached.

You do not exist, Mauritz reminded me, anytime I tried to declare myself an autonomous being. *You are expendable. Your life is cheap.* And it was true, since legally, I was dead.

My parents would have been notified, the mangled body wearing my clothes would have been taken back to Laa An Der Thaya and interred in the family plot.

My relationship with Mauritz had never been about *my* pleasure or convenience. Any time I felt genuine longing for his affection, his touch, he grew distant. Reminding me who was in control. (Not me.)

Old V might say the words, "You're a woman," but that didn't make them true. Words mean nothing. Do they?

Old V sat on the opposite side of the fire cleaning his boots as I lay there, hugging my own boots and watching the flames.

Suddenly I became aware he had come and dropped on one knee beside me, looking into my eyes with concern. I flinched back instinctively, but he didn't touch me.

"Don't be afraid," he said. "I've not been very pleasant, I admit, but I'm not going to hurt you."

I stared at him, the gruff, suspicious policeman who had inspired in me both lust and fear over the last few weeks. It was not the policeman looking at me now, nor yet the tender father I saw interacting with Anton: he was another human, and he had human sympathy for my plight.

"Thanks for my snowflake," he said. He held out his hand, a little stiffly, and I put mine into it, a little hesitantly. "I'm sorry," he said. "For—for being a pig."

His hand was still warm and still strong, and I wished he would never let mine go.

In the morning Anton awoke early, bouncing through camp like an India rubber ball. Between my unspeakable memories and the unsettling emotion I'd seen in Old V's eyes, I hadn't slept well. I did not want conversation. I curled deeper into my blanket and fur wrap, but Anton brought me a steaming cup of tea, and for his sake I rallied and sat up to drink it. Warm and good, I felt it flooding my veins with a curious sort of intensity. I still craved cigarettes and alcohol and opiates at times (though all three cravings had lessened recently), but this simple cup of tea brought me more pleasure than any drink I had tasted for a very long time. I marvelled at it.

I might be of Austrian extraction, but my English upbringing does appreciate a perfect cup of tea.

I lay back down after I finished the tea and stared at the sky, at the birds above, listening to the absence of man-made noise.

I thought about books I had read where people say they feel the earth turning, and I closed my eyes to see if there was anything to it. I couldn't be sure, but something did make me distinctly dizzy as I conducted my experiment.

When I opened my eyes, Anton had returned, dancing and singing me an old Christmas carol I hadn't heard since I'd left England.

> *Here we come a-wassailing*
> *Among the leaves so green;*
> *Here we come a wand'ring,*
> *So fair to be seen!*
> *Love and joy come to you,*
> *And to you glad Wassail too.*
> *And God bless you and send you a happy new year,*
> *And God send you a happy new year.*

I hadn't sung in ages, but I answered Anton anyway.

> *We are not daily beggars*
> *That beg from door to door,*
> *But we are neighbours' children,*
> *Whom you have seen before...*

Anton laughed and reached for my hands and pulled. "Get up," he urged me. "Papá's made something extra special for breakfast!"

And indeed he had. He had broken into the sugar rations and made us a delicious coffee cake. How he managed it with such a primitive cookstove, I have no idea. He really could be magic with food, even if the everyday staples—flatbread and beans, apples and potatoes and porridge and cheese—couldn't be called *normal*.

The cake had chopped apples and raisins in, and a delicate cinnamon-y crumble topping—the most delicious food I'd eaten since joining the Varela expedition, and perhaps even since leaving my mother's house in England. I could have eaten the entire pan myself. He generously let me have some of his portion, and even almost looked as if he was enjoying himself.

We rang in the New Year rather underwhelmingly. No fireworks or confetti, no *Auld Lang Syne* or champagne, no fervent kisses. If anything, Old V seemed more stand-offish than ever. Perhaps stand-offish isn't the right word; he's no longer hostile, but still somehow... *unapproachable*. He may be afraid of a reprise of my drunken proposition and feels a need to keep his distance.

I wonder if he is a bit afraid of me. I certainly am terrified of him.

Not for the usual reasons.

I am more terrified of myself. I want him. And I think he knows it, and that makes me dead ashamed. I don't even like sex, and men are always pigs, but I want him.

This is the longest I have gone in my adult life without having been compelled to have sex (if you discount the six months in Theresienstadt). I should be ecstatic, but in truth I feel only detached. I guess part of me knows Old V is likely to change his mind any time now about having his way with me, and part of me simply doesn't care, but mostly I want him to prove to me he's actually not That Sort of Man.

I don't know what it's like to have proper, ordinary feelings about sex. I had to stoically lie there and allow those men to do whatever they wanted without protest, no matter how unpleasant or distressing it was to me. I had to not cry. I had to "be strong". I had to be cheerful without being exuberant. (Too much happiness would have roused unwanted attention from my ever-suspicious keepers.)

I haven't been mad enough at Old V lately to forget myself and confront him regarding his premarital shenanigans with Anton's mother. But I'm still wondering.

Lago Viedma

10 - 25 January 1952

Leni

YESTERDAY WAS MY THIRTY-THIRD birthday. I did not mention this to either Anton or his father. I did not care to have them think I was seeking attention. I ended up getting attention I had not bargained for, though.

It started when I had a bit of an altercation with those blasted mules. Santiago, the one Anton and I ride, isn't so bad, but the other two look at me as if I am poison, and are inclined to kick up their back legs anytime I come close. Old V asked me to take them to the creek for water, and I agreed. Take three animals to water on leads? Like dogs? Surely even I could manage that. Easy peasy.

Not so easy, actually. I took Santiago first. He was all right; he's used to me, anyway. When I came back for the other two, Pedro lowered his head, and Judas rolled his eyes. I am quite sure if they could have, they would both have spat in my face like disconcerted camels. I gingerly unhooked their picket ropes and instructed them to follow me.

I don't know if they only respond to Spanish, or if they are just as stubborn as... as *mules*... but they both promptly sat down and refused to budge. So I got mad and cursed at them (in German, of course, as it is the only language in which I can curse fluently) and yanked on their leads, expecting them to resist, only they didn't. They got to their feet the exact instant I yanked, which meant I fell hard upon my rear, and I yelled in pain and accidentally let go of the ropes. The mules trotted off in two different directions, and I leapt to my feet and shouted at them. I didn't know which one to follow, so I picked the one that trotted more slowly and ran after it. I think perhaps it was Judas. Anyway, he increased his speed proportionately, and I hadn't gotten far before becoming utterly winded, and I collapsed to the ground and closed my eyes. I was done. I didn't care about these stupid animals. I watered the dust beneath my face with self-pitying sobs.

A moment later a shadow fell over me and I screamed before I took the time to see who it was.

Only Old V, and he looked Very Amused. I scowled at him.

"Having a bit of trouble, are we?" he asked.

"Stupid mules," I muttered. "Water them yourself." I stood up and walked indignantly back to camp.

Naturally when *he* called the truant mules, they meekly followed him to water and back without even needing him to hold their ropes. Of course, he and the mules have plenty in common. That might explain their rapport. Anyway, I glared at him as he came back to camp and wouldn't talk to him. I was very, *very* mad at those dumb animals. Clearly my failure to manage them was the height of hilarity for him.

"Did you see?" he said to Anton. Anton grinned. Even Anton found my ineptitude hilarious. *Well, then*, I thought, *I'll just go to my bed and stay put for the rest of the day.*

Happy birthday to me.

Raymond

MISS MAYER HAS BEEN glaring at me ever since the mule incident of yesterday, and I suppose it was not very gentlemanly to laugh at her. Even so, I was not prepared for her to go into all-out revenge mode about it—after all, we had been getting along better in the weeks since Christmas.

She stewed on her bed for hours, and when I went to the creek for water this evening, she followed me, still glaring. It was funny in the way that a two-year-old glaring is funny, ferocious but harmless, and I couldn't look at her because I knew I would burst out laughing. But when we got to the water's edge, she spoke. One well-crafted, double-edged, sentence.

"Is Anton your son or were you a bloody hero?"

I whipped around and blinked at her, stunned.

"Anton showed me your wedding picture, in front of a Christmas tree. His birthday is in March. Even if he'd been born in April like he was supposed to, there's no way—that's only four months—"

I cut her off. "Antonia was the only woman in my bed, ever."

"Were you the only man in *hers*? I asked if he's your son, and you haven't answered me."

"Of *course* he's my son," I spluttered at her. "You're baiting me. I'm not playing your games."

She charged on. "You treat me like an immoral heap of shit because I've been forced to sleep with men I despise. I didn't do any of the things I did because I *wanted* to. I bet you and your girlfriend had fun sleeping around, didn't you? Guess what, *I've never had fun!*"

I set the pails on the ground with a slosh and stepped close to her. I must have had murder in my eyes, because she shrank back. Our eyes locked and I got a grip on her arms (instead of her throat, admittedly a tempting idea). "Don't you *ever* cast slurs on my Antonia," I hissed. "I was her first. Anton is my son. And even supposing she wasn't faithful? It is *no business of yours.*"

"It *is* my business," she shot back, her voice hoarse with fury. "I have been raped more times than I can count, and the way you treat me, you're no better than any of those swine. What if your precious Antonia was in my place? Would you have blamed her for something she didn't want done to *her?* Would you have taken her back afterwards?"

I tightened my grip on her arms and she winced. But she didn't stop talking.

"You're taking out your frustrations on me, and it's not fair. If you want to fuck me, fuck me. But whatever you do, get your arse off your high horse and stop pretending you've never done anything morally questionable yourself." She trembled with intensity. "None of what happened to me was ever my fault. I didn't ask for any of it. No matter what Mauritz or any of the others said or did. *It wasn't my fault.* Even *you* said that." Tears spilled out of her eyes. "I don't understand real love at all, but it doesn't mean I'm beyond learning. That boy of yours gets it. He didn't learn it from you, though. He makes me long to start over. I was like him once. Trusting and sweet and loving. All it takes is *one assault.*"

"Don't talk to me about my son," I shouted at her.

"I'm not going to taint your precious son," she spat back. "I'm telling you to wake the hell up and realise I have feelings and I want to be treated as if I matter. Not like I'm poison." Her voice sounded high and fierce now. "The first night here, when I got drunk, I offered myself because it's all I know. I haven't owned myself for years. I'm a stupid girl, sure, everyone knows that, but when I lived in England, people smiled and gave my parents sympathetic looks for having produced such a simpleton. Now everyone just... walks over me. Don't I deserve the dignity of *some* kindness?"

Before I could answer her, she'd run away crying, and I sank down to the ground and sat, stunned at the intensity of her accusations. Words came back to mind, words I'd tried to forget, another accusation.

You don't want anything to do with me since Anton was born. Don't I count anymore?

Leni

I RAN BACK TO camp sobbing, and dragged my bed back under the wagon, hiding myself under the blanket, trembling all over. I thought: *I can't breathe. I can't breathe.* I gasped for air and hunched over, burying my face in the ground, ripping out grass as I gripped the fragile stalks in an attempt to anchor myself.

Stupid, stupid, *stupid*. I am an absolute IDIOT.

What I want is for Old V to hold me tightly in his arms, to tell me "You are enough, just as you are." The same thing I long to hear my father telling me.

How to convince him I am worthwhile? I suppose I first need to believe it myself.

And I do not.

I did not know I had passed out until I woke under the flickering shade of a tree. I was dimly aware that I felt more comfortable than I had since running away from Mauritz.

Mauritz. My heart twisted. I was so weary, weary to my very bones. I couldn't move so much as a finger, and my eyelids drifted closed again. *Mauritz.*

When I met Mauritz, I was walking home on Laa An Der Thaya's main street with a basket on my arm, eyes on the ground as always, talking to myself under my breath, oblivious to my surroundings. Minding my own business.

Until I ran into someone. Quite literally, I ran into a black-uniformed SS officer. I stepped back, jerked out of The World Inside Leni's Brain, and smiled by way of apology, curtsied awkwardly, and then skittered around him and hurried on my way. I knew better than to insult Nazis, no matter how much I loathed and feared them.

But his expression had surprised me: a sort of shock in the

eyes, as if he'd seen a ghost. On the steps of Tante Madeleine's, I cast a furtive glance backwards. He stood in the same spot where I'd run into him.

Watching me.

I went into a dither and ran to Tante M to tell her about it. She held me tightly and stroked my hair until I no longer trembled. The encounter had spooked me, and every time I remembered *he had seen where I lived,* I started to panic.

But days went by, and I did not see him again, and I began to relax and move on, until I got caught out after curfew one night walking my bicycle home. I couldn't ride, but it had a permanent puncture and I often used it as a prop when I was out late on one of my clandestine wireless jobs, in case I got intercepted. My simpleton self could get away with a lot. Everyone in town knew how useless Madeleine Mayer was.

I *was* intercepted. But not in the way I'd heard of other resistance agents being grilled and questioned. A hand over my mouth, a knock over the head, and when I opened my eyes I was lying on a sofa with a splitting headache, guarded by some annoying Nazi man who seemed convinced he'd landed a Dangerous Criminal. I refused to answer any of his questions, more from confusion and the residual pain in my head than from stubbornness, and two hours later in walked SS-Sturmbannführer Mauritz von Schlusser.

The man from the street in Laa An Der Thaya.

The man who'd seen where I lived.

Get her for me, for she pleaseth me well.

Now it was my turn to react as if I'd seen a ghost. I sat up partway in alarm, but collapsed back, clutching my head with a moan. He sent out the other idiot with a dismissive wave of his hand, locked the door, and sat across from me, staring at me intently with an unrelenting sapphire gaze that penetrated my brain and read my thoughts.

He was forty-ish then, one of those men who age well and probably had no trouble wooing women. There was a highly attractive charisma about him, and his voice, soft yet authoritative, was nothing short of hypnotic. He acted so officious I felt sure I had nothing to fear, if I would only be polite to him. After introducing himself, he apologised for my head, and stared at me for a long time, contemplative, whilst I kept my eyes submissively downcast. That could be considered my first mistake, letting him see my docility, instead of behaving like any real resistance worker might. I acted neither defiant nor demanding; I just wanted to go home to my aunt, have her hold me tightly until everything had come all right again.

After an interminable silence I looked at him at last, shyly. His eyes were still fixed on me, his leg crossed over his knee, boots gleaming, hat on his lap, short sandy hair going grey. Absolutely nothing threatening about him. I had to admit that.

At last he spoke. "How old are you, child? Sixteen, seventeen?"

It wasn't the first time I'd been mistaken for someone younger. My simpleton air saw to that. "Twenty-one, sir," I murmured.

His eyebrows shot up. "Are you married?"

"No."

"Engaged? Have a sweetheart?"

"Not really." I wouldn't tell this Nazi I loved a Jewish boy, and besides it wasn't a serious or official sort of love. It couldn't be, as long as Jews were treated like subhumans. Why did my love life matter, anyway?

He watched me some more. "A virgin?"

I blushed and stammered out defensively, "Of *course* I am!" And then I straightway wished I hadn't let him in on that. *Too late.*

He posed another question. "Are you a member of the Czech Resistance?"

"No." Partly true. I only helped them in an uninitiated capacity. I had no suicide tablet to get me out of this bind. "I'm a British subject."

"Why is a British woman in Austria?"

"My parents are Austrian by birth. I was born in England. I came here to help my aunt. She's ill. She needs a companion and caretaker until she recovers."

Poor Tante Madeleine didn't have a clue what I got up to in my time off. Neither she nor my uncle ever dreamed their slightly mousy niece sneaked out in the dark to send and receive messages. I was aware it was dangerous, but it was exciting, and I was thrilled to be useful. Why wasn't this man asking me why I'd been out after curfew? He didn't seem at all interested in that.

"And you speak Czech?" he asked.

"Yes."

Another long silence. "I would like to question your aunt and confirm what you are telling me," he said, and before I could protest he had risen to his feet, snapped his hat back onto his head and called in the man who'd interrogated me. "Take her to—" was all I could make out before he lowered his voice to a level I couldn't hear. But the second Nazi escorted me to a bedroom upstairs with an attached bath.

A woman came in, ordered me to strip, and handed over clean underthings and a nightgown. "Bathe and wear these," she ordered me. "We will wash your clothes. The door and windows are guarded." She turned on her heel and left, taking my clothes with her.

The bath was heavenly, because I didn't know yet that I had anything to fear. I soaked for at least an hour, washed and combed my hair, put on the nightgown (the underthings didn't fit), and sat in a chair, unsure if I was meant to sleep in this bedroom. Madeleine Mayer the country girl didn't dare climb into that fine-looking bed without permission. So I curled up in the big chair and fell asleep, naïvely trusting in Mauritz's apparent kindness.

I would never go to sleep so easily again.

In the night the door latch clicked as the door was opened and closed and re-bolted. I was too sleepy to care until a lamp switched on by the bed and flooded the room with soft golden light. Then I realised I hadn't been dreaming, and I squinted in the sudden brightness, trying to make sense of what was happening.

Mauritz had come in. I felt uneasy and hugged my arms over my breasts in an instinctive attempt to preserve my maiden dignity. He set his hat on a table, hung his tunic neatly on a hook, and sat on the edge of the bed to remove his boots. I watched, unmoving, my heart racing. The man acted as if he did not know I was here.

Perhaps if I held very still...

For five minutes I fancied I had succeeded in Being Invisible. Mauritz undid his tie and began unbuttoning his shirt. I squeezed my eyes closed, horrified at the idea of seeing a man in his underthings, especially a man old enough to be my father and whom I didn't even know. Good girls weren't supposed to look at unclothed men until they married, and even then only at their husbands. I was a good girl.

I heard his voice, quite near to me. It said: "Fräulein." I jumped, startled, and screwed up the courage to peek through one eye. He was still mostly clothed, so I opened my eyes the rest of the way and stared at him, mute, stupid. "Get up, please."

I obeyed, trembling, still hugging myself. I felt immensely vulnerable with only that thin layer of muslin protecting me from any invasion of my privacy.

"Do not be afraid," he said. His voice was soothingly melodic, but there was something unsettling in his eyes.

I couldn't make words. I stood frozen in place.

He stepped closer and lightly stroked my cheek with the backs of his fingers. I shuddered involuntarily at the intimacy of his touch. He walked around me in a slow circle, inspecting me. He prised my arms away from my chest, cupped my breasts in his hands appraisingly, raised my hands to his lips, palm up, kissing one and then the other. He looked into my eyes. "You are a little taller than she was," he said, "but that is a small thing." He sounded as if he was talking to himself.

I finally managed to force out some words. "Taller than whom?"

He didn't answer me, only framed my face with his hands. "Have you been kissed before, my lovely little one?" he asked. My mind spun. I shook my head, throat dry and constricted again with panic. I did *not* want this stranger touching me like this; I didn't want to give him any part of myself. I was hardly in a position to refuse, however: too scared to fight, and I couldn't scream. He seemed to take my silence as acquiescence to an unspoken question, because he leant in and closed his mouth over mine. I tried to back away, to wriggle free, but he had me tightly in his grip and I could hardly breathe. He didn't only kiss my lips. He got his mouth all over my face, my neck, my hands, and everywhere in between. Still trying to get free, I tried to wipe off his kisses with my nightgown sleeve the first chance I got, and that displeased him. He frowned and yanked off my nightgown with one quick jerk, the fabric screeching in protest as it tore: muslin more eloquent than its wearer. Then it was his bare skin against mine, my wrists pinned to the bed by his hands, my hoarse attempts to protest all silenced by his suffocating kisses.

I did try to get away, I truly *did* try. No use. He was too strong, determined to have me whether I wanted it or not. Everything about the act revolted and terrified me, and when he had finally done, I rolled away from him onto my stomach and hid my face in the pillow and sobbed, noisy babyish sobs. Josef would never want me now. I was ruined, not a *good* girl anymore. I felt sick.

"Stop that noise." Mauritz's voice, calm but commanding. He lit a cigarette, took a long drag. I could not stop crying, overwhelmed by what had happened. I couldn't even *understand* what had just happened. How could I have controlled my tears?

"I said, stop that noise."

I yelped as he pressed the lit end of his cigarette to my bare arm. I tried to jerk away, but he held it firmly in place. "I will remove the cigarette when you stop the noise." I sucked in my sobs, desperate, and he took away the cigarette. I stared at him in stunned horror.

"You must never cry," he instructed. "Red eyes are very unbecoming." Why did this man, who had seemed so ordinary before, behave now like such an absolute *madman*?

He dressed again when he finished his cigarette and left the room, locking me in again. I slithered to the floor, comatose with shock for a long time. I was in so much pain I could scarcely crawl to the bathroom, but crawl there I did, desperate to wash away the taint of this vile man. But the water had been shut off, denying me even that simple dignity. I collapsed to the cold tiles, too numbed even to cry. Eventually I hobbled to where my rent nightie lay on the floor, wrapped it around myself as best I could, and crawled under that evil bed, smeared with blood and reeking of man, letting the confined space soothe me like a hug from Daddy or Tante Madeleine. It lulled me into a false sense of safety, like a cat eluding the world, whilst I prayed to die. Over and over my brain replayed what Mauritz had done, and each time it felt more repugnant and terrifying.

I don't know how long I lay under the bed, but at some point I did fall asleep, since I woke so stiff I could hardly drag myself out. I was hungry and thirsty and bruised, and the burn itched terribly. Mauritz came in after a while and had another go at me. He seemed oblivious to my pain, my pathetic whimpers of agony muffled by his hand or his mouth. He took great delight in all of this, and again I sobbed afterwards, and again he burnt me with his post-coital cigarette, on the other arm this time. I shut up.

I was utterly muddled by emotional overload and physical pain by the time he blindsided me with the news that tore my entire world apart.

"Madeleine Mayer is dead."

I stared at him.

"Close your mouth, my dear, it is unbecoming to gape," he said. "Madeleine Mayer is dead."

"If she is dead, who am I?" I breathed out. *Stupid thing to say.*

Mauritz raised me to my feet. I gasped from the pain, but he ignored it. "You are Leni von Schlusser. You are my wife." He slipped a ring onto my finger, and I recoiled, shaking my head violently.

"No—no—" I said, but he interrupted me.

"You are a gift from the gods," he said. "You are my Marlene back from the dead. You are wasted as a companion for the feeble."

"You *hurt* me." I didn't know the word for rape in those days, but that's what I meant. "Please let me go home! My aunt needs me."

He took another drag on the cigarette. "She no longer requires your services," he said evenly. (Nothing has ever ruffled Mauritz's composure, except apparently when his mistress defends Jews or his bird escapes its cage.)

Bile rose in my throat. "What does that mean?" I asked him.

He picked a non-existent bit of lint from the shoulder of my nightgown. "Unfortunately, your aunt had some difficulty with her heart. I'm afraid she is no longer among us."

"My uncle!"

"He made the mistake of resisting the officer who came to question him and has been shot through the head."

I stared at him in disbelief. This was a nightmare, wasn't it, only a nightmare? I would wake up, wouldn't I?

"You will do well to obey my every command," Mauritz added. "No harm will come to you if you do."

"My parents," I begged. "Let me go home to England, to my family!"

"Too late," he said.

Was he saying they were dead, too? I couldn't bear to ask.

Mauritz drew me to sit beside him on the couch, took my unresisting hands in his, and spoke quietly. I found myself gazing at him, mouth open, unable to tear my eyes away. I don't remember all he said, but it was something like this:

Madeleine Mayer was found dead beside her bicycle this morning, her bones shattered by bullets. She has been taken to the Mayer burial plot alongside her aunt and uncle, whose house has been marked with the words TRAITORS TO THE REICH in white paint. Madeleine's parents will be receiving a telegram any minute alerting them of their daughter's death.

Now I understood the real reason for the bath, to get my clothes off me, to disguise some other miserable wretch they wanted people to believe was me. Who was the unfortunate girl whose dead body was supposedly mine? I stared in utter disbelief as he said again, "You are my wife. Leni von Schlusser. Madeleine Mayer is dead."

I bent my head and sobbed. I was entangled in a nightmare,

and I longed to die. I had already sent three innocent people to their deaths, two of whom I knew and loved, because of my clumsy inability to carry out a simple errand without being intercepted. The sobs got me two more burns before I managed to get them in check. Once I had gone quiet again, Mauritz whispered promises in my ear, promises irresistible to almost any girl under other circumstances: promises to dress me, feed me, shelter me, pamper me, in exchange for my services as interpreter and mistress. His touch made me want to recoil as though it were the touch of a snake, but in my confusion and distress I couldn't think clearly.

I was in shock, and I hurt everywhere. Weak from hunger, my resistance was down. With no way to go home, the fight left me. I didn't want to be hurt any more, so I gave in.

I am not heroic. I took what seemed the only way; surely the war would end soon and I would be free to go home. Those early days, or months, or whatever, stretched into a grey haze of self-loathing and a stripping away of Madeleine Mayer, layer by layer: first by Mauritz himself, then by Erich and the other guards at Theresienstadt, then by the—that Thing That Happened afterwards. Madeleine withered away in her own head, leaving Leni von Schlusser to emerge from the cocoon.

Leni von Schlusser stopped getting burnt for crying, but she was burnt for other trespasses. Always, always there was yet another thing she couldn't do correctly.

For a few weeks after Mauritz initially violated me, he left me to myself in the room. A maid brought my meals, but she wasn't allowed to speak to me. Solitude pleased me in most ways, but every little noise set me trembling in terror lest the events of the first night be repeated. They gave me no other clothes, and I paced the room wrapped in blankets rather than wear that torn and tainted nightgown.

The solitude gave me time to heal and more than plenty of time to think, to feel the full weight of my situation. I was aghast at the deadly repercussions of my capture. Were they lying to me, trying to scare me into giving them some information?

What was I to do? I was desperate to get out, to find my family, or Josef, or *anyone* who might help me get out of Austria.

Except I wasn't in Austria now. I was in Czechoslovakia, and I was legally dead. My papers had all been confiscated. I had no identity, and no means of contacting the resistance workers who could provide me with fake ID. Not that I'd dare. My Nazi captors did not appear to know of my wireless skills, and I wanted to keep it that way, and I really didn't want to further endanger lives. I'd done enough damage.

One afternoon Mauritz came in with a bundle, which he carefully opened. "Take off your nightgown," he commanded. I let it slide down around my ankles and stood there, incredibly embarrassed to have him see me naked in daylight. He handed me a brassiere and knickers, elegant fine silk ones, which fit surprisingly well. He buttoned me into my skirt and blouse himself, smoothed the silk stockings over my legs, hovering. He supervised me as I tried to fix my hair to his specifications. He hadn't much liked my virginal crown of braids and said he would have someone come in and style my hair properly. He left me as abruptly as he had come, leaving me baffled. What was all this for?

He made good on his word about the hair. A hairdresser came only a few hours later and cut and set my hair. "The colour is not quite right," said Mauritz, "but we will do that next time…"

I heard a rustling sound nearby, but I couldn't make my head turn to see what it was. I felt as immobile as the day I woke to Mengele bending over me, his gap-toothed grin smug as he told me Everything Was Going To Be All Right Now.

My eyes were closed, but my mind could still clearly see him, could still remember the sick dropping in the pit of my stomach, because I sensed everything was *not* all right, that it never would be again. Madeleine Mayer had been legally dead for over a year by then. That day, she drifted away into complete oblivion.

Whatever tendrils of personal morality I had still clinging to me shrivelled and died. I no longer cared how much I drank or cursed or how many men I had to entertain. The haze of my life grew greyer and colder, and my heart grew greyer and colder too.

Coming alive again hurt. I had started to detect flickers of life returning around Christmas: smoking flax, now quenched. I didn't want to get off my bed or even move. And it was my own fault for having felt the need to prove Varela worse than, or at least as bad as, I.

The truth is, no matter how promiscuous he and Antonia were or weren't, they had nothing to be ashamed of in comparison with my load of guilt. *They* weren't responsible for any deaths.

I lay there in Anton's hammock for hours. The gloom of evening thickened. I ran out of tears and had nothing left to summon even the tiniest jump of startlement when Anton came and put his arms around me. Perhaps he had been sitting near me all the time.

I felt dead.

"Your father doesn't want me here," I whispered. I could barely hear myself, and I'm sure I was slurring. "I'm in the way. I should leave."

"*I* want you here," he said, softly, and got into the hammock. He climbed under the blanket and held me more tightly still. The hammock swayed gently. "Papá says when I feel lonely, and I do a lot of the time, to go find someone lonelier than me and make them happy again."

Anton, lonely and wanting me? Me! He went on, "I don't know what it's like to have my mum hold me."

I said, still stumbling over my words, "I miss having my daddy to hold me. I don't even know if he's still alive. I might never know. He might have died, not ever knowing I was still alive."

Then we were both crying, holding each other: two lost children, longing for absent parents.

Raymond

I ABANDONED MY WATER pails and walked to a nearby tree, leant back against it, and stared out over the lake, stinging from the woman's accusations and my own nagging shame.

That I got Antonia pregnant before we were married I would not deny, but we *did* get married. We'd planned to anyway. It was the other jibe that infuriated me more, the bit implying Antonia had slept around.

I didn't want to think about Antonia sleeping around. I chose to remember only good things, like the night she first came to my house.

I had worried I'd never see Antonia again after those stolen kisses in the kitchen, but I needn't have. She turned up unannounced one evening a month later. I stared at her on my back doorstep, a vision within arm's reach, speechless.

"What are you doing here?" I asked when I untangled my tongue.

"My flatmate Jean is on duty tonight and I was lonely."

I couldn't believe this lovely creature had chosen *my* house to come to, and the atmosphere around us felt veritably charged. I struggled again to get my words out. "How did you know where I lived?" Before she had time to answer I asked, "The cleaning girl?"

She giggled. "Guilty as charged. I found a map of the town, and your name's on your letterbox. I had a peek at it before I came round back."

For a moment we both stood there on opposite sides of my threshold, and then she said, "Are you going to invite me in? Blackout, you know."

"Oh. Yes." I stepped aside to let her pass and shut the door quickly behind her. "Sorry. I'm a bit antisocial."

She grinned. "Never mind. You look amazing," she said. I was in shirtsleeves, with my top buttons undone and cuffs rolled up. I hastened to amend these things, but she said breezily, "You needn't bother with that on my account."

I gestured her vaguely towards my front room and murmured something about making tea, and I indecorously left her and vanished into the kitchen to calm myself with a few deep breaths and the comforting ritual of tea-making.

When I brought the tray out, I found her studying the map of Argentina on my wall. It was ragged around the edges and full of coloured pushpins and routes in thread between. "Have you been?" she asked, eyes bright with interest.

"Sadly, not yet. I only dream."

"A pity," she said.

"I like the idea of adventure, but when it comes to actually having any, I never seem quite able to pull it off." I set the tray on the coffee table, poured two cups, and handed her one. She sipped it gratefully and settled into my armchair. I took a seat on the footstool near her. Silence reigned as she sipped her tea and I held mine, untasted, gazing at her. She was so beautiful, and I heard myself whisper, "You look like a queen, sitting there." She beamed, and I went on, "Like a *Polyommatus coridon*."

"Like a what?" she asked, still smiling, but bemused.

I blushed. "It's a butterfly. Common name Chalkhill Blue. It's a soft gleaming blue, like the frock you're wearing. I'm so sorry, I forget nobody else cares for butterflies like I do."

"No, do go on," she encouraged me. "As long as you don't expect an intelligent response from me, I'd love to listen." She didn't seem to be mocking me.

I set my cup down and went to the cupboard and beckoned her over. I drew out a glass-topped drawer and pointed to the butterfly in question. "See?"

She touched the glass lightly with her fingertips, her expression oddly mournful. But she said, "It is very beautiful."

My eyes were on her, and as she gently pushed the drawer back in and turned to look up at me, I heard myself say, "Your hair is beautiful, Antonia." Impulsively I stretched out a hand and touched it: like silk, soft and clean and gleaming, and I leant down and my lips caressed her face, seeking her mouth. Instinct is a powerful thing.

"How many butterflies have you?" she whispered between kisses. We had been stepping backward all this time towards my couch.

"I have a million inside me right now," I whispered back. "Antonia, I feel a bit light-headed."

She gave me a nudge and I collapsed onto the couch and she landed on top of me. She touched my face with light fingers, brushing her lips tantalisingly over mine. My arm circled about her, drawing her closer.

"You're like a flaming candle," I said, "and I am a moth—" She silenced me with a kiss so staggering we tumbled off the couch to the floor. She made a small noise of delight as I kissed her throat, and then I realised what I was doing and pulled away, breathing deeply to quiet my racing heart.

"What is it?" she asked, sitting up beside me, concerned.

"It's not right," I said. "We hardly know each other. I'm too old for you. I don't even know how old you are."

"I'm almost nineteen," she said softly. "I'm consenting. I don't want any old *boy*. I want a *man*. I want *you*."

"I need to think." I closed my eyes to block out the bewitching sight of her dishevelled hair and the way she was practically purring. I suppose her youthful energies demanded release. I understood. I'd never even kissed a girl until her, and I'd been fine, but now I craved her. I wanted nothing more than to chuck propriety to the wind and follow our instincts, but I had seen enough of life to know there were practical considerations a girl of eighteen might not think of. I ran my hand through my hair and opened my eyes to look at her. "I don't want to get you in trouble," I said. "Your parents don't know me. You don't know mine. This is all topsy-turvy."

"You like your life in neat little compartments, don't you?" Antonia didn't seem offended, and she was right. I did. Then she added, "I *am* dreadfully forward. I'm sorry."

I broke a long, awkward pause by reaching for a packet of cigarettes. "Smoke?" I asked, and she nodded. I lit two, handing her one. For a minute we smoked in silence, side by side, and I felt myself calming enough to ask another question. "Did you come here planning to—" I couldn't make myself finish the sentence. She knew what I meant. *Did you come here planning to get me to sleep with you?*

"Not specifically," she said. "But I wouldn't have minded."

I sighed. "You might not believe you're so young, but you *are*."

She laid a hand on my arm. I took another drag and contemplated a while before I spoke again. "I do want it, just—not quite yet, all right? I need to think it over. You deserve better than a one-night stand with anybody. And now we ought to get you on your way back to Bournemouth." I kissed the top of her head, and in a few minutes only the lingering scent of her perfume, and the heat she had ignited within me, remained to prove she had been in my house.

I sent her back to her colonel so easily.

No, I wasn't going to think about that. I wasn't. That was over.

If I could show grace to my wayward wife, why could I not extend similar grace to this fugitive woman who simply needs a friend—someone, anyone, to care whether she lives or dies?

I wandered for hours, until the evening air cooled my temper and numbed my regrets. I went back to camp to make things right, but the woman was asleep in the hammock. Anton was beside her, his hand resting on her cheek, also asleep. Both their faces were tracked with tears.

Leni

THE NEXT MORNING I woke before the sun rose, and I managed to roll out of the hammock without waking Anton. My intention was to try to sneak off someplace before the others woke up, and get myself hopelessly lost or something.

Old Varela foiled my heroically suicidal plan, however. He sat on a nearby stump as though waiting for me. He beckoned to me, and I followed. Why not?

He led me to the creek, and he sat on the rocks at the water's edge, his bare feet in the water, his gaze far away. I eased myself down near him—not *too* near—and watched him surreptitiously.

"I had time to think yesterday, after..." he trailed off, cleared his throat, and went on. "It is true I took Antonia back after she was with another man. I don't know how you guessed, but it's true." Another long pause. "It is also true that I did not treat her as damaged goods afterwards. I know you aren't to blame for the Nazis preying on you. I've been unfair and not at all a gentleman." He glanced over at me—swift, shy. "Please forgive me. I swear I will try my best never to be unkind to you again." He blushed a little, and I decided I believed him.

"I never really doubted Anton was your son," I whispered. "He looks too much like you."

I inched my hand closer to his in the space between us, and his own hand crept towards mine. He turned his palm up, and when I laid mine there, he held it. Lightly, nothing like the vise grip those same fingers had on my arms the day before—and together we sat watching the sun rise with not another word.

Raymond

HER HAND WAS ICE cold in mine, and I realised with a jolt that this woman's heart was frozen solid and needed thawing too. It froze, no doubt, with that first assault, and it has stayed frozen ever since, simply to block out the pain coming to life again would cause. She has by necessity trained herself to be hard and thorny, for protection.

That morning, I really looked at her for the first time. She wasn't classically pretty the way Antonia had been. Striking would be the right word. The morning sun brought out the gold hints in her brown hair and the weary-looking lines about her eyes. Most of all she looked sad. I couldn't remember having seen her smile in all of the last two months. For so long she had known only manipulation and fear, and she had forgotten how to think for herself, forgotten it was an option to try.

Her voice startled me out of my musings. "I hope you weren't too hard on her."

"Hard on—oh, you mean Antonia."

"Yes. You're rather terrifying when you're angry."

I bit my lip and looked out into the distance.

"You were, weren't you?"

"I'm afraid so," I admitted. "But we made up, so it's all right, isn't it?" *Except those final things we said to each other...*

"Perhaps," she said absently, and another long silence fell. "It's not always the girl's fault. You said she was young. I was young when Mauritz—" She cut herself off. "What I mean is, older men aren't usually very kind to young girls." She took a deep breath. "Older men can make a girl feel like she owes them, look on her like a blank slate, and she gets tricked into thinking she has power, only—only she doesn't. It's all an illusion. Who was the man?"

I hadn't wanted to discuss Antonia's infidelity, but Miss Mayer's perceptiveness again took me off guard. She called herself a stupid simpleton, yet she was intuitive enough to read straight through my evasiveness. I decided I had better answer her.

"She was a driver in the war. Her colonel was older even than I was, and with a wife and children. She loved being the centre of attention, and she and the colonel were always bantering, but I didn't know until later he'd been pressuring her all that time, trying to get her alone."

"Before you slept with her?"

"I suppose so. I never asked for details. I guess you could say I wanted to pretend it hadn't happened." *The way I'd rather believe our last conversation hadn't happened...*

Her mouth twitched and she squeezed her eyes closed as if in pain. At last she spoke. "She wanted to have you before the inevitable happened with him. Or possibly someone else had already gotten to her. Your sense of what's normal and healthy is... skewed when your only experience is anything *but* either of those things."

I opened my mouth, but she raised a hand to silence me. "Don't argue with me," she said sharply. "I'm a woman, and I know a thing or two about men. I'm not saying she didn't love you, or that you didn't love her, I have no way of knowing that, but I do know at eighteen, even at twenty-one, there was absolutely nothing about older men to attract *me*. There's a missing piece in all this. I might be a simpleton about most things, but don't assume that makes me stupid about *everything*."

Leni

HIS HAND WAS BLAZINGLY hot, as if he'd been at hard labour already for hours; his grip strong but light. He hadn't let go, even when I'd started explaining to him why I believed Antonia had made the choices she did.

He looked at me, speechless. I knew he hadn't credited me with any real intelligence, and my perception of the situation had unsettled him.

I wondered what he saw when he looked at me. A tired, worn-out whore?

He was so bronzed and dazzlingly godlike, even unshaven as at that moment. His beard was less grey than his hair, which in his wedding photo had looked the same almost-black as Anton's. His eyes were so dark, the pupils were practically invisible; his arms muscled and powerful…

Suddenly he spoke, and I jumped in surprise.

"Will you tell me your story, Miss Mayer?"

"Is this an evasion tactic?"

"No," he said. "I want to understand you, that's all."

Raymond

SHE STARED AT ME, terror flickering in her eyes, and withdrew her hand to hide her face, battling some inner torment.

After a few minutes her hands dropped away, and something like a mask fell over her face. "What do I have to lose?" she said with a shrug. She started off with a few passing words on her childhood in Swallownest, but quickly moved on to her capture and her time with Mauritz. She was clinical and brutal in her descriptions of his seduction of her, of Erich's brutality, how she'd been thrown into Theresienstadt for loving a Jew, and how in the years between Theresienstadt and Buenos Aires she'd been sold to any man who could give Mauritz gold in exchange. My heart twisted in horror at the casual way she related these atrocities. For her, this nightmare had become ordinary, expected. No wonder she was so haunted and feral, so hard, so...

So *cynical* about Antonia.

She began coherently enough, but the longer she spoke, the more frantic she became, and the more difficult it was to follow, as she seemed to be jumping back and forth through time. I noticed one point absent from her narrative: she did not include anything about the dead baby she'd inadvertently mentioned a month ago. She also skirted around the details of how she got out of Theresienstadt, let alone what happened whilst she was there.

"Miss Mayer," I said quietly, hoping to help her focus. "Tell me how you were able to leave the ghetto. Tell me about your baby."

My words were darts that found the chink in her armor. She collapsed as she heard them, and I believe she would have fallen face first into the water had I not caught her arms and pulled her back.

At my touch, or at the restraint, she screamed.

Anton

TÍA LENI'S SCREAM WOKE me out of a nice dream about cuddling with five kittens, and for a minute I didn't know what in the world was happening, and I was scared. I ran towards the sound, calling for Papá, and I found them together by the creek. She was crumpled in a heap on the ground with her arms over her head. He was on one knee beside her, his hands hovering a few inches from her shoulders, trying to get her calm. She didn't move, not even a finger, but she screamed and screamed and didn't stop until she had no breath left, and then she took a breath and screamed again, a horrible sound like nothing I ever heard before. Papá tried to help her, but she was all fists and trying to hit him, crying and speaking mostly in German, and I ran back to camp.

Raymond

MISS MAYER WOULD REQUIRE careful handling, as would any enraged animal.

A mother bereft of her young.

I have never encountered such raw agony in a human being before.

I laid one hand on her mussed hair and spoke in a low, even voice.

"Miss Mayer, nobody here is going to hurt you. Whatever you are fearing does not exist here."

"It *is* here," she moaned. "Everywhere I *go* I take it with me."

"What is 'it'?" I asked.

"My emptiness," she sobbed, barely coherent. "They didn't only kill my baby, they carved me out like a Christmas goose for good measure. *I'll never have a family.*"

Leni

I WRAPPED MY ARMS over my head, hardly able to breathe, my hair in my eyes, my face against the mossy stone, assaulted by the nightmarish mental images of my unconscious body, sliced open, and of the little person inside dragged out and tossed aside to die. It might have been the spawn of Nazi scum, but it was just as much mine. Even though I hadn't exactly *wanted* it, the lack of my consent to killing it haunts me as keenly as if I myself had ripped the babe from my womb and watched it go blue. I'd never have another chance.

"Did you want them to do that?" he asked, his voice softer than usual.

"*Hell* no! I didn't even know they were going to!" I was hyperventilating now. Old V's hand lightly stroked the tear-dampened tangle of my hair.

"Whose was it?" he asked.

"I don't *know*," I wailed. "Five or six of the bastards ganged up on me, drunk, on New Year's Eve. Erich instigated it."

I never knew which days a guard would arbitrarily pick on me at Theresienstadt, but it was not particularly alarming that first time. I'd only been there a week and I didn't know what to expect. I didn't know, on that New Year's Eve, that Erich had told his fellow guards they could have lots of fun with me, and dared one of them to bring me to their party. Serious repercussions would have come from higher up had they picked on a Jewish girl, but I wore no yellow star. They had nothing to lose, picking on me. And Erich had been dying to get his hands on me for months.

They'd been drinking for hours already. Erich, drunk, is possibly the scariest person I have ever encountered. He didn't even claim first dibs. The perverse bastard wanted to watch the others have a go at me first.

The room had no windows, and in the centre stood a table full of bottles in all stages of emptiness, and there were at least five men there, possibly six. I suppose deep down I knew what they were going to do to me, and I panicked. I fought and I tried to scream, but the biggest fellow clamped a hand over my mouth and silenced me. I've blocked out most of what happened after that. All I know for sure is that Erich watched, leering, the entire time, and that each man seemed more brutal than the one before. Everything they did to me hurt like hell, and there was so much raucous laughter. Erich, when his turn came, was worst of all.

Afterwards, they threw me out on the doorstep in the cold, and I believe the only reason I did not freeze to death is because a woman who'd seen them take me risked her life to make sure I got safely to my bed. She propped me up when guards wandered by so they wouldn't notice me, and managed to get me work doing dishes, so I didn't have to move much whilst I hurt so badly. I had to steady myself with my elbows on the edge of the sink trying not to keel over. Not from the physical pain only, but a horror inside, sucking out my breath like a vacuum that I could not make stop.

I was too deep in my misery to ask the name of my rescuer, or even to thank her. I didn't talk to *anyone* for weeks after. I don't know what happened to her.

A month or so later, they pulled me out of line again, but this time for an ordinary interrogation. The guards under Mauritz were inhuman and brutal, but they didn't rape me. They used other methods, doing their damnedest to get me to the point of saying I would do anything, *anything* to get them to let up on me. The guards had been instructed to tell Mauritz as soon as I capitulated to his demands.

Mauritz's men worked *so hard* to brainwash and bully me. That first session, all I could see was Josef's brown eyes giving me one last heartbroken glance before the life went out of them. They'd held my head in place so I had no choice but to look. But I would have looked. It was the least I could do. I do so hope he understood, that he forgave me.

But as the months wore on, the image of Josef's eyes became blurred and distorted. I held out for a very, very long time, but eventually the arbitrary torture and hunger and constant cold and exhaustion and the maddening unpredictability of the guards' whims wore me down.

I wanted out. I wanted to be a human being again. I would die here if I did not escape soon, and getting back to Mauritz would at least mean food and clothes and warmth and a roof over my head. It would be the first step towards a real escape. I suppose I started to look on Mauritz as a beneficent saviour, a way to regain some sense of security.

It would mean I'd be a collaborator again, but Mauritz could keep me alive. It was a means to an end.

"All right," I told my tormentors, at last, weeping with exhaustion. "I will do anything Mauritz asks, only let me go."

They made me sign a document with a lot of jargon I didn't understand, but I got the gist of it. I was Mauritz's slave for life. They'd tried to get me to sign it for months.

As soon the document was signed, Mauritz ordered me disinfected and brought back to his house, but he did not come to see me. I was left in solitude in my room, a battleaxe-like housemaid acting as guard, seeing to it I ate and drank and bathed. Ravenous and exhausted, I mostly slept and ate. Those flutters in my belly that I'd started feeling a few weeks ago, the ones I assumed were from hunger, had intensified despite now having plenty to eat. And as I lay in bed one night after turning my lights out, I ran my fingers lightly over my belly and felt, as clearly as could be, something kicking from inside.

I bolted upright, my hands pressed to my belly. There it was again.

In a rush I realised *I had a baby in there*. Instinct alone told me; I knew only the barest rudiments about growing babies, let alone how they got started.

I hadn't questioned missing my cycles, because I overheard some women in Theresienstadt say they didn't have them anymore. I thought, naïvely as usual, that being in a ghetto automatically took them away from everyone.

I collapsed back into my pillows, overwhelmed and terrified. Who was the father? Which brutish guard on New Year's Eve? It had to have been one of them, and how would I ever know for sure, even after the child was born? *O God, please don't let it be Erich's baby,* I pled silently, staring wide-eyed towards the ceiling in the gloom above me, my hand frozen in place over my squirming middle. I struggled to breathe normally, struggled to not remember the cruel laughter and the way the bastards had held me down to make it easier for their friends to have fun with me, but it was no use.

For me, the memory of horrible events is often worse than the experience itself. It takes me so long to process what happens that the emotional response is delayed, and that response is invariably ten times worse than the event which caused it.

My mind whirled with questions. What would happen now? What would Mauritz say? I searched my memory desperately, hoping there might be a chance it could be his, rather than Erich's or any of the other Nazis'. I convinced myself Mauritz had surely slept with me shortly before going to the camp, and I comforted myself that he would be happy at the prospect of fatherhood, that he would be kinder to me now. Perhaps I could earn his love this way. Didn't Hitler want all women to be fruitful and multiply? If nothing else, he would surely have sympathy for my condition and not require me to do anything strenuous that would endanger the baby. He would never ask me to interpret at interrogations in this condition! These naïve dreamings gave me hope to eclipse the panic of only a short time before, and I fell asleep with my hand over the little kicking mystery.

For the next several days I spoke to no one, just quietly processed the development in my own head, and waited for Mauritz to send for me, trying to decide how I should break the news to him. I had so thoroughly convinced myself now he was the father, was so sure he would be pleased, I actually began to be impatient that he should come to me. I wasn't so much excited about becoming a mother as I was at the idea that this would surely create some tenderness between us, and that Mauritz would become a true lover to me. It would gentle and soften him, and we could become truly happy together. After all, Mauritz had a few good points, didn't he? Compared to Erich, he was Most Benign. And it didn't seem as if I would be able to go home to England any time soon. I might as well be a dutiful wife and mother in the interim. Even though I wasn't his wife in any *legal* sense.

Finally I couldn't bear to wait any longer, and I asked the maid to go get Mauritz for me. She rolled her eyes, but she rang a bell and asked another servant to tell him he was wanted.

He came in several hours later, after I had had my supper. I felt excited and shy and I ran to him as he came through the door.

"Mauritz!" I exclaimed, trying to throw my arms around him. He held me at arm's length and surveyed me, narrowing his eyes suspiciously.

"Why are you so giddy?" he asked.

"I'm so glad to be out of the ghetto," I said. "Thank you for getting me out. I'm so glad."

"You would do well not to forget your discipline," he reminded me.

"I won't forget," I vowed earnestly. "It's—Mauritz—I've discovered something important."

He cocked his head and fixed his gaze on my face. Probably I looked stupid, and sounded stupid too.

"I've just learnt I'm having a baby!" I squeaked out.

He leapt back as if I'd slapped him, and the reaction surprised me so much my mouth fell open.

"What's wrong?" I stammered, as his hands appraised my belly. Not in the way I wanted him to touch it. His reaction alarmed me: even when inflicting cruelty, he was always so *calm*.

"Damn," he said sharply, and he seized my arm and said fiercely, "Whose is it?"

"Well—yours, I think," I said, baffled. "Whose else would it be?" I didn't want to remember the rape. I had thoroughly convinced myself by now that this baby couldn't possibly be anyone but Mauritz's.

"*God*, woman," he spat out, and he whipped around and headed for the door.

"Where are you going?" I asked, my voice high. "What's wrong?"

He turned in the door and shook his head slowly, his taut face pale, his eyes cold. "It's not mine, and you're not having it," he said, and he shut the door. I ran to it, but he'd locked it from the outside.

"Mauritz!" I wailed. I felt deflated and scared. Why was he not holding me, fussing over me, offering me suggestions for names, the way Daddy did when Mama was expecting my little brother?

I didn't see Mauritz again for a time after I'd shared my news with him, and asking for him brought no result. My foolish, delusional heart kept hoping he would come back and love me. When the bolt on my door clicked a week or two later, I was brushing my head at the mirror (I can hardly say I was brushing my hair, as it was still extremely short from a shearing at one of my torture sessions), and I turned about quickly with a shy smile, thinking that at last it was Mauritz.

It was not.

Erich sauntered in, closing and locking the door behind him as if he had every right to be here. I turned back to my mirror to avoid looking at him.

He stood behind me, and I tensed, my arm frozen mid-stroke as his hands lightly circled my throat.

"You ugly bitch," he said with a lascivious grin, and he dragged me off the seat by my neck and ripped off my robe. I struggled desperately to get free. The hairbrush flew out of my hand and shattered the mirror, and he held my shoulders so tightly I could scarcely breathe. He smirked at my round belly. "Told him it was his brat, did you? Bet you didn't tell him it might be *mine*."

I still struggled, terrified. I opened my mouth to scream, and he covered it with one hand. Instantly I lost all sense of time and place; it was New Year's Eve again, his friend's hand silencing me.

"No—no," I tried to say, my words incomprehensible against the hand. He let go and turned me to face him. His eyes glittered and he unbuckled his belt, whipping it off with a crack that sounded like a shot in my pounding ears. "No, Erich, *please*—"

"Shut your ugly trap or I will hit you with this," he said. I sucked in my breath, swallowing my cries as best I could, but before I knew what was happening, the belt cracked around my shoulders in a stinging, serpentine embrace and I cried out in spite of my resolve.

The next few minutes were a nightmare dance of me trying to fend off the lightning strike of that evil strip of leather (futile of me), darting from one corner of the room to another, never quite able to escape. His last strike caught me around my naked waist, and I collapsed at his feet sobbing that I would do whatever he asked, only please not to whip me any more. I mustn't let anything happen to my baby. Whatever else I might be, I was not going to have the death of my unborn child on my conscience too.

Grovelling at his feet was exactly what Erich wanted. Inflicting pain turned him on, and my begging for mercy the final incentive for him to finish what he'd started.

"I'll tell you a secret," he whispered sneeringly in my ear as he stretched himself over me. "I got to shoot the elder in charge of your house at Theresienstadt today, for not reporting your pregnancy."

"No," I moaned, with another sob.

"And here's another secret." He gave me a nasty pinch. "Your Sturmbannführer can't make babies."

I have blocked the rest out.

I woke the next morning with my welts throbbing, and the rest of my body stiff and aching too. I never understood how Erich did it, how he could make my entire body hurt. I spent the day crying and scared he would come back, or that he had hurt my baby, but the baby wriggled within as before, as if to reassure me it would be all right. I didn't get out of bed.

When my door next opened, a day after the incident with Erich, I started up violently, trembling like a leaf, fearing he was back.

But it was Mauritz, his usual composed self again.

"Erich came here," I said without preamble. "Look what he's done to me!"

Mauritz stood there unblinking. "What did you do to him to make him that angry?" was all he said. I burst out sobbing, pressing my fist to my mouth trying to stifle the sound. I didn't want to add burns to my current injuries.

But he didn't burn me. He jerked his head towards the door, indicating I should follow him, and I obeyed, shrugging on my dressing-gown, wincing at the soreness of my beaten shoulders. I pressed my hand to my belly and received a reassuring kick. *I'm all right, Mummy*, said the baby.

I'll keep you safe, I told it in my head. *I won't let them touch you.*

Leni, you naïve *idiot*.

Mauritz led me at a brisk pace to the kitchen, brightly lit. He bolted the door loudly behind us and I stood, hugging myself in my thin robe, trying not to shiver, my eyes darting about suspiciously.

A man I didn't know sat there in a chair, calmly smoking. He wore civilian clothes, but he oozed self-important power. I sensed evil in this charming, ordinary-looking fellow with his gap-toothed grin, and I shrank away as he stood and shook my hand with a gallant little bow.

"Good evening, Frau von Schlusser, I'm Dr Mengele," he introduced himself, stubbing out his cigarette. "Friend of your husband's. He asked me to come specially, and this is the first chance I've had. I understand you are in some trouble?"

I was speechless, mistrustful, and I backed further away from him with my hands over my belly. "I'm not in trouble," I said, confused what he meant. "Except for Erich beating me, I'm—I'm just fine."

"Now, Frau von Schlusser, there's nothing to fear, I promise you," said Dr Mengele. "Your husband tells me you have gotten yourself pregnant."

"It takes two for that," I heard myself retort. "I didn't do it to myself."

Dr Mengele threw back his head and laughed. Mauritz stood erect and narrowed his eyes at Mengele disapprovingly. I caught a glimpse of a coil of rope in Mauritz's hands behind his back and my blood went cold. I shook my head violently.

"No—no—" I protested as Mauritz stepped closer to me.

"We would like you to lie on the table, Frau von Schlusser," Mengele said. He had stopped laughing, and his voice was calm again as he took my arm.

"No," I breathed, trying to worm out of their grasp, but I was still weak from my months of deprivation, and the two well-fed men easily overpowered me. Between them they tied me to the table, securing me by my wrists and ankles, immobilising me. I wanted to scream, but I had no voice.

They leant over me from either side, eyes fixed on each other's for an eternal moment. Their mouths moved, but I heard no sound. The chloroform pad came at my face. Someone held my head in an iron grip. I couldn't turn away.

The last thing I remember before everything went black was one final flutter from my baby.

I opened my eyes again.

The light in the kitchen dazzled me, and I squinted and tried to turn my head. My mouth felt dry as the Sahara and I couldn't move. The first thing I saw clearly was Mengele's face as he bent over me, grinning like a demon.

"The operation was successful," he assured me, his eyes glinting with pleasure.

"What... operation..." I managed to ask out of my dry throat.

"We've removed it," he said casually.

"Removed—it?" I stared at him, uncomprehending. "What is 'it'?"

"Are you really such an idiot or do you just like to make people *think* you are?" He stepped back and sat again in his chair watching me with the disinterested analysis one might bestow on a lab specimen. *Cold, calculating monster.*

I began to remember now, being tied down. I was still tied down, I realised, when I tried to move my hands. I began to panic in a way I had never panicked in my life up to that point. I struggled desperately to burst my bonds; when I could not accomplish that, I burst into tears and began to scream. Mengele stood and slapped me across the face with the back of his hand. "Shut up," he said, "and stop squirming. You'll tear open your stitches."

"What stitches?" I asked, my voice cracked and quavering.

He turned on his heel and walked out of the room, leaving me immobile and fraught with terror.

Old Varela looked at me, his forehead creased, his attention riveted on me. "That's criminal," he said. "When did they tell you?"

I bent myself nearly double, clutching my violated belly, shaking with the horror of revisiting my living nightmare. I felt him encircle my shoulders with his arms and hold me, lightly. I slumped into him. My tongue was thick, my entire body ice cold. My teeth chattered as I forced myself to keep spitting out these words I had never dared speak aloud before.

"They *didn't* tell me."

After a few hours, or maybe a few minutes, Dr Mengele came back into the kitchen, shot me up with a sedative, and untied me. He didn't carry me to my room. He made me walk. I remember that bit. He whistled cheerfully the whole way, whistled bits of *Ride of the Valkyries*. There was a bandage around my middle, soaked through with blood: some of it old and stiff, some parts soft with fresh red. He didn't change the bandage or even remove it to check on the wound. He left me dazed on my bed, and it wasn't until the next morning that I began to understand. But only *just* began. I knew they'd taken my baby; they'd cut me open to do that. But I didn't know what else they'd done until much later.

I spent the next several days suffering as my breasts, cruelly unaware that they had no baby to feed, ached with milk, reminding me constantly what I had lost, and the next weeks tending and washing my own wound, since nobody else saw to it. My belly had become a squishy, uneven thing, and the stitches started to get overgrown by skin before I finally summoned the courage to remove them myself. I was sick twice whilst taking them out, and the incision flamed red and sore for a long time after. I'm surprised I didn't die of infection. Lucky or unlucky? I don't know.

They gave me *nothing* for the excruciating pain. And I waited for my cycles to come back and they never did. I asked Mauritz about it one night when he came in to see me, and he explained what exactly Mengele had done in a tone one might use to remark upon a good bargain advertised in the paper. And when at last I understood, the last piece of Madeleine Mayer died. One day I'd had naïve and girlish golden dreams of this baby. The next day I was just a shell, a body around an empty void. I couldn't manufacture any happiness for myself. That was why I sought oblivion however I could get it. Drugs or alcohol could deliver. Sleep could not. Sleep was my enemy; sleep brought me dreams, and my daddy wasn't there to hold me and sing to me until I felt at peace again.

"I'm no woman, I'm a barren tree," I said to Old Varela bitterly, and let out a bark of a laugh. "It made it easy and safe for me to provide favours to anyone who could pay him. He didn't let Mengele *experiment* on me, he insisted very specifically what he wanted done and he stayed there to make sure his orders were followed. I so wanted to be like my daddy when I grew up, and just look at the mess I am now!" I gulped down more sobs. "No babies for me, *ever*. And I wanted babies someday. When I got away. I wanted to be *ordinary*."

Anton

TÍA LENI'S SCREAMING FRIGHTENED me, and I wanted to help, but Papá shook his head when I tried to come near and mouthed *Wait.*

So I went back and sat a little ways away from them, far enough I couldn't hear what they said, but I could see them through the bushes. It took a long time for her to finish whatever she was saying to him, and at the end she curled up into herself like a hedgehog, still making those frightening little sobs.

Then I crept over again, and that time Papá didn't stop me. I laid my hand on one of hers, the one she had clenched over her face, and I tapped, *Tía Leni, take Little Cat.* And I pushed Little Cat close and sat back to watch. Her arms swallowed up the cat like an anemone sucking in a fish. Almost immediately she became quiet. Papá looked at me in surprise and whispered, "How did you *do* that?"

I looked at Tía Leni, whose face had gone grey. Her entire body unclenched and she went limp. Little Cat tumbled to the ground. I glanced at Papá. "Is she dead?" I asked, frightened.

He reached for her wrist and felt for her pulse. "No," he said. He scooped her up and hurried back towards camp. "Get me all the blankets," he told me. "Fold them in half and make a bed out of them in your hammock."

I hurried off to do as he asked.

Raymond

LISTENING TO HER BITTER confessions, my own insides wrenched. I remembered Antonia's growing belly and the delight we'd both shared as Anton grew inside her, feeling him kicking and squirming and responding to our voices. It made me angry that a young, naïve girl had been forced into such an irreversible procedure for no reason other than Mauritz von Schlusser's wounded ego and obsession with control.

I wanted to be like Daddy, she'd said. I hadn't thought about the fact she'd have parents wondering what ever became of her, and the pricking of my conscience intensified. I'd made no effort at all to really help this woman, beyond making sure she didn't die, which I realised now was as selfish a motive as anyone could have.

Whilst Anton went to prepare the blankets as I asked, I held her close to my chest, willing her to be all right. I wanted to kick my own teeth in for having been so unkind and unsympathetic towards her. For the first time I understood with clarity that Nazis remotely bombing Bournemouth was hardly the worst they could have done to Antonia. This woman had survived *so much*. She needed and deserved only kindness.

When Anton had finished preparing the blankets, I laid Miss Mayer on them and brushed her mess of hair from her face. She remained slack and unresponsive. Anton lay beside her and wrapped his arm over her shoulder, one hand against her cheek, and he tapped against it. Suddenly I understood how he had gotten her to calm down before. He'd gotten her attention with *Morse code*. I watched him closely. His message was a short one. *Please wake up, Tía Leni*. But she didn't move. Whether she was still passed out or simply couldn't make herself respond, I could not tell.

Anton looked at me. "What happened?" he whispered.

I stared at Miss Mayer and, unbidden, tears slid out of my eyes. For a long time I stood there, one hand over my eyes, struggling to absorb what she had told me, and Anton reached one of his hands to my arm and stroked it, waiting.

At last I dropped my hand. But what should I tell him? "I asked her to tell me what happened to her, what the Nazis did to her. Anton, they—they killed her baby."

He blanched and glanced at Miss Mayer and back to me. Anton was soft on babies, and I knew that bit would help him appreciate the extent of the horror to which Leni had been subjected, without telling him all the gory details.

"Can't she have another one sometime?" he asked. I shook my head.

"They made it so she can't ever have a baby of her own."

I heard him start to cry too, and I scooped him out of the hammock into my arms and held him tightly. When he'd quieted, he asked slowly, "Is she married to that Mauritz?"

I shook my head. "No. He made her false papers with his name and gave her a ring, but they've not really married."

"Why would he want to kill his own baby?"

Anton *would* ask that.

"I don't know." I decided not to clarify it hadn't been his baby. "He has no love in his heart for anyone."

"No wonder she's so scared all the time," he mused.

"Yes," I said. "No wonder, indeed."

Leni

WHEN I OPENED MY eyes I saw the piercing blue of the cloudless sky overhead, and I moaned and closed them again. I didn't want to face light. I couldn't move. I tried to remember where I was. Strapped to the kitchen table, freshly dissected?

Tía Leni, please wake up. Wake up, Tía Leni.

Who was talking? I didn't hear a voice, but someone had spoken. Then I felt the small, soft fingertips tapping against my cheek. *Anton.* A sob escaped my throat, and tears ran out of my eyes to pool coldly in my ears. I could not move.

"Miss Mayer," I heard Old Varela's voice speaking gently near my ear. "Miss Mayer, you will be all right. We won't let anyone hurt you again."

"Not ever," Anton added, firmly, to make sure I understood.

I reached out for his hand and managed to tap out, very slowly, *Thank you.*

I went into another slump after that, immobile and uninterested in staying alive for a week or so. Dredging up those memories had been like taking dynamite to a dam. I again begged Old Varela to just let me die, to throw my useless body in the lake, simultaneously cursing him for keeping me alive and sobbing with pathetic gratitude that he had chosen to look after me.

He was no longer merely tolerating me. Something had changed.

In the end, though, I came out of it. Anton and his father tirelessly looked after me, and I liked the sensation of being cared for. And by some unspoken understanding, Old Varela never touched me without telling me first what he was going to do.

He is far more sensitive than I gave him credit for.

ANTON

TÍA LENI HAS BEEN having one of her sad times again. I've sat with her a good deal. Papá told me not to ask her any questions about her baby, and I didn't, until today.

I guess I know now why sometimes Tía Leni looks at me with an odd look in her eyes. Like sadness, or like need. Like she wants to hold me tight and never let go.

Today, though, I *had* to say what was in my head. "Can I tell you something?" I asked her as we lay together on her blanket watching the birds pecking around nearby and fluttering in and out of the notro bush.

"What is it?"

"I think your baby was a girl."

She was quiet a bit. "I think so too."

"Did you get to see it?"

"No." She reached up to the bush and picked off a few leaves, nervously picking them to pieces. Her lips trembled and she didn't look at me. "Anton," she said, "it's like an ache that just never goes away. I see children, other people's children, and something twists inside to remind me I'll never be so lucky. Do you have any way of understanding that?"

I did. "It's like me and mum," I said. "I don't remember her, but something feels out of place anyway, and even more when I see all my friends with their mothers. A jigsaw puzzle with a piece missing right in the middle."

"Yes," she said. "That's it exactly."

Another long silence. "What would you have named her?" I asked.

"I've never thought about it. I really couldn't let myself or I'd have gone madder than I already am."

"You know what I'd like to call her?" She didn't answer, so

I went on. "I want to call her Inocencia. And when I am home I'm going to make a memorial stone for her like the one I made for Papá's cat Mariposa, and put it in the garden so she's never forgotten."

She rolled onto her side and wrapped her arms around me, held me tight, kissed the top of my head. "I love you, little one," she said. She sounded fierce, and somehow I *knew* I couldn't ever let her go.

Leni

INSPECTOR VARELA'S SHADOW FELL over me as I took my last bite of breakfast, and I looked up. "Come to the creek with me," he said. "I'll show you how to do the washing."

I was very willing. After all, I had proved astonishingly inept at almost every other task around camp. Perhaps, if I could make a success of doing the washing, I would stop feeling such an utterly useless sponge.

I gathered the bundle of clothes and dropped them in a heap where he directed me to put them. He casually took off the shirt he wore and added it to the wash pile.

My mouth dropped open at the sight of so much of his rather amazing body, startled afresh by how superior he was in every physical way to all the members of the so-called Master Race I had ever known. He saw me gaping, gave me a half-smile and a self-conscious shrug, and knelt beside me.

He wore a gold chain about his neck. At first I thought the thing attached to it, glinting blindingly in the sun, might be a medal. Was he Catholic? We'd never discussed religion, and he didn't seem to ascribe to anything particularly. But as he turned back towards me, I saw it was a ring.

"Hers?" I heard myself asking.

He glanced down, as if surprised by the thing hanging from his neck. "Yes," he said.

I reached for it and lifted it closer to my face in the open palm of my hand. A marquise-cut topaz, modest but perfect, with tiny diamonds on either side. He didn't protest my examination. "It reminded me of her eyes when they flashed," he said softly. "They were topaz. Like Anton's."

I let the ring fall back against the dark hair of his chest and met his eyes. It made Antonia less of an apparition somehow, having touched the ring she once wore. "I took it off her before we buried her," he went on. "In case Anton might like to have it someday. This one was my father's." He held out his right hand, showing me a very masculine onyx ring. He didn't show me his left hand, the hand with his own wedding ring still firmly in place. I didn't mention it. Somehow I felt he wouldn't want to talk about it any more than I wanted to talk about mine.

"It must be nice to have such things," I said wistfully. "My family wasn't very well-to-do. My mother had a simple ring, even more so than that one—" I indicated Antonia's—"and all I have is this spurious wedding band and those lovely but ill-gotten pearls."

"Ill-gotten?" He sat back on his heels and studied me, puzzled.

"Mauritz got rich off the Jews at Theresienstadt. Gold rings and whatnot—he pilfered *so much*. The Jews brought all their valuables with them, and Theresienstadt was their stop-off place before being shipped to Auschwitz or Treblinka or wherever, so Mauritz got first choice on a lot of the goods." The shameless magpie. "For all I know, those pearls he claims he bought for me once belonged to some murdered Jew. But considering what I am, well—" I trailed off, and my gaze turned away from him over the green-blue waters of Lago Viedma.

I felt his hand on mine, light and warm. "What you *were*, maybe. You aren't a whore now. You don't ever have to be again. And it wasn't your fault, what happened. None of it. Don't blame yourself, Miss Mayer."

When I didn't answer, he removed his hand and said briskly, "Now let's get you washing these."

He worked patiently with me whilst I struggled to hang on to the slippery soap and manoeuvre the clothes. He didn't scold me or make me feel inferior. I felt as if he *wanted* me to succeed, and that gave me a sort of strength.

After everything had been scrubbed and rinsed to perfection, I laid the wash on the rocks to dry in the sun with a profound sense of satisfaction. At last, I had found a Useful Thing I could do.

Anton, meantime, had finished washing up the breakfast things and came out to join us. His father put an easy arm around the boy and I looked at my hands in my lap, feeling like an intruder, but stealing frequent furtive glances over at the pair of them.

Their hair was getting long, curling under—such thick, beautiful hair, both the grey and black versions of it. I wondered if the father's would be as soft to run my fingers through as the son's.

He caught me peeking. I sat up more stiffly than ever, ill at ease, until Anton broke away from his father and came to sit in my lap. I blushed furiously (why?) but I put my arms around him and kissed the top of his head, hiding my face in his hair. It smelled of woodsmoke, a scent which clung to all of us constantly. I liked the smell: homey and comforting, like Mama's old cookstove at home.

Raymond

MISS MAYER AND ANTON have gone walking together, and it's astonishingly quiet here at camp. I've made a few radio calls and caught up on my field notes, which lately have become a little haphazard. I keep starting to sketch flowers or foxes and find I'm sketching... other things instead. I find myself constantly distracted thinking about Miss Mayer's history, and about Antonia, and lying here in the grass under the trees in the silence, Antonia's memory feels very close.

On Antonia's nineteenth birthday, I went to Bournemouth.

We had seen each other in passing a number of times since her surprise visit to my house, but only long enough for me to stammer greetings at her. I'd written to her twice and she'd replied, all very proper and aboveboard. Nice, newsy letters on her end, all about her colonel, her flatmate Jean, and wickedly funny comments about everything and everybody. My letters were boring in comparison.

I suppose I thought that if page after page of writing about my cat, my father, my Argentine friends, butterflies, and how strange my family thought I was hadn't scared her away, my showing up on her doorstep uninvited probably wouldn't either.

When I arrived, she was ecstatic that she did not have to spend her birthday alone. Jean was on duty all day, and her family was too far north to go spend the day with. "Give me a few minutes to get ready," she said, and I waited outside by the door until she emerged in a flowery dress and a white straw hat and white sandals that showed off the rosy red nail varnish on her toes.

"You look good enough to eat," I said, taking her hands, and she winked at me.

"Go on, take a bite," she dared me, and for a moment nothing else in the world existed outside our kiss.

I leant in close to her ear and whispered, "I really want to be alone with you."

She invited me in and we fetched things from her room: blankets and supper from her secret hoard of provisions, and set out comfortably side by side, my arm about her shoulder, tentatively, afraid she would shake me off. (She did not shake me off.)

She knew of a rowboat we could borrow, and we set off down the river until we found a secluded and lovely little cove where we tied fast the boat and sat on the grass to have our lunch. It was hardly a glamorous repast: cold tinned beans and hard-boiled eggs and a bottle of Coca-Cola between us. But we were each too keyed up by the presence of the other to notice what we ate. When she'd consumed the last crumb, I put my arm around her again and she leant her head on my shoulder. I confided, "I've thought of you all the time. I can't seem to stop."

She replied, "I can't stop thinking of you either. And also feeling frightfully embarrassed over last time. You were right to turn me away."

"Have you changed your mind, then?" I asked. "About wanting me?"

"Not a bit," she assured me fervently.

I pulled away from her and lay back on the grass with my hands cradling my head, watching the rustling green of the canopy over our heads. For a long time I was quiet until she plucked a stem of grass and tickled my face with the end of it. "Tell me what you're thinking about?"

I propped myself on one elbow to be closer to her. "I wrote you how I've been the despair of my mother and sisters, trying to tear me away from my real butterflies and match me up with social ones."

"Yes. It made me smile."

"I bored them all to tears in no time. I'm not witty or charming. I don't know how to talk to people, outside an official capacity sort of way."

"You talk to me."

"You're different somehow." A pause. "You were so kind and interested in me from the start, I felt if I could only be brave enough I might have a chance with you—and then you came purring into my house like a cat in heat and I *turned you down*. I can't decide if it was really my sense of duty or merely cowardice. I have never met any woman who *wanted* me. I'm not sure why you do. I am very boring."

Whilst I spoke she listened, thoughtful, combing her fingers through her hair slowly. "I'm boring too," she said. "The real me. The one I don't let most people see. But there's something about you, Raymond. I can't explain it, but you really *do* seem the most dependable, steady sort of person. And you *are* gorgeous—don't argue, it's true! Don't you ever look in the mirror?"

"I just see the tweedy failure my mother and sisters not-so-secretly think I am."

She shook her head and lay down beside me. "Shame on them. How old are you again?"

"Thirty-four."

"That's younger than many of the men who chase after me."

"You seemed—seem—so *sure* of yourself."

She smiled brightly. "I've dated a lot of fellows. I like the attention. But not a single one of them has been someone I felt I could really trust or count on, you know? I like a handsome face, but you've got that *and* character. And a sort of... unpresumptuous innocence I like too. You're not being nice to me just to get into my knickers—not that I'd mind, you understand—"

That made me laugh in spite of myself, and then we began swapping funny stories of childhood antics, of our nieces and nephews, our parents. She was charmingly idealistic and opinionated, and the more we talked, the more I wanted her. We lay side by side, not quite touching, watching the leaves above us. During a lull, she turned towards me and laid one hand on my chest as she said, "You are far more talkative and charming than you give yourself credit for."

"You make me brave."

"I should think you'd be brave on your own. You're a policeman!"

"Booking drunks and thieves and chasing off loitering young people is *nothing to this*." I let my hand rest lightly on her thigh, stroking it with my thumb. Her breath came faster; her eyes brightened. "What about you, Antonia? Doesn't anything ever flap you?"

"The idea that some policeman might come along and chase us off for loitering does," she said, a ridiculous gleam in her eye. She leant in close and whispered against my face, "I know you want some snogging and so do I. Kiss me, Raymond."

Abruptly the mood changed from easy camaraderie to crackling electricity. I tried to speak, but I couldn't make a sound. She kissed my mouth to save me the trouble, and I kissed her back until we were both breathless. My hands found their way down her lovely body and up her skirt, and she squeaked delightedly when I worked off her knickers and reached for the fastenings of my trousers. For one brief moment I hesitated, my lips pressed to her cheek. "I shouldn't do this," I said.

"Don't stop," she whispered fiercely. "I need you *now*."

I really couldn't bear the idea of stopping, and I let myself go. It was unpractised and ungraceful and utterly mad, but also so easy. In only a minute we had finished; I lay my ear lightly over her heart and both our breaths came shakily. She trembled in my arms. "Did I hurt you?" I asked, brushing the hair away from her eyes, beyond besotted now.

She shook her head, face shining.

I laughed. "You're like champagne, my darling. Delicious and sparkling and going straight to my head." I drew her closer and kissed her mouth again and she giggled.

"This is madness," she said, "and I want more."

I may be a man of honour and integrity, but I am a man, not a saint, and she was so full of softness and curves and passion, and my mind as muddled as if I was drunk. For a long time we just touched one another, experimenting, exploring, learning what we liked, before we made love again.

"How are you so *good* at it?" she asked me.

"I don't know."

I was too preoccupied to wonder then how she knew I was any good.

We spent two hours afterwards lying on the blanket on the grass under the shifting green light and shadow of the leafy branches overhead, face to face, earnestly talking, occasionally kissing or touching. We fell asleep for a bit, and when we woke the setting sun told us the time had come to go. She attempted to fix her hair and put her clothes back on (an ivory dress with red poppies all over it; I'll never forget that dress) and we stepped into the boat and turned back the way we had come. The pinky-gold of the sunset made her hair and skin glow, and I stopped rowing to touch her face.

"This light makes you look like an angel," I said. I still felt the glow inside me from our union, and had an irrational urge to revisit that intimacy. She beamed at me and tossed her head, setting free one of her curls down to her shoulder. I was speechless with longing, and she, always perceptive of my feelings, winked and leant in close to whisper, "I dare you to make love to me in this boat." Her hands gripped my knees and her mouth hovered tantalisingly close to mine. The earthy mossy scent lingered about her yet, and it only increased my longing.

I glanced around. We were still in the countryside, outside town, and our only witnesses would be cows, but I hesitated. Whilst I hesitated, she straddled my lap and kissed me in a way that stirred me to action. We didn't undress, except for the bits that absolutely needed to be out of the way, and went at it. The process felt more natural already, and Antonia was very vocal in letting me know how much she loved what I did to her.

We lay together in the bottom of the boat afterwards, spent and very, very happy. I spun a strand of her hair lightly around my fingers and I said, "I will love you and be true to you until the day I die, Antonia." She responded by snuggling in closer to me, her smile bright.

It was very late by the time we made it back to her place and

I left her at her doorstep. We stood there, unwilling to part, for fifteen minutes, holding each other tightly.

"If Jean wasn't probably back and trying to sleep," she confided, "I'd sneak you into my room and we'd have another go in my bed."

"I loved every minute of today," I whispered, and I reached into my pocket and drew out a key, which I rather impulsively pressed into her hand. "So you can let yourself in next time you're in Tangmere," I explained.

Her surprise was evident. "You *are* serious, aren't you?"

"Aren't you?" I asked. She met my eyes and her expression was wistful.

"I take you very seriously," she said. "It's men taking *me* seriously I'm not used to." She clasped her fingers around the key, the warmth and affection in her eyes as clear as the surprise had been moments earlier.

"I want to marry you," I said.

"I'll think about it," she promised. And she kissed me again, whispered goodnight, and disappeared into the house.

It hadn't occurred to me to find it odd that she hadn't once said "I love you" to *me*. Our afternoon together had been more than a little intoxicating to my muddled, passion-fogged brain, if I am honest. Men can be appallingly short-sighted when in the arms of a beautiful woman. All that matters in the heat of those moments is how good it feels to be there. I was hopelessly in love with her. I assumed she felt the same for me.

But it was also true I really didn't *know* her yet.

Leni

INSPECTOR VARELA HAS BEEN so much nicer ever since that morning at the creek when I told him about Mengele, genuinely nicer. I think he believes me now, truly believes I am innocent of any collusion with Nazi ideals. If anything, he has become almost too solicitous, too eager to make up for all his previous grouchiness.

Even so, our truce still feels fragile, and I hardly dare say anything, afraid he will get angry again. I suspect he's afraid to say much too, for similar reasons.

But I feel so much better, cleaner somehow, now that someone else knows what happened. As long as I had it trapped inside, it ate away at me like rust, but now I know that if someday the Nazis do find me and kill me, someone else knows the truth. Someone else can make sure it gets out if I am never able to do it.

Tonight I went to wash my hair in the creek, and when I came back to camp I sat and stared at the fire instead of combing it. I had the comb in my hand, but I didn't feel like tackling the straggly, tangled mess my hair had become. I'd not had it set or coloured in so long that I looked like a crone all the time. I just couldn't be bothered trying to do anything with it between washings. I found myself trying not to look in the mirror. Last time I had, I'd spotted a few dozen grey strands that years of colouring had veiled from my eyes until now.

Inspector Varela surprised me by taking the comb from my hand, and he knelt behind me and teased out the weeks' worth of tangles and knots. He kept combing until my hair was softer and shinier than it had been in months. I closed my eyes, imagined I was still stylish and attractive, enjoying the gentle pressure of the comb against my scalp, and when at last he finished, I let myself relax back against his solid chest.

To my surprise, he did not pull away. He rested his chin on top of my head and put his arms lightly around me. We watched the fire and I thought how I would have stiffened in dread had Mauritz behaved this way, but Varela didn't frighten me at all. He might be softening me up so I would provide him with favours later, but somehow I doubted it. I had begun to believe Raymond Varela really wasn't that kind of man.

Whatever his motives, I will take it. I will take whatever crumbs of affection anyone is willing to drop for me.

Lago Viedma

16 - 25 February 1952

Anton

TÍA LENI HAS BEEN doing much, much better. I am very glad. She started reading me *A Voyage Round the World*. Papá still has all his Jules Verne books from when he was a boy. Some of them even belonged to *his* father! Anyway, I brought several of them with me. She hasn't read any of them before, except for a copy of *20,000 Leagues Under the Sea*, in German—*her* father's! And this one is new to me too, and part of it takes place in Patagonia! Imagine that!

Papá has been lingering around the campsite to listen to the stories, too, instead of wandering looking for foxes and rabbits to talk to. He *pretends* he's writing notes in his boring old journal, but I know he's really listening to the story, because sometimes I sneak peeks later and he's written nothing new, only doodled something that was in the story. Or even sometimes me and Tía Leni.

I am glad he and she are getting along so much better.

Leni

THE REGULARITY OF OUR daily routine calms me, makes me feel safe. In Theresienstadt, what kept me sane was the reliability of the schedule. Anyway, I think if I could only spend the rest of my life feeling as secure as I do here at Lago Viedma, I would be the happiest woman alive.

Anton and Inspector Varela invited me to come along exploring with them, but I declined, because I longed to go have a thorough wash in a nearby pond I'd found, and I wanted to be sure of my privacy.

It was heaven, soaking there. I scrubbed myself all over, and after I dried off, I knelt at the edge of the water and I gave myself a critical and thorough examination in my reflection before washing my hair.

I already knew my willowy-ness had gone. Adequate feeding had brought me back to my proper weight, but I *felt* fat, having been used to being a skeleton. Not much I could do about that. I couldn't even fit into the clothes I'd worn when I joined the Varelas. I was making do with a skirt I'd sewn out of empty bean sacks and one of Inspector V's shirts tied around my waist with twine I braided into a belt. So classy. Mauritz would die of embarrassment at the sight of me in that getup.

Anyway, somehow, seeing my reflection just then, something clicked.

I had spent the last four months looking like a tired old harridan. My battlescarred figure might be forever dumpy, but surely I could at least make my hair pretty?

I was once proud of my hair; it might not have been thick like my older sister Hanna's, but it was long and gleaming. I'd never cut it, and I could sit on my braids if I wanted to. I liked winding them around my head like Mama did, imagining myself a queen with a crown of hair instead of gold.

I doubted my hair would ever grow so long again, and I didn't really want to wear it in braids like I did in my youth. Too juvenile. But I was determined to find something I *could* do with it, a grown-up style befitting a woman of thirty-three with grey hairs manifesting. I went back to camp, dug out my long-abandoned hairpins, found Inspector Varela's shaving mirror, propped it against the wagon seat, and set to work.

I ended up with a simple chignon, as Hanna liked in her hair, and which I'd watched her do hundreds of times. It was different doing it on myself, but after nine or ten tries and some frustrated tears, I managed to pull it off.

It astonished me almost immediately what simply looking tidy can do for one's morale: having clean hair, and having that hair out of my face, made me look and feel like a new person. I looked from the mirror down to my ragged fingernails and thought, *I need to stop biting my nails, too.* I'd started that during the awful weeks of withdrawal, and it had become habit.

And then I sat with my back against a tree and stared at the clouds scudding across the sky and remembered my sister Hanna, seven years older than me, pretty and sophisticated and smart. I idolised her, even though she was frequently bossy, and grumbled at me for trailing after her everywhere she went. I wanted to look like her, to *be* her. "Leni," she'd say. "I don't know why everything you wear looks grand until it's on you."

It was true, though. My sisters were short and shapely, even as children. I was always a twig, too thin for my height. We didn't have the money to buy me clothes that fit properly, so I made do with the frocks my sisters outgrew. Mama did her best to alter my Sunday clothes, but she didn't have time to fuss with what I wore to school on ordinary days.

When Hanna wasn't complaining about how I looked, she complained about how I walked. "Look up, Leni!" Hanna said, reproachful, bossy. "All this beauty, and all you want to look at is the dirt at your feet!"

The day she said that, I was six years old, tired and cross, and I'd already fallen on my face twice trying to do exactly the thing Hanna insisted I ought to do now. I sat down in the middle of the path and began to wail, loudly and full of rage. I was far too old to behave like this, but Hanna had pushed my button once too often, and I'd had enough.

Daddy came hurrying back towards me and tried to pick me up, but my body was doing that trick peculiar to young children of being simultaneously limp and stiff.

"Leni, Leni," he said soothingly.

I kept screaming. It felt good to scream, to point at Hanna and tell Daddy how she was picking on me again. I can't have been very coherent, but somehow he always seemed to understand me.

Hanna slunk away during this tantrum, aware that she was in the wrong. Daddy reassured me that I could walk however I wanted, and if I wanted to watch my feet, that was perfectly acceptable. Mama was furious that he didn't strap me for such behaviour, but Daddy never strapped me. Hanna got the strapping instead, and later that night when she crawled into bed beside me she was sniffling and begged me to forgive her.

Hanna got nicer to me as I got older and less of an annoying baby sister. She started to help me more and complain at me less. We were just getting to be real friends when she married her sweetheart David and moved to Manchester where he worked. By the time Mauritz captured me, Hanna had two babies already, a boy and a girl, and was expecting another.

I wonder where Hanna is now, what she did during the war. What David did. Whether the third baby was a boy or a girl. What if they'd all been bombed, and they were all dead now? It could have happened. Anywhere in England, outside of sleepy little Swallownest, *they might* have been bombed.

I can still see the last family photograph we had taken, the Christmas before I went to Austria: Mama and Daddy sitting on a couch, with the five of us children lined up by height behind them. Only Frederick was taller than me, and Hanna the littlest.

Of all my siblings, it is Hanna I miss and long for the most.

Raymond

ANTON AND I CAME back tonight to find Miss Mayer looking unusually well put together. It took me a moment to recognise what had changed—her hair. She had pinned it up, and the difference it made in her appearance was staggering, after having seen her uncombed locks in her face for so many months. She clearly felt self-conscious, without her curtain of hair to hide her blushing face behind, so I said nothing. But I smiled.

Later as I lay awake on my bed looking at the stars, my mind was inexplicably still on Miss Mayer, and it unsettled me how such a small thing as fixing her hair should make such a difference to the way I viewed her. Just with that one little thing, she'd transformed into a grown woman, instead of a distressed wild animal, or a child with no impulse control.

Antonia used to wear her hair in an elegant, elaborate pile of fluff which seemed to defy gravity, just as she herself never seemed quite to touch the ground, a thing of heaven rather than earth. Miss Mayer's chignon was sensible, solid. Nothing remotely of ether or angel about her.

After the Incident in the Rowboat, Antonia came and went as she could, never once having a chance to use the key I'd given her. It was usually a quick cup of tea in town or at my house, never more than an hour or two.

My jealousy kicked in almost at once, though. It was very black and white to me that we now belonged only to one another, but I quickly came to see I never could be completely sure what *she* got up to when she wasn't with me, and it baffled me. It wasn't that I assumed she would marry me, necessarily, although I wanted her to. It was the utter lack of commitment on her part that had me worrying.

Men of all ages piled at Antonia's feet like moths zapped by flame, and she thrived on the attention. She didn't want the wider world to know we were an item until we were really engaged. I complied with her wishes, all the while fretting over her fidelity, and jealous particularly of her Colonel X. I wrote long letters to her, baring my soul, and then tore them up, too afraid to actually send them. I needed her. I didn't dare drive her away.

One night I came home from work to find Antonia in her underthings in my armchair, one of my family photo albums in her lap.

I was so stunned, both by her beauty and the unexpectedness of her being there, that instead of greeting her, I called Mariposa. I had a particular call for her: not quite a whistle and not quite a click, and she'd come trotting out. I scooped her up. With my cat in my arms, I felt less shy, and we walked over to Antonia.

"Mariposita," I said, "this is Antonia. She's part of our family now too." Mariposa purred and butted her head against my chin in obvious delight, paying no heed whatsoever to Antonia, who stroked her gently.

"I'm staying the night," she informed me casually.

I sat on the armrest of the chair. Mariposa purred drowsily in my arms as I scritched her furry tummy, hesitating to respond to Antonia.

"Do you not want me to?" Antonia asked, uncertainty in her eyes.

"I feel very much as though I've cheapened you," I said slowly. "You're so precious to me. I wish we didn't have to keep our relationship so terribly secret. It feels illicit, and I don't like it."

"I haven't decided if I want to marry you yet," she said.

"Any particular reason you're unsure?"

She gave a little shrug. "The war. Your work, my work. We wouldn't be together much more than we already are."

"You could leave your job with the colonel," I pointed out. "You're not military. You're under no obligation to stay there."

She sighed, staring at nothing. "When I do decide," she said, finally, "I'll be the proudest girl in the world to have everyone know about us, truly I will. But I need to be sure it's what I want."

She got to her knees in the chair and began kissing me, leisurely and seductive, distracting. She was expert at distracting me. Her arms twined around me; Mariposa chirruped in scorn and leapt out of the way, and I let myself be distracted.

My head knew something wasn't right between us, but my body had other, seemingly more pressing, needs than trying to work out such complex problems. Having once (or thrice) succumbed to her charms, it was very easy to keep on as we'd begun. I was so in love with her. I lifted her into my arms and carried her to my bed, and we didn't go to sleep for some time.

In the morning I felt such warm pleasure at finding her still beside me, curled into me contentedly on one side, just as Mariposa had curled against my legs on the other. "I'm rather trapped," I whispered against Antonia's hair. She smiled and wriggled in closer, and for a minute we lay there tangled together not speaking, my arms full of her softness and her hands doing things to me that left me quite breathless.

We pulled apart at last and I said, "Let's have breakfast." I tossed her my robe and she put it on, lighting a cigarette and leaning on the windowsill to smoke it whilst watching me go out to the back garden.

At that time I had it divided in half: five pristine rows for vegetables down one side, and scratching ground for my hens and my animal graveyard down the other. Every morning I would let my hens out of their house and crouch to talk to them and pet them and trade them some cabbage leaves in exchange for the eggs they'd left me. Usually my resident fox would show up too. She leapt to greet me like a dog, and I'd hug her and throw her a treat or two. None of this seemed odd to me, until I stepped back inside to find Antonia merry with giggles.

"You *are* an odd duck, Raymond," she said fondly.

"Because I talk to my chickens?"

"And foxes! Don't foxes bother hens?"

"Not my fox. I give her things to eat. We have an

understanding—don't laugh, it's true! She comes inside sometimes to play with Mariposa, only she *does* make rather a mess—"

"Any other creatures around here I ought to know about?"

I considered. "Well, the little brown bunny, Ladrón. He's far more trouble than any fox. He has a family, the little scamp, all thieving rascals. And there's a flock of doves that comes and goes. Eat out of my hand. So do the squirrels."

She stood on her toes to kiss my cheek and disappeared into the bathroom to comb her hair. I set to making breakfast and in a moment I heard her call. "Why do you keep a dish of water in your bath? It can't be because the tap is leaky, it's at the wrong end."

"It's Mariposa's," I called back.

"In the BATH?"

"If I forget to put it back after washing it, she'll sit in there and stare at me 'til I do."

"She's trained you well," Antonia said. She joined me in the kitchen. To look at her then, all trim and pristine, I'd never guess she'd been sitting in my chair in her underthings less than twelve hours before.

"Do butterflies come flying into your net as cheerfully as your other creatures come into your garden?" She glanced towards the sitting room, and I knew she was thinking of the dozens in their glass-topped tombs.

"They do land on me quite often," I said. "But I try not to touch them. They're so fragile. The only way to keep a butterfly intact and still enough for study is to kill it, I'm afraid."

"How do you do it?" she asked.

I sighed. She had unwittingly trodden on a very sensitive subject. "You get it in your net, and stun it so it doesn't damage itself battering about, and imprison it in a jar with alcohol-soaked cotton and wait for it to die. Then you impale it on a pin and mount it on a wall for everyone to see, or in a drawer—"

"Like the ones you showed me?" Her face was serious now, hesitant.

"Those are the ones I've murdered. As a boy, originally, and in university."

She laid a hand lightly on my arm. "I'm sorry I brought it up. It was foolish of me." Then, "You have a good heart, Raymond."

"I'd have no qualms about turning a gun on a human and shooting to kill if necessary, but I cannot bring myself to hurt an animal, or let someone else, even for food, as long as I have other options."

Antonia sat quietly a long time. "I guess people have the sense not to get into trouble if they want, but animals depend on us to make those choices for them. I never really thought about it before." She looked into my eyes, clearly wanting to reassure me. I gave her a half-smile and a swift kiss on the head and said:

"Let's have breakfast."

Antonia said being seen with me was like walking around with a sign saying *Trespassers Will Be Shot*, but I felt insecure about my standing with her nonetheless.

"Do you love me, my Antonia?" I asked her, holding her tightly in bed later. "You've never told me you do."

"I think I do," she said softly.

"Are you sure you're not in love with someone else?"

"Of course not," she said quickly.

"Not even Colonel X?" I asked, deliberately. She stiffened, and I said, "I've heard the way you banter. And he's married—am I your fallback because I'm not married, so you have someone *available?*"

She burst into tears. "How could you *dare* insinuate I'm cheating on you? You're my lover, my safe haven! I hate Colonel X! Don't be cross with me—don't go all suspicious policeman on me—"

A heavy silence hung between us. Mariposa, with the impeccable timing inherent to cats, jumped onto the bed and turned in circles about ten times before settling into the hollow between us, purring.

Antonia sniffled a long time, her back to me. When she

quieted, she asked stuffily, "Would I be *only* Mrs Varela if I married you?"

"What do you mean?"

"I mean I can't decide if I want to throw away all my independence. Maybe I want to do more than be a wife and mother. Go to university. Travel. I don't know."

"Do you not want children?"

"Sometimes I think yes, sometimes no." Another long silence. "I like you and trust you and we get along all right. I can be *me* with you. But is that enough to marry someone on?"

"I'd be happy to build a marriage on that," I said, thoughtful now too. I had completely forgotten our unresolved dispute of a few moments before. "I believe we could make it work, find an outlet for your talents and energy."

On the other side of the firepit, under the wagon, Miss Mayer moaned softly in her sleep. She often did. Her dreams troubled her, no doubt. I turned to my side and looked in her direction. *Miss Mayer understands your insecurity, because she shares it. Antonia never really understood you,* came a Thought.

No, I told myself sternly. *Antonia was my one true love. Nobody else matters. Nobody ever will.*

But you are *insecure, Raymond Varela,* persisted the Thought. *Admit it. If you'd admitted it to Antonia, maybe you'd never have lost her.*

I huffed and pulled my blanket up to my ears, hoping to block out the invasive Thoughts. Why should I be thinking of some other woman, in any way whatsoever? I'd failed miserably with the one chance I'd had.

The Thought had a point.

LENI

TODAY I AGREED TO go exploring with the Varelas, only at the last minute Anton decided he wanted to stay at camp and Do Things by Himself instead. He handed me a bag with our lunch in and some other sack to carry, whilst his father draped a variety of things about his neck (binoculars, camera) and slung a sack of his own over his shoulder. Explorer Things, I supposed. I wanted to ask him what it all was for, but I was too shy.

I was somewhat nervous setting off alone with Inspector V at the outset, but I soon forgot myself in my enchantment with the way he saw living creatures where I saw only rocks and grass. He forgot everything else in his delight. He told me the names of many of the plants and creatures we saw, recording every sighting in the little notebook that was always in his shirt pocket. I sat and watched him conversing with a rabbit, hardly daring to breathe. The creature looked into his eyes and cocked its head as if it understood every word, and sniffed at his outstretched hand before loping away. It had no fear of him.

Out of nowhere a flaming orange butterfly landed on my hand. I gasped, then I held myself as frozen as an icicle.

"Oh!" he exclaimed softly, alight at the sight of the insect. He came close, telling me what kind of butterfly it was, but I heard his words only as a distant hum. I stared, transfixed, at the slowly moving wings, stunned immobile by a memory, and I heard myself talking over him, saying in a low murmur:

> *I want to believe that the fluttering flame*
> *which chose her hand to light on*
> *Is a promise of better things to come:*
> *That we too will fly away from this place of death*
> *and sorrow, of filth and endless rain...*

"What's that?" he asked, and I raised my eyes to him slowly. "German?"

"Czech," I whispered. I let him coax the perfect little creature onto his own finger. I started to close my eyes so I did not have to watch him kill it, but he only raised his hand and let it go.

"Aren't you going to keep it?" I asked in surprise.

"No," he said. He looked at me, and our eyes locked. "It's good luck when they land on you. What was the Czech?"

For a moment I couldn't speak, and he sat beside me and waited.

I repeated the lines again, in English, and he bent close to catch the words.

"A poem? Did you write it?"

I shook my head. "Rodak Martínek, a fifteen-year-old boy at Theresienstadt. Don't ask me now."

He nodded, stood, and gave me his hand to help me rise. He didn't let go as he and I looked into each other's eyes, searching for... for *something*.

Unlike my sister Hanna, Raymond didn't seem to notice or care that my eyes were perpetually scanning the ground around my feet as long as I was walking, and his hand, warm and firm, did not let go of mine.

As we walked away, for the first time on this journey, instead of me struggling to keep pace with his long strides, we walked together.

Raymond

WE STOPPED TO EAT our lunch at the top of a hill where, theoretically, we could have seen our camp below if not for the trees in the way. I lay down and closed my eyes and thought I might doze a bit, but I kept opening one eye to peek at my companion, who sat ramrod straight, staring off into something that wasn't Patagonia. She didn't look angry or sad or happy, but she *did* look very intense.

"What are you thinking about?" I ventured to ask, but she didn't seem to hear me, so I sat up and asked again. She startled a little and shrugged.

"Would your wife have liked it here?" Miss Mayer asked after a while. I didn't have a ready answer, but she didn't seem in a hurry for one.

"I don't know," I said at last, truthfully. "She wasn't much of an outdoors person. I mean, not long hikes or any real exertion. She liked to be fresh and pretty always, and I somehow don't expect cold lake baths would be her idea of a good time."

"I like it here," she said, her tone wistful. "If I didn't want to find my father, I would like to stay here forever. It's so pure, it makes me feel there's hope for me."

"I admit I'm tempted to stay here myself," I said. "But I can't. At least not yet."

Another long silence. "Tell me about a place you went you wished you'd never gone," she said.

I laughed. "Does out of the sweet shop with a pocket full of unpaid-for sweets count?" I asked.

She looked at me askance. "You? You have a criminal record?"

I couldn't tell if she was serious or making a joke, so I answered seriously. "I was four years old. And yes, that's my criminal record. One of my earliest memories of my father was him marching me back to apologise and pay the shop owner and then me having to work hard to earn the sweets back, since he'd loaned me the money to pay for them."

She didn't smile, but her eyes lightened at my story. "And you?" I said. "Any juvenile criminal records for you?"

"No," she said. "I was a dull, good girl who never did anything really bad." After a moment she added, "But one place, one time—" She seemed to gather her thoughts and went on, "The October after Mauritz stole me, when I was twenty-one... I'd been coöperative—it wasn't too terrible just then between us; I was obediently translating, I was going places, being introduced everywhere to his friends as his wife, and Erich hadn't gotten to me yet—Mauritz took me to Berlin, to show me the sights—"

"Did you meet Hitler?" I interrupted.

"Mauritz took me to a rally, yes. Hitler scared me. I did not meet him personally." She paused again. "But the highlight of the trip was going to see *Das Rheingold*. I'd never gone to the theatre before, let alone opera. Daddy didn't approve of such entertainment, even if we could have afforded it, but he'd take us to concerts when he could. He liked Bach." She drew her knees to her chest and rested her chin on them. "Anyway, I had the jitters, scared that God would punish me for setting foot in an opera house, but also excited, because Mauritz had just bought me my first evening gown. It was dark grey velvet with silver trimmings, so beautiful. I felt like a crow dressed as a peacock in such a lovely thing. And we sat there for four hours, listening to a story that had me spinning in confusion. Do you know Wagner?"

"I'm afraid I'm not very knowledgeable about music of any kind," I admitted.

"It's all pagan gods and killing and things. It horrified me so, I didn't even want to look. It was so hard for me to not cringe the whole time, thinking of how Daddy would never approve of such rubbish. But Mauritz seemed so enlivened by it. I didn't understand then, about Wagner and Hitler, but I do now. The music is like a drug. One ring to rule them all. One race to rule them all. It's inherently corrupt and evil. I hate Wagner, and I hope I never have to hear anything from that horrible opera again in my life."

Her fiery eloquence surprised me. She didn't usually have so much to say at once without tangling up her sentences, but she was fierce about this, and forgot her natural tendency to stumble for words.

"It sounds like you've thought a good deal about it," I said.

"I've had nothing else to do," she shrugged. "I had to keep reminding myself the Nazi party was evil. It would have been so much easier to let go, let myself be indoctrinated, give in. But I couldn't, not completely, anyway. Remembering Daddy helped."

She lay back in the grass and folded her hands over her chest, heaving a sigh.

"Who is your father?" I asked her.

"Dr Tobias Mayer," she answered, and shot my question back at me. "And you, Inspector Varela? Aside from childhood sweet shop thievery, surely you've regretted something as an adult."

"Not having kept my son from visiting a zoo," I replied promptly. Her eyes popped open again and she looked at me startled.

"But you're a scientist," she said. "And you love animals."

"Exactly the reason I can't bear to see them dragged away from their homes to a climate that's not right for them, and put in prison cells where they pace their empty lives away until they die of boredom and sorrow. I'd *never* have taken Anton myself. My mother had him in London for a weekend and took him, about a year ago. She knew perfectly well what she was doing, and he was very upset by seeing the animals trapped like that. I wouldn't talk to Mum for a month afterwards, and I've never left him alone in London with her again since."

She sat up, watching me closely. I went on. "It's one thing to rescue an animal that is hurt, help it get better, and return it to its home afterwards. But capturing an animal and condemning it to a life in a zoo is ten times worse than trophy killing. I hate trophy killing like I hate Nazis, but at least the trophy animal is put out of its misery."

She looked at me quietly, her brows drawn together. "Is that why you didn't kill the butterfly today?"

I nodded.

"I'm glad you didn't," she said.

"I used to kill them pretty lavishly," I confessed. "As a boy… and I had to at college. I have drawers full of them at home. But then I stopped. I need a pretty good reason before I'll kill one now." I looked at her. "What was that poem about the butterfly?"

She lay back in the grass again and closed her eyes. The words came out musically, as if she had perfected their delivery. Soft and lyrical, even though I'm sure some of the original rhythm got lost in translation.

> *I don't know the name of the lady on my right*
> *at the end of our row.*
> *She is always there: every morning, every night.*
> *I think she is alone here,*
> *the only one left of her people.*
> *I see her at work in the house where I live*
> *with the other children,*
> *But nobody speaks to her*
> *as she endlessly washes dishes.*
> *I have never heard her voice, but I know she*
> *weeps when she thinks nobody sees.*
> *Her tears drop like crystal into the dishwater,*
> *Like the raindrops forever dropping*
> *off the edge of the roofs here.*
> *She must have been lovely once.*
> *Now her eyes are no colour at all,*
> *And her dingy kerchief hides*
> *whatever might be left of her hair.*
>
> *This morning I pray for her.*
> *Even here, surely, God can see.*
> *Send her some hope, I plead silently.*
> *Send her something to smile about.*

And in a moment, He answers me.

A beam of bright flame catches her eye
and she glances up.
We are all hungry for colour here,
but I think she is starving for it.
The ghost of a smile touches her face
as ever so carefully she crooks a finger.
Please, God, I beg, don't let the guards see.
And I watch something come to life
in the sad lady's colourless eyes.

The butterfly is weightless
upon her raised finger, resting.
The pearls it wears on its orange gown
rival any queen's.
Its existence in this moment means more
than the wealth of a kingdom.
The fragile creature rests there,
Catching its breath
before once more taking the air.
When it flies away her eyes follow it,
growing dull again.
I think it has taken part of the lady's soul with it.
I want to believe that the fluttering flame
which chose her hand to light on
Is a promise of better things to come,
That we too will fly away from this place of death
and sorrow, of filth and endless rain.
I pray that soon will come her day, to no longer
crawl but fly away to a safe place
Where she will no longer
weep silently into her dishwater,
And someone will love her
and bring her eyes once more to life.

She fell silent and I watched her. There was at least a foot of space between us, but I was very conscious of her presence. I could have reached for her hand if I'd wanted to. I *did* want to, inexplicably. But I didn't.

"It's so beautiful," I said. "And a fifteen-year-old boy wrote it?"

"Yes." She sighed. "A few days later someone passed me some toilet paper with the poem carefully written out on it. Toilet paper was like gold. We got five sheets a day. A precious gift." Her voice caught. "I memorised the words as fast as I could—the paper wouldn't last long before it disintegrated or got stolen, and as soon as I got out of that place I wrote it out on typing paper and hid it on the inside of the endpapers of the prayer book Mauritz gave me. He never found it, and every now and then I'd slit it open so I could read it again, even though I knew every word."

"I'll bet it was an *Issoria lathonia*," I said. "A queen of Spain fritillary. I'll bet your poet boy recognised it, too, since he compared it to a queen."

"All I know is it was beautiful. I wonder whatever became of that prayer book."

I turned my head towards her. She twirled an escaped strand of hair around a finger absentmindedly. "When you said you came here for the butterflies," she said at last, cautiously, "back when I was first here with you, that poem came back to me with a slam. *Someone will love her and bring her eyes once more to life.* And I don't know, but..." she turned and met my eyes, fleetingly. "Well. Anton."

I understood what she meant. "He likes you a great deal," I said. "You know how he has so much to say sometimes he's not coherent, goes down so many rabbit trails it's impossible to keep up with him?"

She made a soft little sound, almost a laugh, and her eyes softened. "Yes."

"All he does when we go out is talk about you. He loves people generally, but I have never seen him so fixated on anybody before. I've been thinking how hard it will be for him to have to—well, say goodbye to you when we get back to England."

"It's occurred to me too," she said. "And then I shove it out of my mind because I can't bear it. I keep trying to *not* love him, but it's just not possible."

"Anton wants you to come live in Tangmere," I said. "I told him you probably want to go home to your family, but he insists you'd be happier in Tangmere."

"He has a point," she said.

She closed her eyes and went quiet. Perhaps she fell asleep. I watched her a while, and my mind, unbidden, wandered unexpectedly to the notion that it might be nice to hold her in my arms, right here in the grass.

Anton

TÍA LENI AGREED TO come out with us today. She looks SO PRETTY with her hair combed. Like a different person, sort of. But then I thought, I want her and Papá to go be by themselves a bit and who knows. I doubt if Papá will even notice her once he gets butterflies in his sights but it's worth a try, even though I *did* say I was done trying to get him interested in anyone. I'm going to be really, really sad when we go home and don't have her with us any more. I will miss her so much. Maybe if I ask Papá he'll help her find a place to work and live in Tangmere and I can go see her sometimes. Though she might want to go home to her family.

I never liked any woman so much as I like Tía Leni. Even if she can't have any more babies. She's the one I want to look after me when Papá's working.

They've come back. Papá says tomorrow we are going to the GLACIER.

Raymond

MISS MAYER AND ANTON stood with me on the edge of the lake. She hugged a blanket to herself as she glanced across the water.

"It's a lot of water," she said uneasily.

Anton dropped the picnic basket to the ground and threw his arms around her. "We'll keep you safe, Tía Leni," he vowed.

"I can't swim," she said.

"Papá can," he answered promptly. "Like a fish. And so can I. Look, I'll get in first. It's easy. You'll see." And he stepped in and held out his arms triumphantly.

"Stop showing off and sit down," I ordered. "You'll fall out, standing in a canoe."

I put the provisions in, got in myself and held out a hand to Miss M, who still hung back. "Perhaps I'd better stay behind," she said weakly.

"Nooooo," said Anton. "It will be so much more fun with you, Tía Leni!"

She looked sceptical, but put one foot into the canoe and quickly retracted it, with a strangled sound. "Are you sure it won't sink with another person in it?"

"It won't sink." I grasped her hand and told her to shut her eyes, probably not the wisest advice I have ever given. She made it into the boat, but narrowly missed tumbling into the water over the far side. She really is very accident-prone. She hunkered at my feet in the bottom of the canoe and looked approximately as relaxed as a wet cat.

"You'll need to move to the front, Miss Mayer," I said. "To balance it."

She pressed her lips together and crawled over the crossbar to the front of the canoe as I instructed, then stuck her face between her knees and didn't move again for some time.

I rowed us across the narrowest bit of lake to get to the glacier. Miss Mayer eventually raised her head a little, still far from enjoying herself, but she made it across without having any meltdowns.

We spent hours exploring the glacier. When it came time to start back for our campsite, Anton lay down in the front of the canoe and fell asleep. I decided to row out into the lake instead of taking the more direct route back to camp. Miss Mayer relaxed against my knees as I rowed; I think she felt safer there. I splashed her occasionally as I switched sides, but she didn't seem to mind. She looked up and I smiled at her.

"Feeling better in the boat?"

"Yes," she said. "Much." There was a long pause. "It's not so much the boat, you see. It's the water. Like I told Anton, I can't swim."

"I could teach you," I said.

"I don't think so."

"It's a useful skill to have," I said.

She shook her head. "I don't want you to see my scars."

I tried to apologise, but she pointed to the sun setting behind the teeth of the Andes, and for a moment its glory arrested our full attention. I laid one hand lightly on her shoulder.

"Sometimes at Theresienstadt, the only beauty in a day was the sunset," she murmured. "They couldn't touch the sky. Even with aeroplanes and bombs, they couldn't defile the sky, not really."

I didn't know what to say to that. Finally I said, "You were there six months, you said?"

"Yes."

"And Mauritz worked there?"

"Yes. He did a lot of record-keeping and questioning, which is why I was useful. Many of the Czech prisoners didn't speak any German, and some of the ones who did pretended they couldn't. I filtered the information they gave me or confused it as much as I dared without it being obvious. I hope at least some got through alive. But I'll never know." She sighed. "Mauritz's house was half a mile from the ghetto. Everything in Theresienstadt was greyness and grief behind a false front of humane fairness, but Mauritz's house with its pretty painted shutters and neat flowerbeds and lawns—you felt like you had gone into another world. I had my own little suite of rooms on the first floor, which had barred windows I couldn't open. That's where I lived after... after the... after Mengele. Mauritz acted as though nothing had changed, but suddenly he expected me to provide favours for other SS men seeking relief. And most of them weren't too terrible, honestly. It was emotionless and I hated it, but they didn't *hurt* me, not like Erich and Mauritz did."

Another long silence. "I don't understand why he had Mengele go to such drastic lengths," I said.

"It wasn't his baby, and his pride would never have let him raise another man's child as his own. It didn't matter that I'd been raped; it was still my fault, just for being a woman dragged into a room full of drunken brutes." Her voice caught, and I squeezed her shoulder gently. "So *stupid*. All of it. He sold me to other men, yet still I was his mistress, his *property*. All so irrational. Why did he even want me? I guess because he was so obsessed with recreating his dead wife."

I remembered the conversation I'd overheard in El Calafate, and felt surer than ever that Mauritz's need for a wife went far deeper than Miss Mayer suspected. I wondered if we'd ever discover the truth of it.

"You don't have to tell me these things if you'd rather not," I said. "I mean, I'll listen, it doesn't bother me, but only if you *want* to tell me."

She nodded, solemnly. "It helped, telling you what Mengele did. I don't have as much trouble sleeping or so many nightmares now. I need to get it out." She bit her lip and glanced up at me, then away again. "You know what I want, all I ever wanted? A baby of my own. I didn't know it until it was too late, but it's true. I will never be satisfied until I have a child, yet I know it's physically impossible. It's an obsession with me, the way Mauritz's dead wife was to him."

There was another tiny catch in her voice, and she said, "Tell me about your home." Clearly she had finished with confessions for the evening.

I balanced the oar across my knees and let the canoe drift. "It's tiny," I said, staring into the distance, picturing it in my mind. "White clapboard with blue shutters and a red front door. That was Antonia's doing, the door. She loved red. And a white picket fence that needs repainting badly. Anton is supposed to do it, but he comes up with all kinds of excuses. I'll likely have to pay him before he'll get it done."

"Does your gate squeak?"

I smiled. "It does, actually. Anton likes to swing on it a few times, coming and going every day. I park my car under the lean-to attached to the side of my house. It's a dark blue 1934 Morris Cowley Six. I got it a few years after finishing university. I don't drive it much, though. I walk or bicycle most days instead."

"You would." Was she teasing me? "Anton says you run marathons for fun." *Definitely* teasing me.

"It *is* fun," I said, a little defensively.

"I think it's wonderful," she said. "I can barely walk without falling over my own feet. It must be nice to have such self-control and grace. Go on."

"Two apple trees in front. Garden and chickens in the back, and my little animal graveyard. Mariposa is there."

"Your cat?"

"Yes."

"Tell me about her?"

"Sometime. Not tonight. You'll think I'm overreacting, being so sad about a cat after all the horrible things you've gone through."

"Grief shouldn't be measured in comparison with someone else's troubles," she said. "Only in proportion with your own experience." She looked up, and impulsively I planted a kiss on the top of her head. Her soft hair smelled of warm grass and lake water.

"Have you ever had sex in a canoe?" she asked, in an unexpected topic switch.

"Not a canoe. I wouldn't recommend a canoe. Too tippy. Antonia and I borrowed a rowboat once and—" I stopped, feeling my face hotting up as I realised what she was asking and what I had so carelessly started to spill.

"You're blushing." This time there was indisputable mischief in her voice.

"And what if I am?" I asked, my cheeks burning.

"Is that the most unusual place you've ever done it?"

"Why are you asking me these things?" I said, trying to put her off.

"We're adults," she pointed out. "Anton is asleep. And I'm curious. What do ordinary people do when they love each other?"

"I can't speak for everyone, but—"

"Where?" she demanded, and I sighed and answered her.

"Against the wall of a station one dark night when I had only fifteen minutes and thought I would combust if I couldn't have her right that instant."

"Against a *wall*?" she asked, bewildered. "How does that even work?"

"There's more than one way to make love," I said.

She was speechless for some time. "Not only one?"

"No," I said. I explained it to her and she made a face.

"It doesn't sound remotely comfortable."

"I was younger then. A bit mad. Loving Antonia was a whirlwind of madness from the minute I met her until the minute she died."

"If you enjoy it, it's all right to be a bit mad." A wistfulness replaced the mischief in her voice, like a cloud drifting over the sun.

"Have you really never once made love?" I asked. "I'm not meaning the act itself. I'm talking about all that goes along with it that makes it fun."

She shook her head. "I guess *they* had fun. I never did."

"Then it was only sex and not lovemaking. It can be beautiful, I swear it can."

"Are you going to combust if you don't get to show me all about it right this instant?" Her voice was light, but I felt her shift away ever so slightly, and her fingertips tapped restlessly on the edge of the canoe. I recognised that a switch in her brain had flipped from calm to agitated and I backed off.

"No, I won't combust," I said softly. "And it doesn't have to be me. I'd just like to see you happy, that's all."

She went silent. I secured the canoe on shore and carried Anton to bed. When I came back a few minutes later, she still sat hunched in the canoe, face hidden behind her hands. I didn't think she was crying, but I could tell she was in the depths, and I did so hope it wasn't because I'd unintentionally insinuated that we should sleep together.

I helped her out of the craft, but she staggered so much trying to walk that I scooped her up and carried her to her bed. I lay her there and covered her and brought my own bed nearer hers—near enough that I could be there for her in the night if she dreamed.

As when Anton had difficulty breathing, I found myself hyperaware of Miss Mayer's emotional distress. I did not sleep much.

She tossed restlessly, clenching her hair in her fists, scratching her mosquito bites (she was a compulsive scratcher of wounds), and making small noises like an animal in pain.

Her lightning mood swings had ceased to alarm me some time ago, but it distressed me to think she would likely live the rest of her life battling these demons of anxiety, compulsion, and addiction. I did not want her to have to face them alone.

I lay there in the inky darkness, and my mind drifted to Anton and how much I feared losing him. He was part of me, but my role in his making hadn't involved nurturing him in my own body for months. Whatever I felt, the way a *woman* feels for her child must surely be a hundred times more intense.

I couldn't fathom living with that sort of pain. It made me sad that there was absolutely nothing I could do to ease it for her. I couldn't bring back her child. I couldn't give her another.

Or…

Anton was almost the right age, and he adored her and she adored him. I sat up, alarmed at the unexpected train of my thoughts.

It might be a poor substitute, and perhaps she wouldn't even like the idea. But if I married her, she would have Anton.

Me, marry Madeleine Mayer? The idea was so far-fetched and impossible that I started to laugh aloud at myself, but the laugh caught in my throat.

I wasn't even in love with her. I mean, I was fond of her, like a friend. But marry her? She would probably laugh at me, or retreat back inside her silent shell of fear.

But Anton.

Maybe some things were more important than my self-imposed consecration to my dead wife. Mauritz's obsession with *his* dead wife had brought Miss Mayer so many of her troubles, the greatest of which was the loss of her baby.

It all circled back to that baby, and to Anton. He and Miss Mayer needed each other. I resolved that somehow I would test the waters and see whether she would be receptive to the idea, before I made an ass of myself and asked her outright.

Lago Viedma and Lago Argentino

10 - 31 March 1952

Leni

WE ATE OUR SUPPER under a threatening sky.

Inspector Varela kept looking at it with obvious concern, and he asked if I wanted to sleep in the wagon or under it.

"We can all fit in the wagon," Anton said, artlessly, from where he sat doodling some highly dramatic story about a tarantula and a scorpion in his journal. "I'll get sick if I sleep out in the wet, and it would be mean to make Tía Leni sleep in the wet."

I exchanged glances with his father. He came and sat beside me and whispered, "He could sleep between us. But I don't want to make you uncomfortable. I can sleep under the wagon and let you two be inside, if you like."

I looked at him and I said, "With Anton between us, I don't mind."

So we all moved our bedding into the wagon. We laid three blankets across the wagon bed, and we each had our other blanket to roll up in. We had barely finished the task before the first drops began to fall.

"I'll finish cleaning up," Inspector V said. "You two go in the wagon."

Anton bounded around camp, gathering myriad scattered things he didn't want to get wet: his journal, his cat, some of the tatty paper snowflakes still fluttering on the notro bush, several books. We got into the wagon and he bundled up whilst I read to him a bit. The rain pattered on the canvas, but we stayed dry. I lay there and he snuggled against my shoulder and soon fell fast asleep, nose whistling softly near my ear.

His father laughed at the sight when he joined us. "He does that to me too," he said.

"It's like he's trying to absorb himself into whatever source of warmth happens to be nearest," I said, fondly.

"Like a cat." Inspector V took off his boots and stretched himself out, or tried to. He had to prop his ankles up on the tailboard. "He's like his mother that way," he told me. "I used to tell Antonia she was a cat in human form. No other explanation for how such a small person could take up so much room."

"He's so snuggly," I said. "I love it." I glanced at his feet. "I gather you weren't planning to sleep in this wagon?"

"I was hoping I could avoid it," he agreed. "I knew if I had to, I'd be uncomfortable. Nothing is ever long enough for me. At home my bed has no footboard. Otherwise I'd never be able to stretch out."

"You could drop the back of the wagon down and extend the canvas," I suggested. "It would open it up to the wind, but at least you'd have more room for your feet."

"I might do that," he said.

We fell silent, but I sensed the edgy alertness of the man on the other side of Anton. Inspector Varela wasn't sleeping, and I wondered what he had on his mind. Somehow I didn't think it had anything to do with having to sleep with his feet propped up.

I extracted myself from Anton's clinging and turned towards him. "Can't you sleep?"

I heard him turn to his side to face me. "Miss Mayer, please do not call me crazy for saying this, but—" He stopped, and I was struck with sudden fear that he was going to send me packing back to Buenos Aires. I couldn't speak for my heart in my throat.

Finally he went on, "I wondered if we could—for Anton, you understand!—we could—get married."

I sucked in a breath, alarmed. "You are crazy."

"I won't ask anything of you," he said. "I swear it. I just—you and he are so happy, and you said yourself you don't know what you'll do when you have to say goodbye to him. You don't have to decide right now," he added in haste. "Think about it, maybe?"

I was stunned. "Are you in love with me?" I asked, incredulously, when I could speak. "I thought you hated me. Or were just tolerating me. Or something."

A short pause. "Well, no, I'm not in love with you," he admitted. "I've become rather fond of you, but mostly it's Anton I'm thinking of."

Not flattering, but that part didn't matter to me. To not have to part with Anton would be a grand thing indeed, but having to take on his father as part of the package? I wasn't so sure.

"I'll think about it," I promised.

He went to sleep after that.

I never did.

Inspector V didn't mention the topic of marriage again. I knew I hadn't dreamed it, but ignoring it seemed the best course of action. I couldn't fathom actually marrying the man. Sure, he'd been very nice since we laid all our cards on the table, but *marry* him? It sounded so frighteningly permanent, and surely as my husband he would expect certain things of me, things I wasn't keen on.

Still, for Anton, I might be willing. And at least his father wasn't likely to be a violent, manipulative sadist.

We continued to sleep in the wagon together for a few more nights, and spent a good deal of our days in there too. Inspector V did tinker with the wagon as I had suggested, which I found oddly touching.

The rain poured relentlessly. It wasn't terribly cold, but when you can't ever get dry, you feel colder anyway.

Anton did not relish confinement at all. He came out to eat, but he didn't want to wear his bandana to keep out the smoke, and he became utterly drenched, his hair plastered to his head and dripping in the wet. But he was in reasonably cheery spirits, until he burst out laughing about something and it turned into a horrible attack of coughing that nearly gave me heart failure. He couldn't stop once it started, and he gasped and wheezed so hard he passed out.

Inspector V took the boy to the wagon, stripped off his wet clothes, and I hunted for the driest things I could find to change him into. Inspector V kept his voice calm, but his eyes betrayed that he was frantic. There wasn't much he could do to really help the poor lad, except to watch and pray that Anton could get one deep breath, just *one*, and then one more, and one more, until he was all right again.

I could not bear it if anything happened to Anton out here and we lost him. I felt tense all over; my heart was heavy and I couldn't stop the streaming tears. I couldn't imagine how much more shattering this must be for his father.

Anton did get through it, but it left him white as a sheet, exhausted, and shivering. I held him close whilst his father rubbed his hands and feet briskly until, warm again at last, he had fallen asleep. I laid him down, and his father hovered over him, one hand holding the boy's hand and the other clenched at his side. The crisis might be over, but he was still terrified he might lose Anton. Only after an hour or so had passed without further incident did he begin to relax. He buried his face in his hands, in some silent, personal hell.

When he finally looked up, his face haggard, his eyes bottomless pits of pain and agony as they met mine, he said unsteadily, "Madeleine, if anything happens to my boy, I believe I would die."

I reached for his hand. He didn't even seem to notice as I clasped it in mine.

I thought of my baby, whom nobody missed because nobody had had time to know it, yet had left a permanent gaping tear in the fabric of my life. And I glanced at Anton, frail and vulnerable and colourless, and I *understood.* If I could still feel so keenly the death of a baby I never met, of course this man would feel a thousandfold more keenly the loss of a child in whom he had invested so much of himself over the last nine years.

...Madeleine.

He'd called me Madeleine.

Raymond

I'VE SEEN ANTON LIKE this before. Evenings are always his worst time, especially when he's exposed to too much damp and smoke and gets to laughing too uproariously. But who wants to discourage a child's happy laughter? And sometimes, he's fine.

Not so tonight. Fear has absolutely drained me, but I cannot sleep. I keep laying a light hand on his chest, leaning in close to listen, to be sure I can both feel and hear him breathing.

When he was a baby and caught cold (and he often did), I used to sleep upright in my armchair, holding him on my chest so he could be warm and breathe more easily. I never trusted that task to anyone else. In the years since, we've tried steam tents and breathing exercises and eucalyptus oil and every medicine the doctors have to offer. None of these are of any lasting benefit, but he is still here. Really, apart from his troublesome lungs, Anton is as healthy as the next boy.

I wonder if the fact that Antonia smoked like a chimney has anything to do with the fact that smoke is his worst trigger.

I never smoked as much as she did, but I gave it up as soon as I realised it made my son's breathing worse. My love for him is stronger than the longing for any indulgence.

Would Antonia have stopped her smoking for his sake?

Of course she would have.

Wouldn't she?

I must have drifted off to sleep eventually, because I became aware of Miss Mayer removing my glasses and hanging them on the little loop I'd made for them, tucking in my blanket around me.

"He'll be all right," she whispered.

In the morning I woke in the dim pre-dawn light to find Anton breathing normally again, and Miss Mayer's tousled head nestled close to his. Sleep had erased all care from her face, and I imagined this was how she must have looked before the Nazis got her: quite lovely, actually.

The sun rose, with not a cloud in the sky. We could dry out and warm up at last.

I wonder if Miss Mayer has given any consideration to my marriage proposition. I'm half afraid to mention it again.

Meanwhile, Anton is in an uncommonly grumpy mood and I'm at my wits' end what to do with him.

Anton

TÍA LENI SAYS I look like a STORM CLOUD and she is probably right. I sure feel like one. I don't want to write any more in this stupid notebook either, but Papá insists, says I'm being such a grouch I ABSOLUTELY MUST. That it's better for me to grizzle at my notebook than at him.
SO! I AM GOING TO GRIZZLE!

Things I'm Tired Of:

1. The cold. The only way to get warm is in front of the stupid smoking firepit. Which makes me cough. (Coughing like what happened last night stinks. It makes my hands go funny, like they're blocks of wood or something, and I can't feel *anything*.)
2. The rain. It's as bad as at home. Why travel halfway across the world just to come somewhere in a similar latitude and rainfall average as home? Why not go somewhere DRY AND WARM AND SUNNY.
3. Being outside. I don't care how nice it is, I want my room back.
4. The campfire. I want a nice normal coal stove like at home. It doesn't smoke and it doesn't make me cough.
5. Da

Tía Leni sat beside me before I could finish writing out Complaint Number Five, and she asked if she could see my notebook, and I felt bad because I didn't want her to see how mean I feel right now. But I handed it over anyway, and she paged through it. Some of it made her smile. When she got to what I wrote up above, she didn't say a word, which is worse than if she was cross about it. She just handed it back to me, hugged me, and went to crouch in front of the fire to warm her hands. She looked tired.

I watched her a while, and then glanced at Papá, who was shaving over by the wagon seat. He uses his father's old straight razor with the horn handle, which I am not allowed to touch or play with (not that I would, the blade is scary), and he looked tired too.

I guess I am not the only one not in the best mood today. Maybe if I cheer up they will too. I wonder what I can do.

I could catch up on my schoolwork from the past few days without being asked. I bet that would make Papá more than happy, because I've refused to do it the whole time we've been stuck in the wagon.

Oh! I know what I can do. I will pretend I am Papá for a minute.

> Today the weather is very weathery and there is no sign of weather ever letting up in this place. I have observed a substance at my feet which is the colour and texture of sand. On closer inspection it is sand. Here is a drawing of the sand.
>
> It is cold. Except by the fire. And it is windy. And no matter where I go the wind blows the smoke in my face.
>
> There are two odd animals in camp. Closer observation indicates the bigger one to be a Raymondus varelus, a Greater Spectacled Curmudgeon, and the other a Lenii mayerus (Grey English-Austrian-Argentine Fritillary). Their behaviour is very alike even though they appear to be different species. Here is what they look like.
>
> The R. varelus feeds on beans and cheese and observation and insists on lifting heavy things and running around.
>
> The L. mayeris feeds on beans and cheese and communicates best in Morse code.
>
> Intrepid Observer Anton would like to bring these specimens home to England for further study and

observation. But he will have to be very clever to trap them! Haha! He will lure them with RADIO PARTS and CHEESE! Not even such a creature as the L. mayeris can resist radio parts and cheese!

Leni

WE HAVE BEEN BUSY the last couple of days. Inspector Varela wanted to move to our next camp site, so we had to break everything down, make sure we left the place as we'd found it, and then walk for several days. As before, Anton and I took turns on Santiago, but neither of us found it as difficult as the original trek.

Inspector V showed me the location on his map. We were a little further south and west than before, closer to Lago Argentino, the most southerly of the Three Lakes, the Tres Lagos. It was colder there, but the mountains were closer, and *so beautiful.* Since there wasn't a creek near our campsite, we had to do all our bathing in the lake.

Today I lay on a rock, sunbathing a while to dry off before dressing and returning to camp. It felt odd, being in the nude so openly (secure in the knowledge that Inspector V had better things to do than spy on me), and yet also be so far removed from people that it didn't matter. I was quite calm and charitable with the world when I got back to camp.

"Papá's making another coffee cake!" Anton announced excitedly as I approached.

"What's the occasion?" I seated myself on a rock and began to comb out my hair. Anton dropped his notebook and ran to fetch the mirror for me, holding it so I could see what I was doing. He didn't keep it very still, but his intentions were the best, and I didn't mind.

"No particular occasion," his father said. "I just thought it sounded nice."

"My birthday is in nine days and I'll be NINE," Anton said. "It's for that. We'll have a party every day until I'm nine, won't we, Papá, like Las Posadas in Mexico, only for my birthday?"

Inspector Varela laughed. "Not sure about that, sonshine," he said. "But I'll give you a treat on your birthday. What do you want? Nine raisins?"

Anton burst into giddy giggling laughter, and the clouds above got a good look at themselves in the mirror. "Silly Papá," he said. "I want apple tart."

"Apple tart you shall have, then," he said, and he threw his arms around his son in a tight hug. He met my eyes over Anton's head, and something in his expression made me blush unaccountably.

I wandered through the trees in the waning light to fetch some water to be ready for the next morning. I knelt by the lake and dipped my fingers into the silky water, flicking up sparkling droplets and sending ripples circling ever outward towards... more endless wilderness? The vastness of the solitude here felt marvellous. I had stopped worrying that Erich would find me. In fact, I had almost stopped thinking of Erich entirely. I was safe and cared for, for the first time in years, and I was *happy*. I really was.

"Hello, Madeleine." I heard Inspector Varela's voice and whirled around, startled out of my daydream. "Is it all right if I call you Madeleine?" he asked, seeing my reaction. He stood there with his hands in his pockets, watching me.

"Oh! Well—" I quickly filled the bucket and stood. "You already did, the other night."

"I did?" He seemed surprised, and I didn't want to remind him of Anton's asthma attack, so I brushed it off.

"It's fine! Or Leni is fine. My family called me that too, long before Mauritz ever entered the picture. It's my misfortune his dead wife's name was similar—"

He nodded gravely, looking out over the shimmering surface of the lake. "It's a lovely night."

"Yes," I agreed. He stood *so close* to me. I could reach out and touch him, if I dared. I couldn't take my eyes off him.

His hands came out of his pockets and he looked as though

he might turn and leave. Impulsively I snatched his hand to stay him.

"It's not as cold as the last time," he said, as if to himself. His thumb stroked my palm, and I experienced a sudden prickle of anticipation. That surprised me. Was it possible I had the latent ability to respond to a man's attentions after all, to *want* such attentions?

He lifted my hand to kiss my fingers. I closed my eyes, held my breath, savoured the feel of his warm lips pressed to my hand. I would take whatever scraps he was willing to give me, and I would treasure them. He had asked me to marry him, hadn't he? Perhaps he would give me more than scraps, if I would say yes.

He stepped in closer. "Are you all right?" he whispered huskily, peering into my eyes with questioning. "I won't hurt you."

"I know," I said, barely audible, transfixed. I couldn't take my eyes off his face now. He let go my hand, took my pail of water and set it aside, and rested his hands lightly at my waist. Not like Erich, squeezing until I shrieked; not like Mauritz, with his sense of entitlement and possession. Inspector Varela held me lightly. I could leave if I wanted to. Did I want to? My mind raced in circles.

I would give myself to this man without any hesitation, because that's what I do. But I don't suppose it's what he wants. I don't know what he does want. I'll let him decide. I'll let him lead. I don't know what I want either, apart from asking him what he's thinking, but talk would spoil the purity of this moment.

He smiled crookedly, and lifted my chin. His lips hesitated, for what seemed aeons, just shy of touching mine. I didn't dare move, and his mouth didn't ever make it to a kiss,

because he, Varela,

the stick-in-the-mud, sourpuss policeman,

suddenly

got the giggles.

After he got done giggling (and I couldn't help but join in, it was *so infectious*) he said, "I've never seen you really smile or heard you laugh before." He stroked my cheek with the backs of his fingers, a fondness in his eyes that made me warm and quivery inside. "It's—it's rather lovely to see you look happy."

I think maybe I said something, but whatever it was no doubt came out a tangled, incoherent mess, so I'm better off not remembering it. But then he said to me, quite seriously, "Would you mind if I kissed you?"

It shocked me so much that he bothered to ask what *I* wanted that, for a moment, I stared at him speechless. He ran a hand over his face and added a touch ruefully, "Of course, you might not want to at the moment. I could do with a shave. How adventurous are you?"

I wanted to say, *I don't mind at all and I probably wouldn't mind if you never stopped.* But I couldn't. I felt strung tight, the dread that he might not stop with only a kiss stronger than my wanting. I stared at him, uncertain. His hands still rested at my waist.

"I've never kissed a man with a moustache before," I said, neither smiling nor laughing now. I was deciding if I dared to do this.

"Funny you say that," he said contemplatively, his eyes fixed on some distant memory. "One of the first things Antonia said to me was how the first lad who kissed her had a moustache like mine and she liked it."

"She didn't waste any time, did she?"

He turned back his gaze to me and gave me a funny half-smile. "She never wasted any time once she'd decided what she wanted."

"I'm not like that," I said. "Does that make me inferior?"

"Hardly," he said. "You've been burnt too many times to dive into something you're not sure about. I'd like to kiss you. But I'm not going to unless you tell me it's all right."

I bit my lip, unable to meet his eyes. "Swear one thing to me?" I asked, timidly.

"What is it?"

"You'll think I'm very silly—"

He shook his head. "What is it?"

"No tongue?" I squeaked. "Erich—" I couldn't make myself

finish the sentence, but the shudder that passed over me said it more eloquently anyway.

He didn't laugh. "Agreeable enough," he said.

And then we stood there for minutes, not saying anything, before he bent down close again.

Inspector Raymond Varela may never have touched a woman in the last nine years, but he had not forgotten how to kiss one. His lips were warm and gentle and persuasive, and I felt myself going to jelly. His arms tightened around me, keeping me from falling, and I suddenly didn't want to stand any more. And somehow we were sinking into the low-crooking branch of a nearby tree, and my head was exploding with the simple delight of having a request respected, the freedom to enjoy one thing, without being required to tolerate the rest of the things.

His fingers strayed nowhere beyond my face, his lips nowhere lower than my shoulders. I decided quickly I liked the moustache. I went positively giddy, the way it brushed lightly over the sensitive skin of my neck. I couldn't believe he could kiss me like this and not also tear off my clothes and—no, I wouldn't think of *that*—

Too late.

I froze and pulled away, pressing my back to the tree trunk.

"What's the matter?" he asked me, his eyes soft and concerned. He let go the minute he felt me stiffen.

I sat there, staring at the sky, trembling.

"Did I do something I oughtn't have?"

"No," I said, through chattering teeth. He rested his hand lightly on mine, waiting.

"I don't understand," I said, when at last my shivering subsided, "how you can kiss me like that and yet not take any more of me. You aren't like any other man I've ever known."

"You didn't give me permission to go any further than kissing," he said. "If I wanted more, I would ask you first."

My eyes flooded at this reaffirmation that my opinion mattered. I forced a calm into my voice that I did not feel, and whispered, "*Do* you want more?"

Raymond

I TOOK A BREATH. Emotion beat down reason in my brain and I had to make an effort to regain control. "I would be lying if I said no." She didn't answer, so I added, "I am giving you the reins, Madeleine. You decide when and what and how far."

She looked at me. "What kind of man *are* you?"

I shrugged. "I try to be decent. But I *am* only a man, and it would be so easy to…" I trailed off, my hand tightening over hers. For a moment we sat there with hands clasped. I didn't need to finish my sentence. She understood.

"I am a hideous monster under my clothes," she stated, flatly. "Somehow I don't expect you'd be turned on by marks of violence, like Mauritz or Erich." Her voice lost its hard edge and her tone became hesitant and vulnerable. "I've never told anyone this, but—"

What now, I thought, groaning silently in my head.

"It hurts. I mean, sex does. It hurts me."

"Always?"

"Yes." She turned her face to me, her eyes fearful, as if she was afraid I would punish her for admitting imperfection. "I dread—" she hesitated. "I don't know what all the proper words are for what men do, especially in English. The bit where they go in. I dread it so much I get tense, and I *think* that only makes it worse, but I can't help it. I'm so scared of the pain I know is coming."

It struck me as odd, her pervasive innocence about things she had been experiencing for ten years. I laid a hand to her cheek and I said, "Most likely they are all just terrible lovers. But we'll find you a doctor when we get back to Buenos Aires and find out if there's anything actually amiss."

"Why are you doing all this for me?" she asked, a hint of the old bitterness in her tone. "What are *you* going to get out of any of it, if I don't decide to marry you?"

"I don't need to get anything out of it except the satisfaction of knowing I've put things right," I said. "I'm a police inspector. It's what we do. Put things right, if we can."

Another long, contemplative silence. "I still don't know if I should marry you."

"You don't have to decide now."

She turned to face me again. "Are you my friend?"

"Of course I'm your friend."

"And if we're only ever friends, is it all right for you to kiss me like you just did?"

"We can be friends who do, as long as you are happy."

She let out a long breath and gave me the tiniest of smiles. "I'm glad of that, because you kiss beautifully. Do it some more. Please?"

Leni

HIS FINGERTIPS TRACED LIGHTLY along my neck, around my ear, twined with my own. His hands moved down to my hips, held me tight, but didn't wander; he didn't try to slip under my clothes to bare skin. He murmured lovely things to me in Spanish. It was like nothing I had ever experienced, and a tiny part of me wished he would go just a little further. But most of me was content to have exactly this for now. I wove my fingers into his hair, so thick and utterly unlike Mauritz's or Erich's close-cropped styles, and relished the *difference* of this man.

When we finally parted ways to go to sleep, I flopped onto my bed, heart racing. I could still feel the warmth of his mouth on mine, still feel the wistful hunger in it, but most of all I focused on the *mutualness* of it. He wasn't only kissing me. Not after the first few minutes, anyway. I'd kissed him back, with the same hunger. I hadn't known I longed for this, that I *could* long for it, let alone reciprocate.

The undemanding purity of Josef's affection was what I'd always dreamed of finding again someday, somewhere. Raymond Varela was not like Josef. He was prickly and prejudiced and set in his ways.

But he *had* accepted me, even if that acceptance was a long time coming, and now that he had, I believed nothing would sway him from it. The lone wolf and his offspring had adopted me into their pack, and that was that.

Raymond

WHEN SHE LEFT ME to go back to camp with the water, I sat alone by the lake for a few minutes, trying to collect my unruly thoughts and calm my unexpectedly intense emotions.

Madeleine was taller and more angular than petite, curvy Antonia. She hadn't *looked* like she'd be soft. But she was, intoxicatingly so.

It had required great restraint to keep myself from going further than she was comfortable with. She was not Antonia; I would have to be patient. But she was trusting me, inviting me so far. I didn't take that lightly. Madeleine Mayer, that well of hurt and secrets, had *let me kiss her*.

The wilderness might have been going to my head, but I was beginning to believe marrying her would not, after all, be strictly for Anton's benefit. Was I losing my mind to think I might actually be falling in love with a woman I actively despised only a few months ago? Was it merely lust or instinct, reaching out to her because she was available?

I got to my feet and strolled along the lake edge, analysing my lost wife with an impartiality that I'd somehow never managed before. Antonia had been very available, almost too available. How much of our relationship had been nothing but a lust-fueled fling? All of it?

We'd been walking in the woods near my house when Antonia dropped her bomb on me. She'd been unusually jumpy, and she startled me by snatching both my hands in hers and saying, "Raymond?" An uncharacteristic timidity in her voice gave me pause, and I stopped walking.

"What is it?" I asked, alarmed.

She locked eyes with me (I'd always found that a little

unsettling about people in general, but nobody more so than Antonia) and she said, "I have a confession to make." She swallowed, but she did not avert her gaze. "You thought I was cheating on you with Colonel X," she said. "And I got angry when you said so, but mostly I got angry because—because I felt you were trying to get a confession out of me. I—he—" she lowered her voice to a whisper. "I have slept with him."

I jerked my hands out of her grasp as if hers were poison and croaked, "Damn it, woman, am I not enough for you?" My voice shook.

She plunged on. "He's been after me for—for as long as I've worked for him. In the beginning he was charming and fun to flirt with, and for a while I thought he would leave it there. I was flattered. You know I like admiration. And then he got pushier. I told him I wasn't a virgin, hoping that would put him off, but he said he would be glad to have a girl he didn't have to break in." Antonia sniffled miserably. "One day I was driving him somewhere and he had his hand on my thigh, like he'd been doing an awful lot, and the car stalled. Out of petrol. He'd tampered with it somehow. I got mad, but he started touching and kissing me and I—it felt so good, Raymond. I hadn't seen you in such a long time and I forgot myself completely. I'm so ashamed—"

"I cannot believe this is real," I said, turning my back on her. She was pulling my entire world to pieces. What did she count as "such a long time"? A month? Two weeks? A day?

"Don't go! Please!" she begged. "Please let me finish." And I stood still, albeit facing away from her. "Colonel X is an old bastard and I was—I felt so trapped. Once I'd let him have his way once, then I had to again, and again, and I'm so miserable about it." She laid a hand on my arm and I twitched it off.

"He's *married*," I said. "And what about me?"

"I didn't *mean* to," she said.

The idea that she had lain in my arms, in my bed, after she'd slept with another man, revolted me, filled me with speechless fury. I couldn't look at her. How could she do such a thing to me? To us? How could Colonel X do this to his wife? *You could have quit your job*, I wanted to say. "Stop," I said. "Just... just shut up." Every word she spoke twisted the knife of betrayal deeper into me.

"I have to confess," she said. "I have to get you to forgive me, or I'll never be able to live with myself again."

"No, we're through," I said to her shortly. "Go."

I walked away, and as I turned a corner on the path I caught a brief glimpse of her standing there in the trees, pale and colourless and drooping—a spooky, ghostlike sight—and I shuddered and hurried away. I felt as though my heart had been ripped to bits and scattered at the foot of those trees.

The first thing I did, after the initial shock of Antonia's confession wore off, was to go to Bournemouth and pay a not-so-cordial visit to Colonel X. I told him exactly what I thought of him with a well-aimed blow to the jaw. He lost his footing on the polished floor of his foyer, and took a fall.

"WHAT THE HELL DID YOU MEAN BY SLEEPING WITH MY GIRL?" I raged. He struggled to his feet, one hand to his jaw. He was older, but I was bigger, and he knew he deserved it. His wife screamed as she fluttered in from the back of the house—at me, until she realised why I had punched her husband. Then she turned her rage on him. I walked out, leaving the chaos behind, satisfied that my prior claim on Antonia had been asserted, even if I had said I was through with her.

Antonia, meanwhile, was relentless in her quest for absolution. Her impassioned letters of apology and fruitless attempts to phone me went on for two months. Finally I agreed to see her so we could talk. I went to Bournemouth again and found her at home with Jean.

It was an awkward encounter, as if none of our previous intimacy was enough to compensate for this breach. We walked to the park and sat on opposite ends of a bench, and the usually loquacious Antonia seemed hardly able to speak. At last she said, "I've missed you so much. I can't tell you how sorry I am for not telling you right away when he—when he did what he did."

"I know. You said that in your letters."

"Do we have a chance?" She hadn't tried to touch me at all, but her eyes pleaded with me. "I'm sure that I love you, now I've thought I lost you. I want to marry you, if you have it in you to forgive me and love me again."

I stared out over the park and considered. *When he did what he did,* she said. As if she hadn't admitted to it having felt good and allowing it to happen more than once.

"Are you with child, then?" I asked.

"No!" she said. "I... I took care to make sure that didn't happen."

"Taking care to make sure it didn't happen rather indicates premeditation, don't you think?"

She bit her lip, not answering, and I stared out over the park. My pride was not a small hurdle to get past, but I *had* missed her more than words could say and I longed to have her back and know again the joys of loving her.

"I quit working for him two weeks ago. I've found a job at a stationer's instead. And I swear I will never be unfaithful again as long as I live."

I turned to her and I said, "You'll really marry me?"

"As soon as you want," she promised.

"I guess that's all right then."

We went to a pub for a drink, and as the evening went on we became our old selves again. We made plans until the owner of the pub grew fed up with us and shooed us out into the street. Then we wandered towards the train; I had to go back to Tangmere.

"Let's not set a date until we've talked to my father," she said, as we clung to each other against the wall of the station. The words came out fragmented, the spaces between filled with intense kisses.

"All right," I said, kissing her again. "When shall we talk to your father?"

"We'll go together. As soon as you have time off."

"Antonia," I breathed, "all I want right now is to carry you off somewhere and make mad love to you and I only have fifteen minutes and—"

"It's dark," she said, her hands eloquent and suggestive.

"We'll get arrested," I objected, not very authoritatively. "You're so loud."

"Arrest yourself afterwards then," she said. "I *can* be quiet, I swear."

"I don't believe you," I said, laughing shakily at her touch.

"Try me," she said, and right there against the wall with the stationmaster only a few feet on the other side of it, she proved she could.

How easily she had always swayed me into doing whatever made her happy. I wonder if any of it was real for her, ever.

Madeleine has never been anything but proper since she's had her senses back. It would be unfair to count her propositioning me against her; she was drunk and on withdrawals. When she's in her right mind, she's always scrupulous about keeping her clothes on. Sleeves down, collar buttoned. Far more reserved and prim than Antonia ever was, and I do not believe it is only because she's ashamed of the burns on her arms. I believe that's just how she *is*, when she's allowed to make her own decisions about what to wear and how to be. She's not naturally promiscuous. I don't think, even if we married, that I'd ever walk in and find her waiting for me in my chair, clad in nothing at all, or almost nothing at all, like Antonia loved to do. She would probably melt with embarrassment at the idea of making love in a public place, even in the dark.

Why *had* I taken Antonia back? What was it about her that made me cling so tenaciously?

When I finally walked back to my bed, with none of those questions answered, I found Madeleine waiting there. Fully clothed, but *alight*.

I opened my mouth to speak, but she whispered, "Don't talk, just hold me, please."

We didn't do anything but hold each other tightly, yet it was exactly what we both needed. I forgot Anton slept only a few feet away. I forgot all except the soft warmth of her in my arms and the silken strands of her hair between my fingers as I combed through it lightly.

Most of all, I forgot Antonia.

Anton

I WOKE UP THIS morning to find Tía Leni already up. Usually she sleeps a lot later than Papá and I do, but she crouched by the fire with him as he showed her how to cook the oats. But something was different. He was SMILING. I mean, REALLY SMILING, like he couldn't keep his happiness in, and Tía Leni's eyes shone bright and she was laughing, and I stared at them for a long time wondering if these were the same people I kissed goodnight only last night, or if I got dropped on some other planet with people who just look like Papá and Tía Leni.

I went to Papá for my morning hug, and then Tía Leni reached out for me. She held me tight and her hair, which still hung loose, smelled of Papá's cologne. I took a deep breath and it filled me with happiness, too.

"You smell nice," I whispered, and she turned pink and giggled.

What is going on with the grown-ups?

Raymond

I CANNOT CARRY A tune, but I can whistle, and whistle I did this morning. I whistled Miss Mayer awake (she fell asleep in my arms) and even the mules looked at me askance. I want to burst with the joy left over from last night.

One is less inclined to succumb to impulse in the fresh light of morning than under the bewitching spell of moonlight, but her sleepy, unimpressed face was so adorable when she cracked open an eye at my noise that I took her hands and pulled her to her feet.

"You ought to stop that racket, you'll wake Anton," she scolded. I didn't stop, and she stood on her toes and shut me up very effectively.

Everything is cheerful this morning. Everything is wonderful.

Leni

INSPECTOR VARELA HAS LAUGHED a real laugh several times today, and his eyes sparkled, and oh, it makes me so happy and wistful and achingly sentimental inside. I can't quite believe it is really *me* who has done this for him. It surely is the magic of Patagonia, and nothing to do with me.

I want to believe it is me. But if I hope for things, I risk disappointment, so I will live in the moment and wait and see what happens.

All I know for sure is: I don't want to ever be another man's blank slate. I want to be Madeleine Mayer. Whoever she is, I want to find her and be *her*. Not Marlene von Schlusser or Magdalena Sanchez or Leni Varela. I just want to be *me*.

Several days went by after our kisses by the creek, during which neither of us mentioned it or tried to make it happen again. But I knew it had been real, because a wall seemed to have crumbled like Jericho. I saw Raymond with new eyes; he seemed softer, shyer. I often caught him looking at me, and then he'd blush. I felt exultant and foolish in turn, and the air between us crackled whenever we came close to one another. A gaze held a little longer, or his hand lingering on my arm an instant longer than necessary, or a fleeting caress of the backs of his fingers over my cheek when Anton wasn't looking.

In the evenings, Raymond has been unusually chatty, and I listen whilst he expounds on, say, the comparative visual merits of every butterfly known to inhabit southern England—in alphabetical order, which pleases me. And I don't mind listening. In fact, I find it a soothing accompaniment to my unravelling and untangling the black wool, the wool still in my bag from Mauritz's socks that I am reworking into a scarf for Anton, to keep his throat warm and pull up over his nose and mouth to soften the effects of wind and smoke.

Anton is less impressed with his father's monologue. "Papá, can't you talk about *normal* things?" He lay on his back, stretching his toes up as high into the air as he could.

Before Raymond could answer, I spoke up. "It is normal, for him. We all have our own normal."

Things are very, very lovely. Anton is bouncier and happier than ever. His father and I haven't had many chances to be alone; we're so busy during the day, I've found I'm actually ready to sleep when night comes. It is unusual and refreshing.

It was probably just as well to be too busy, however, because although I had moments where I wanted nothing more than to kiss and be kissed by Raymond, I had more moments of just wanting to be near him and sneaking looks at him like a besotted schoolgirl. Mooning, Hanna would have called it.

I am a little more cautious now, more conscious of what he might think of me. In the pre-Nazi-mistress part of my life, it seldom occurred to me how my actions appeared. Now I'm so paranoid, it is impossible to *not* be at least a little self-aware. My well-being depended so critically on being able to pick up cues from Mauritz.

Raymond is different. He gives me no cues. I have to figure it all out for myself.

"Want to watch the stars a bit tonight?"

Anton had been asleep some time, and I sat picking through tomorrow's beans for stones, another task I had found myself adept at. I liked the feel of the smooth beans in my hands, digging into the sack and letting them slide through my fingers like pellets of silk.

I smiled shyly. "I'd love to, Inspector Varela."

"You know you don't have to keep calling me that."

"I know," For some reason I was shy about using his name. It felt wickedly intimate. I'd had the same trouble with Mauritz. It had taken me years to stop feeling impertinent addressing him by his name.

Inspector V sat beside me whilst I finished picking. There weren't many bits of gravel in this batch. It was a new sack, and the gravel was always thickest at the bottom.

"You said your Argentine papers have your name as Magdalena," he said. "Do you know what magdalena means in Spanish?"

"The only thing Magdalena makes me think of is Mary Magdalene," I admitted. "Patroness of Sexual Temptation?"

He ignored that. "A magdalena is like a muffin."

"And in what way, exactly, am I like a muffin?"

"Well, you're sweet. And soft." He said it so matter-of-factly, as if he compared women to baked goods every day, I had to bite back a giggle.

"I'm done now," I said, and he poured water over the beans for me and covered them with a plate to keep out curious creatures. Then we took one of my blankets to spread on the ground in a clearing a short distance from camp, where we had a fantastic view of the stars. We lay shoulder to shoulder, fingers laced together, gazing upwards.

"What are your sisters like?" I asked. If I was possibly going to become part of this man's family, I really ought to start preparing myself for what to expect.

He said, "They look a good deal like me, only Lucinda insists on hiding her grey hairs with dye and Matilda has by some genetic quirk gotten the green eyes of my father's aunt. We're all tall. My mother, too."

"Would they like me?" This was what worried me the most. Would they *accept* me?

He was silent a long time. "I don't know," he said. "My strangeness doesn't sit well with them, and I'm not sure what they'd make of you."

"You're brutally honest."

"Well, it's better I am brutally honest now rather than later, don't you think?"

I sighed. "I suppose."

"They loved Antonia. I... I think maybe they hoped she would 'fix' me."

"You don't need fixing," I said softly, adding, "Why are we different? You and me, I mean."

He squeezed my hand. "I don't know. But I'm awfully glad there's at least one person in the world who understands. My mother and sisters, they're not truly awful. They mean well. They just... I perplex them, that's all."

It was a clear night with no moon, and the stars were a light show extraordinaire. I'd never paid much attention to stars before coming to Patagonia, and these hung so low, like fat diamonds, I found myself reaching up, longing to grab one.

"That's Canopus," he said, his hand pointing with mine to a particularly bright star. "What would you do with a star, if you could get one?" he asked me.

"I'd wish on it," I answered readily.

"What would you wish?"

Again I answered with no hesitation. "That I could see my father again. What about you?"

He took a long time answering. When he did speak, his voice sounded shy. "I would wish I could spend the rest of my life watching the stars in the wilderness with you."

I considered this. "You really wouldn't rather be here with Antonia?"

He exhaled, and I felt his hand grow tense. "There's something I should tell you," he said. "Something I've been denying and trying to forget for nine years. Maybe you can help me sort it out."

"About Antonia?"

"Yes. Her and me."

I waited quietly. He raised himself on one elbow and looked out into the darkness. I could just make out his profile in the starlight. "We quarrelled the day she died."

"What about?"

"Anton came early, as you know, and we had to be very careful of him once we brought him home from hospital. I was exhausted because I was so worried about him. Losing sleep. Being the one to make sure he stayed alive overnight so Antonia could sleep. And she wanted me to make love to her, and it felt so wrong to even think of such a thing when our son was so fragile."

I laid my hand lightly over his; his fingers were anxiously picking at the pilled wool of the blanket on which we lay. Eventually he went on. "Aside from that, I was just so damn tired, you know? I still had to work. And the doctors told us to wait at least six weeks, and she barely waited for three. I didn't want to hurt her." He laughed, a short, humourless sound. "Six weeks to the day, she demanded I quit holding out on her, and I—I am afraid I was, ah, a bit... unpleasant."

"In other words, furiously angry," I said.

"Yes." He lay down again and laced his fingers together over his chest. "I told her all the things I just told you and that I didn't feel like she cared and maybe she could try growing up a little? And then she said—she said I'd hardly noticed her since Anton was born, and if he was all I wanted, she'd jolly well leave him to me and go find someone who *would* shag her." His voice broke, and I nestled into him, laying my hand on his. "She got dressed up and walked out. Didn't say goodbye to me. I didn't say goodbye to her, either. I was so angry and hurt by the whole thing. I didn't know what to do, but I took it for granted that we'd work it out. And then a few hours later Jean telephoned to say Antonia was dead."

I winced, picturing it all, feeling the heaviness of his own regret and self-loathing, his fear and guilt. He sniffled a few times whilst I absorbed what he said, and finally he collected himself enough to ask, "What happened, Madeleine? What should I have done? How do I live with it now, all these years later? I *would* have apologised, made it up to her, but..."

"You couldn't. I understand." I squeezed his hand, and he waited, knowing I'd answer when I'd had time to think it all through. Finally I said, "You weren't really secure in her love, were you? I mean, deep down you always feared she had a wandering eye."

"Yes, unfortunately."

"I think," I said, "that she was insecure too. She was afraid of losing you as her lover. She wanted to be more than just Anton's mum in your eyes, but she expected you to know that without telling you. Men don't pick up on subtleties very well. I know. And you less than most."

"Yes," he said, with great feeling. "That's it exactly. I was constantly guessing what she actually meant and I never knew if I was getting it right."

"Perhaps she didn't know how much it would have meant to you to be brutally honest all the time, or how much you needed it. Her wanting you to make love to her was probably indicative of a deeper insecurity that maybe she didn't even know how to communicate."

He turned to his side, facing me, his voice earnest when he spoke. "Why could I not have met *you* in 1941 instead?"

I laughed nervously. "You sound like you're more in love with me than you've let on!"

"Maybe I am." He paused, then took my hand. "You've just plodded along all these months, mostly not complaining, no matter how unkind I was to you. I was an insufferable ass from solitude and clinging to my bitterness so long, but I want to do what I can to make up for all you've had thrown at you, if you'll let me."

"I have been quite scared of you sometimes," I admitted. "I'm still a little scared of you."

"I had started to come apart at the seams a bit back in England," he confessed. "It was a terrible time for you to get a proper impression."

"Mauritz seemed nice to start with. A lot of men do. Then they sleep with me and turn into monsters."

"I won't turn into a monster," he promised.

"Are you planning to sleep with me, then?" I asked.

"No. Not at the moment, anyway."

"You wanted to the other night."

"I did." He kissed my forehead lightly. "But I am determined that I will not get carried away. If you ever decide you want to go further, I want to show you what it is to make love. Not just clinical, cold 'having sex'."

"Is it bad, me not being like Antonia?" I had to hear him reassure me again.

"Not at all," he said emphatically. "You're not ready to get so serious, and honestly, in my less hormonally charged moments, neither am I. But I do want you close to me like you are right now—if you don't mind, I mean."

"I don't mind," I whispered, and I laid my hand against his cheek and stroked it. Our lips met, briefly, warmly. I traced over his bare forearm with a light fingertip.

"Oh, that's lovely," he said, halfway between rapture and groan, and the next thing I knew we were kissing again, starved.

"Leni," he said, when we came up for air, his voice thick and indistinct, "Leni, I do love you."

"Have you gone mad?" I asked.

"Maybe," he said, "but it's true."

"Is this a hormonally charged moment?"

There was a pause, but he did not let go of me. He seemed almost desperate to anchor himself to another human, his big beautiful hands framing my face. "It is, but also…" He went silent, quietly breathing, before at last continuing, "Antonia is dead. She was good for me, and I loved her and I needed her, but she is dead, and you are not. It's you who's right for me now, whom I need now." He leant his forehead into mine. "I do want to marry you, and Anton would love it if you did, but even if you don't want to, you could still be my friend and I'd be content with that. I love you," he repeated.

I want to go all the way and then some. But I'm afraid to let go, afraid to trust, afraid of losing Madeleine again when I've just started to get her back. I hadn't imagined I'd ever feel anything pleasant out of physical contact with a man, and here I was in the arms of the most gorgeous man I had ever laid eyes on and he *loved* me? Not only that, but I liked being there. I felt safe and happy and content.

Aloud I said, "You're very sweet. Maybe it's you who's the muffin."

"Have you thought about it, Leni? About marrying me, I mean?"

"I have," I said, and I told him how I feared becoming another man's blank slate. He listened, playing with my hair, and when I'd finished, he said:

"What *would* you like to do when you go home? You said once you'd wanted to be a doctor."

"I don't know," I said. "It still doesn't seem real that I actually *will* go home. I'm not there yet. I don't know that I should make any concrete plans until I get back alive."

"That's a little morbid," he said.

"I know. But you get that way when you live for ten years believing each day might be your last."

We lay quietly a while. His hand sought mine again, and finally he said, "I will support whatever choice you make, whatever you want to do with your life. That's how I love you."

"You're very sweet, Inspector Varela," I said again.

"Say my name," he begged. "Please?"

"You're very sweet, *Raymond*," I said, stumbling over the word, and changing the subject as quickly as I could. "Tell me how butterflies mate," I said, and snuggled closely into him to listen to a discourse on the habits of his favourite thing in the world. I found his obsession utterly adorable. I wondered, were I to spend ten years with him, as I'd done with Mauritz, if I would ever tire of every conversation circling back to butterflies. Somehow I didn't think I would. "Is it superior to how humans do it?"

He laughed and tightened his arms around me. "There's at least one regard in which their lovemaking is inferior," he said. "They face away from each other. We can do it face to face. Look into one another's eyes, if we want to."

"I don't suppose they care much about eye contact," I said.

"The male likes the way the female butterfly looks. She likes how he smells. They're wired differently from one another, just like people. And they do make a lovely picture when they're coupled, tail to tail. Sometimes the male flies away with the female still attached. Showing off, probably."

"A typical man, in other words?" I quipped. "I like the way *you* smell. Honestly, any woman in her right mind should be falling at your feet."

"The world must be full of millions of women out of their right minds, then," he said, sounding self-conscious.

"Less competition for me," I said. "I'm scared to death of committing myself to you, but please know it has nothing to do with anything but me. You're dead sexy." The night air emboldened me. I usually wouldn't have said that. But I didn't stop. "I *do* want you. I'm just scared I still won't like it, and that would be terrible."

"I understand," he said. "Believe me, I do understand."

Lago Argentino - San Carlos de Bariloche - Buenos Aires

14 - 30 April 1952

Leni

IT HAS BEEN GETTING colder at night, and the three of us have been sleeping in the wagon again.

Tonight I stood by the fire, braiding my hair before climbing into my third of the bed, and Raymond came up and wrapped his arms around me from behind. He does this fairly often of late, these unsolicited displays of affection, and I have come to treasure them. It has been unspeakably wonderful to experience the joys of non-sexual human touch these last several weeks. For a while he just stood there hugging me, and I closed my eyes and smiled.

"We need to talk," he said suddenly, "about what comes next."

I turned in his arms and looked at him, brush in hand, plait undoing itself. "What does that mean?" I asked. "Like am-I-going-to-marry-you what-comes-next, or something else?"

"No, I mean going back to Buenos Aires." He guided me to the rock we liked to sit on and put his arm around me. "I had originally planned to stay here until the end of June, but I hadn't counted on having a third person. There aren't enough supplies. I've taken inventory and we need to break camp in the next few days and head back north."

"So soon." I felt oddly deflated and empty at the idea of leaving this place I had come to love so much. I had known our idyll here would have to come to an end, but I had not prepared myself for it to be *now*.

"I don't want to leave either, but it's not just the supplies I'm concerned about," he went on. "I don't know how long it's going to take to sort you out at the embassy and get you some proper papers again. I want to make sure we have plenty of time to tend to all that before the last minute, so you can come home with us."

I fell silent for a long time, and he didn't say anything else either, only sat there lightly stroking my arm with his thumb.

"I'm scared," I said finally, the sum of everything I was feeling.

"You won't be alone," he promised me, and when I opened my mouth to speak, he laid a finger on my lips to silence me. "If you're about to ask me why I'm doing this for you, don't."

I had to smile at that. "I was going to." I snuggled in closer to him. "I'm cold."

"You're always cold," he said, fondly, but he wrapped me in his arms and we sat there quietly holding each other until I fell asleep.

We set to packing the next day. We'd been burning the sacks and crates as we emptied them, and the wagon, full to overflowing in November, was now so empty Anton and I could have ridden in it if we wanted to. By the morning we left, everything had been returned as closely as possible to how we had found it, and we started on our way back to Tres Lagos.

Anton and I were both considerably sturdier than we were only a few months before, and although he did ride Santiago sometimes, mostly he walked with us, and he didn't seem too terribly winded by it either. He did wear the bandana. He hadn't argued about it again since that last horrible attack in March. We arrived back at the humble home of Señora Ríos by the end of the third day. She was pleased at how happy and healthy her mules looked. She didn't recognise me at all.

The next morning we climbed into the truck, and this time I did not have to ride in the back.

Being in a motorised vehicle shocked my senses. The slow pace of life in the wilderness had calmed me, and driving even at thirty-five miles per hour was enough to make me ill. Anton looked a bit green as well, but of course Raymond was Perfectly Fine. I'd have given him a hard time for his smugness, only I knew if I opened my mouth, I would be sick.

We slept in the back of the truck that night, and late the next night (after a number of prolonged pauses during which

Raymond went chasing butterflies) we arrived in San Carlos de Bariloche.

To begin with, I was all right. The three of us slept together in a bed that was wider than the wagon. Sweet, innocent little Anton offered to sleep on the floor to give Raymond and me more room, but I quickly shut that down. I would have preferred to continue hiding indoors as long as we were in the city, but Raymond said we must act like an ordinary family being touristy. So we spent a few days seeing things, mostly quiet things, and shopped for some clothes that fit me.

But sometimes in the night, Raymond's hand found mine in the space above Anton's head, and I fell asleep knowing no harm could come to me as long as he was nearby.

The day we left San Carlos, Raymond exchanged his wilderness garb for ordinary city clothes, and he and Anton got their hair cut. Anton fussed over having his luxuriant mop of curls shorn off, but his father was adamant. I sat on a bench, watching but not seeing, my fingertips tense and tapping. Anton brought me a particularly fine curl he gleaned from the pile on the floor, which distracted me from fretting for a few minutes. I folded it safely into a scrap of paper and tucked it into the secret pocket of my handbag where I used to hide my pharmaceutical reserves. Raymond looked so different in a suit and tie that I had a little difficulty processing that he was, in fact, the same man.

My ability to cope with being in public vaporised completely the moment we stepped into view of the station platform to get on the train for Buenos Aires.

I felt I was again in the mad crowd that had unwittingly helped me to escape five months earlier, felt as if Erich or Mauritz or Hitler himself was breathing down my neck. Aside from Señora Ríos, I had had no human contact with anyone but Anton and Raymond in all the intervening time.

too
many
people

Raymond more or less had to physically push me onto the train, drag me to my seat, and hold on to me whilst I had hysterics for a full hour. Who knows what the other passengers thought of the crazed lunatic sharing a coach with them. Eventually I was too exhausted to cry and sat as unblinking as a fox in headlights for hours.

(Seeing the station platform again, I *did* wonder how in the world I managed my getaway. There's nowhere really to hide. In my heels that day, I would have been taller than Mauritz, and we aren't particularly short people.)

Buenos Aires, though.

If I had panicked in Bariloche, I became an atomic explosion of disaster in Buenos Aires. Raymond and Anton had both their hands full, trying to keep me from falling apart.

It wasn't any one definable thing.

It was the memories of what had happened to me here.

It was knowing that at any time, at any place in this city, I might meet someone who knew me (or perhaps worse, be seen by someone I didn't see), and all I had gained in the last several months would have been to absolutely no purpose whatsoever.

I *looked* different enough. Señora Ríos hadn't recognised me, after all. The clothes Raymond had bought me in Bariloche (before the Great Station Platform Meltdown), were second-hand and hardly the peak of fashion, especially when paired with my now-faded floppy hat from El Calafate. My hair had grown out and I wore no makeup and I wasn't a limpidly white skeleton anymore. Maybe I could make it to the embassy without anyone recognising me. *Maybe.*

"It's been almost six months," Raymond reminded me. "Surely they've given up on you by now. Surely they won't still be watching the stations."

I wanted desperately to believe him. But he didn't know them as I did. They were insidious and omnipresent when it came to sniffing out their own.

I waited with Anton whilst Raymond found us a cab to take us where we needed to go. I held the boy's hand tightly, as if the waif of a child beside me could protect me from harm, and scanned furtively for any familiar faces from beneath the shield of my ridiculous hat. I didn't see anyone I recognised, but that didn't mean much.

I heaved a huge sigh of relief as the three of us climbed into the cab together. First stop: the embassy. I'd have rather gone straight to our hotel, but Raymond insisted and I didn't argue. I couldn't leave the country without papers, I *knew* that, and I worried about having enough time, but I was *so drained*.

I followed Raymond meekly up the steps, and Anton clung to my hand. We sat in chairs to wait our turn. I perched on the edge of my seat, fingertips drumming my handbag nervously as it balanced on my knees. I didn't see anything suspicious, although my eyes darted compulsively over the people around me, still convinced I must be on constant vigil for Nazis who might recognise me.

I was so intent on my Nazi Watch, I nearly jumped out of my skin when I heard my name.

"Madeleine?"

A man had stepped forward and stood before me, tentative. In his gaunt old face I saw a ghost, the ghost of my father. My quaking turned me into something more akin to jellyfish than human, and I fell backwards into my seat. My voice was hoarse. "Daddy?"

The man dropped to his knees, reaching for me. "Madeleine," he said again. I closed my eyes and listened. His voice was the same, the arms wrapping tightly around my shoulders were the same. He too shook with emotion as he held me, and I hid my face in his shoulder and said nothing at all.

After a few minutes I looked up. I allowed myself, through the blur of my tears, to look at the man kneeling before me: an old, tired man, his kind eyes full of a familiar love. He said, "My darling girl, your friend sent for me to come. You cannot imagine my joy to know you are still alive, that you're safe."

"Daddy." My mouth moved, but I don't know if I made any

sound. I felt too stunned to do more. I leant into him again, crying. "Where's Mama?" I sobbed out, although I suspected I already knew the answer.

"She died two years ago," he said quietly. "Very sudden. She never gave up hope that you would come back to us one day. She never believed for a minute you were dead."

"Did you?" I whispered.

"I knew you didn't die when they said you did. But when you never came home, I didn't know what to think..." he trailed off. Then he laughed a tiny laugh and laid one hand against my face. "You see, they said they found you by your bicycle, and *that* could never have been our Leni."

I laughed, but it turned into a sob as soon as I let it out. It's true. I am far too uncoordinated to ride a bicycle, and I never did learn. For several minutes we just held each other, until Raymond's gentle hand on my arm jerked me out of my bittersweet reverie, telling me that the embassy man had called us and it was time to go talk with him. Supported by my father and Raymond and followed by Anton, I somehow made it to the office and sat down.

I couldn't have survived that interview without Raymond and Daddy's support, though the man was nice, and he promised he would do his best to sort out the tangle of my identity. I was legally dead, after all. They took fingerprints and a handwriting sample, and of course my father vouched for me. "If there's any chance you could find your passport from 1939," the man said, "it might help."

"I don't suppose they kept it," I said sorrowfully.

When we finished, we all went back to the guesthouse Raymond had found for us. Just being in the same car with my father was too unbelievable, too overwhelming. But Daddy was a very wise man. He had not forgotten how to handle his peculiar child. He sat beside me with one arm securely over my shoulder and the other hand stroking my hair, and didn't try to make conversation as long as I sat there with my face on my knees, jittering as if I'd lost all control of my body.

I collapsed on the couch and passed out cold for at least an hour.

When I woke, I had another cry. "I'm supposed to be happy," I wailed. "It's DADDY."

"Shh, muffin, you're not *supposed* to feel anything," Raymond said. "Just let yourself feel whatever you feel. It's all right."

Raymond

EVERYTHING ABOUT THIS DAY was wrong and overwhelming and draining for Leni, but once we'd said goodnight to her father at his room I took her to our room. (We'd agreed to stay together as we have been; there's a bed and a couch, and since we both have wedding rings nobody questioned the arrangement.) I told Anton to go to bed and took Leni to her couch. Sat beside her, holding her whilst she sobbed and shook. I tucked her in with extra blankets, knelt beside her and lay my head on the pillow beside hers, stroking her hair. "We'll get through this. I'm here for you, whenever you need me," I whispered. She reached for my other hand and held it, wordlessly, and we lay there breathing together until her hold on my hand loosened and she had gone to sleep. I kissed her forehead lightly, dimmed the lamp, and went to my own rest.

LENI

I DIDN'T WAKE UNTIL nearly noon the next day. My emotional distress, the long journey from Bariloche, the unexpected appearance of my father, the ordeal at the embassy, all left me utterly drained. When I did wake, Daddy was sitting in the armchair near my couch, watching over me with loving concern. For a moment after glimpsing him there I snuggled deeper into my heap of blankets and smiled with my eyes closed, feeling safe.

He laid a hand on my head and stroked my mussed hair. "You've slept such a long time, my dear girl. Would you like some breakfast now?"

"Not just yet, thank you, Daddy." I sat up, feeling as lucky as a queen to luxuriate under the weight of so many soft blankets after months of the stiff wool ones. I looked into Daddy's eyes, and tears rose in my own. I didn't know what to say, where to begin telling him about these past ten years.

Finally I stammered, "Have you spoken to Raymond—Inspector Varela?"

"Some. Why?"

I began to tremble involuntarily, to think perhaps I was still not ready for any conversation at all, and I hid my face in my hands. Daddy came swiftly to sit beside me on the couch, took my bundled self into his arms to still my shaking, soothing me with quiet assurances that everything would be all right now we were together again. Nobody could hurt me now. Finally I did cry, sobbing until I could scarcely breathe. When I was too exhausted to cry any more, I went slack in his arms, sighing shakily and sniffing.

Daddy kissed the top of my head. "Have you the strength to talk?"

"Maybe you start," I said. "Tell me how you came to be here?"

I snuggled into the curve of his arm and he took my hand, the one with Mauritz's ring still on it, looking at the gold band a while before speaking.

"Your police inspector sent a wireless message to a friend of his two months ago, someone here in Buenos Aires, I believe, who passed it on via telegram to me. My heart about stopped when it came. Your sister Hanna was with me that day with her children. She opened it and read it and burst into tears, but she was smiling too as she pushed it towards me."

"What did it say?" I asked.

He reached into his breast pocket and pulled it out. "I've carried it everywhere ever since. I had to show it to all our friends, and it was such a comfort to me."

He handed it to me and I unfolded the little paper.

> 29 March 1952
> Dr Tobias Mayer, Swallownest, England
> Pleased to inform you I have located your daughter Madeleine in Argentina. She has been in Nazi captivity. Have her safe with me in Patagonia. Will be returning to Buenos Aires late April. If you are able to meet us there would be pleasant surprise for her. Please confirm receipt of this message to Delfina Regalados who can relay it to me where I am.
> Inspector Raymond Varela
> Home address Tangmere, England

"I was overjoyed," Daddy said. "I sent a message back right away and booked passage to get here at the time he said. I also went and did some paternal detective work to learn who this Raymond Varela was. I wanted to know who was looking after you, whether he could be trusted. You know."

I smiled in spite of myself. "And?"

"I couldn't learn much. The superintendent at his station told me Raymond was asked to take a year's leave, and he'd packed off to Argentina almost immediately and hadn't been in touch since."

Asked to take leave? My curiosity was piqued. I tucked it into a mental pocket for later. "What else?"

"His neighbours proved more talkative. Said he kept to himself since his wife died, that he was a decent fellow who loved animals and had a son everyone adored."

"Anton," I said fondly.. "I am so glad you came, Daddy."

"It was a gamble, but it would have been worth it just to have a *chance* of seeing my girl again."

There was a long silence, and I broke it at last. "They declared me legally dead. Threw me in the ghetto for six months and tortured me until I agreed to do whatever they asked—" I stopped, my sobs rising again to cut off my voice.

He held me tightly. "I know," he said. "My poor darling. I see it in your eyes. I know."

The four of us stayed in our room that day. We had our meals brought in, and I savoured being shut in away from the noise of the city and from people. I didn't want to talk to anyone, not even Anton. I still cherished the luxury of lying in as long as I liked, even all these months later. Didn't yet take it for granted.

Anton

OVER THE LAST FEW days, we've mostly just stayed in our rooms, except Papá, who can't bear to not go run for miles or something else ridiculous like that every day. He started getting restless and pacing the room after only the first day or so, until finally Tía Leni shoved his satchel of Explorer Things into his arms and shooed him out the door to go hunt for butterflies outside town, and he has been much happier ever since.

Tía Leni and her father and I don't mind waiting for him. Tía Leni's father is so nice. I am glad Papá didn't tell me he was sending for him. I couldn't have kept the secret.

Anyway, the place we are staying is not quite a hotel, more like a boarding house. Dr Mayer has the room next to ours, and so we see a lot of him. Today Papá asked Tía Leni to come out with him to hunt for butterflies, and I think she *wanted* to go, but she looked sort of hesitant about the idea and said she'd stay behind.

I think she wished she'd gone with him for sure when her father and I talked her into going out with us for a walk. There's a market not far from here, and we decided it would be nice to pick up the developed photographs Papá ordered from his film. So she put on her funny floppy hat and the three of us went out. She really doesn't ever relax when we're outside our room. She was constantly looking around for familiar faces, and I got lost for ten minutes while she paid for Papá's photos, but I found them again. Tía Leni hugged and scolded me and her eyes were wet and she said we needed to go back. She didn't let go of my hand the whole way after that, and then she slept for two hours, after ordering me to leave the photos in their envelopes until Papá gave me permission to look.

Buenos Aires

2 - 11 May 1952

Leni

I WENT OUT WITH Daddy this morning and had coffee across the street from the house where we are staying. It took a good deal of coaxing on his part to get me to come, after the incident at the market the other day, when we lost Anton for a few minutes. Anton was safely in his father's care, however, and there was no reason for me to not go.

Still, my eyes scanned everywhere, my ears straining for familiar voices, until Daddy distracted me by seating me at a corner table.

"You always did like corners and tight spaces," he said, fondly, reaching for my hand and squeezing it. "I remember you as a little girl, if we couldn't find you, always having to search under the beds and in the closets…"

I smiled and relaxed just a touch. "My favourite place was the cupboard under your sink in your surgery," I said. "I was so sad when I outgrew that."

"Your mother thought it was odd," he said, eyes twinkling.

"I know," I said. "None of the other children was so strange. I don't suppose she ever quite knew what to do with me."

"Maybe not, but she did love you." He took a sip of his coffee and changed the subject. "Are you going to marry your Inspector Varela?"

I ducked my head, blushing in spite of my best efforts to remain cool and collected.

"He's a fine man. I'd trust him with my girl in a heartbeat."

"Well," I said, "he did ask me to, but I said I didn't know, and mostly it's for Anton, but we haven't said anything to him—he'd be heartbroken if I decided *not* to marry his father, and—"

Daddy raised an eyebrow, and I became defensive, my voice going a little high-pitched. "If you'd been treated by men like I have, you'd hesitate too, Daddy! It's not that I don't like him, I just don't know up from down."

"He's definitely up," Daddy said calmly, returning to his coffee. "And you might not know it at the moment, but you *do* love him. I see it in your face every time he comes into the room. It's like you've just seen an angel."

My face flushed even more and I wished I could sink into the floor. Was I so obvious? How could I betray an emotion I didn't know if I felt?

Of course, my brain and my emotions were as out of sync as my feet when I tried to dance, so maybe that wasn't even a valid excuse. I felt *some* things when Raymond was near. Confidence. Security. Comfort.

"And he's very much in love with you. Have you slept with him?" Daddy asked me next.

"No..." Being talked to frankly as an adult by my father was clearly something I would have to get used to. "Not... not that way."

"Maybe you should."

I swallowed and worried my napkin in my lap. "Daddy—"

"Yes?"

"How much did Raymond tell you about—about what the Nazis did to me?"

"Not much." He watched me, waiting. "What I know is what you told me the other day."

"I had a baby coming." I took a deep breath. I could tell Daddy this. He was a doctor. "Dr Mengele, Josef Mengele, he came to Mauritz's house as a special favour and he—he—got rid of it. For Mauritz. Not because I wanted to. He strapped me to the kitchen table and took my baby. Cut me open and made it so I couldn't ever have any children—"

Daddy's face went white and his eyes flashed. He set his cup down with a clatter and stood. "This you must show me," he said. "Come at once."

I paid for our coffee with trembling fingers and we went to Daddy's room. I showed him the scar, and his hands, which had cared for so many people over the last forty-odd years, were light and gentle.

"What a horrible job he did stitching that." His voice was quiet with fury. "Did it get infected?"

"I think it did, a little. I had to take the stitches out myself. The skin had started to grow over them and nobody was bothering to do anything."

"You say Mengele did this?"

I nodded and sat up, swinging my feet to the floor.

"The authorities at the Nuremberg trials said he was dead."

"Well, he's not. He's here in Buenos Aires. I've seen him dozens of times."

Daddy's eyes flashed again. "He is here and alive? I will kill him myself."

"I don't know where he lives," I said. "I don't know what name he uses here, either. You're unlikely ever to find him."

"When did this happen?" Daddy gestured to my scar.

"July 1941. Almost exactly a year after they captured me."

"What else have they done to you?"

I unbuttoned my blouse and shrugged it off, to show him the burns on my arms and Erich's lash marks on my back. He shook his head, speechless, and gathered me into his arms and wept with me.

He didn't say, "I *told* you you shouldn't go to Austria." He didn't say, "You got what you asked for." He said, "My precious daughter, if only I could turn back time."

After a few minutes, I buttoned myself back up and Daddy asked, "Does your police inspector know of this?"

"Anton saw my arms once, by accident. I haven't shown Raymond the damage. I've told him what happened, but I'm dead ashamed to let him look. I'm like a... a sideshow attraction."

I stood, and Daddy hugged me again, and he said quite seriously, "You should show him."

In the night I woke and my brain instantly leapt into action, thinking back to Daddy's advice. He wanted me to marry

Raymond. He even thought I should sleep with him. He hadn't said in what order he recommended these two things, but the fact that he'd left it open to interpretation rather surprised me.

I got off the couch, made sure the connecting door was locked, and turned on the light. Taking off all my clothes, I forced myself to look in the mirror, turning to get a glimpse of my reflection from every possible angle. I hated my body, not only for its scars, but also because I felt fat.

Raymond had told me many times I wasn't fat, I was a perfect weight for my height, but I couldn't accept that. I'd been kept too thin for so long, anything heavier than skeletal looked awful to my eyes. It wasn't so bad when I had clothes on, but naked I was appalled at the sight of myself. I closed my eyes and whispered what Anton had said to me once, a month or so ago: "You're so much softer to hug now than you used to be." It was meant as a compliment, but I burned with shame nonetheless. And Raymond calling me a muffin—

I turned on my heel away from the mirror, threw my robe on, and switched off the light. Unlocking the connecting door, I padded across the floor, past the bed where Raymond snored softly beside Anton, and out to the balcony. I leant on the railing. It was piercingly cold through the thin fabric of my robe, but I didn't care.

The city was still awake, even at two in the morning or whatever it was, but not in the same way as during daylight. I could hear passing automobiles, and tango music drifting from some distant dance hall. The clouds hid the moon and stars, but there were still enough lights on in the city that I could see around me. I closed my eyes and felt the breeze in my hair, and imagined I was back in that great wilderness, that it was the wind coming off the lake lifting my hair.

I had liked Patagonia, I really had: so untouched and pure, everything I wished I could be myself. Town felt claustrophobic in comparison to that freedom. I liked enclosed spaces, I felt safe in them, but the city held no comfort for me as had the arms of the earth. Not anymore. The future, too, felt like a vast, howling wasteland, and I did not want to think of it.

Instead I focused on Raymond. Our path was united now, at this moment, but if I did not marry him, would it diverge once we got back to England? What would I do? Daddy was old. I couldn't count on him living forever to care for me, and the idea of trusting myself to my sisters was frightening. Except for Hanna, I'd never been very close to any of them. I didn't want to think of what would happen if I found myself alone in the world again.

I remembered Raymond's wish on the theoretical star and thought how lovely it would be if it came true, if somehow we could be together always, watching stars in the wilderness. Tears flowed silently from my eyes at the pure simple loveliness of having such a friend. He did love me. He loved me enough to demand nothing of me, even though he might want more than I had given him. Maybe Daddy was right, and I should let myself dare to love Raymond, or at least have a go at trying.

My mind was so consumed with Raymond that I felt little surprise when he materialised at my side about twenty minutes later. He stroked my wet cheek, tucked my windblown hair behind my ears, and instinctively I reached for him.

Raymond

"TEARS?" I ASKED, CONCERNED. I put my arms around her and she rested her head against my chest, just breathing.

She whispered to me, "What happens when we get back to England?"

"Anton and I go to our little house in Tangmere, and you decide whether you want to stay with us or embark on a life of your own." I toyed with a lock of her hair, soft and clean, so different from the bedraggled tangle of our early days together.

"Daddy wants me to stay with you."

"*I* want you to stay with me."

"I know."

There was a long silence and I felt her sigh. "What could I ever do for you?" she asked. "You've seen what a terrible cook I am, and I break things, and I don't know how to do laundry without a—a creek and a scrubbing stone, and I can't give you children. I'm of no possible benefit to you."

I took her firmly by the shoulders and gave her a gentle shake. "Leni, I've fallen in love with who you are, not who you aren't. You've brought unpredictability and life back to me, and I don't ever want to go back to what I'd become when I met you. As for children, we have Anton. Isn't that enough?"

"We have Anton," she repeated in a whisper.

"Yes, we," I said. "He adores you. You know as well as I do he'd be over the moon if you were going to be his mother."

"You really don't care that I'm a barren tree?" Her voice was genuinely disbelieving.

"I really, really, *really* don't care. First of all, supposing you had a baby now, I'd be ancient and decrepit by the time it turned twenty."

I felt her giggle soundlessly and she turned up her face to say softly, "Sixty-five isn't so ancient and decrepit, Inspector Varela. Not for someone as fit as you."

I ignored that comment. "Second, I don't have room in my tiny house for more than Anton, and I like my house and I'm not planning to leave it as long as I'm in England. Third, there is such a thing as marrying for the simple joy of it. A woman's worth is not determined by how many babies she produces, nor is marital happiness. Get that idea right out of your head." I leant in close to her. "I know you feel deprived of something you wanted, and I wish I could change that. Giving you my son is the closest I can come."

She stood on her toes and gave me her lips to kiss and for a few minutes neither of us spoke. When she pulled away she looked into my eyes and said solemnly, "I don't think it would be fair of me to say yes when you don't know what you're getting."

"I know what I'm getting."

"No, Raymond. You've endured my tantrums and moping and you know I'm damaged, but you haven't seen it. I'd consider myself dishonest if I didn't give you the opportunity to thoroughly examine the goods before you commit to them."

"*Madeleine Mayer*," I said, exasperated and despairing at her conviction that she was unworthy. "You are a woman. A *woman*. Not a bolt of cloth or a basket of turnips."

She took my hand and we walked back inside. She led me into her little sitting room, shut the door behind her, and flicked on the light. Before I realised what she was doing, she had let her robe drop to the floor, and she stood bare before me.

Leni

HIS EYES WENT WIDE as saucers, but they gazed nowhere but at my face. "Look at me," I commanded fiercely. Pain flickered in his eyes, his mouth twitched a little, but he *looked*. He walked in a slow circle around me, and he looked. His fingertips lightly traced every burn on my arms, every mark on my backside where I'd been beaten, until he got to the angry scar on my belly, and he dropped to one knee and kissed it. Actually kissed it, and then he stood again, wrapped my robe around me, took me in his arms and held me close.

"You see," I said, "why I—"

He cut me off. "No," he said. "I see only a warrior. And I am unspeakably proud of her." He pulled me onto the couch with him, and held me, and I felt safe, and I wanted to stay like that forever. But he broke the silence by whispering, "I suppose I should go back to bed and let you sleep."

"You don't want to stay?" I asked, genuinely surprised. He'd seen the damage and been unmoved and he wanted to marry me, and now he was going to leave without taking what every man ultimately wanted?

"Of course I *want* to stay," he said, brushing the backs of his fingers against my cheek. "But is that what *you* want?"

I hesitated. I was hot and breathless, but was that panic or longing? My chest felt constricted. I hugged my knees, hiding my face. Not crying. I just needed a moment to think through it.

Raymond straightened beside me. "I want you to know if you do marry me, you can say no to me and I'll listen to you. Even if all you want out of me is friendship. *I won't own you.*"

There was a stumbling, endearing earnestness in his tone, and as his fingers lightly combed through my hair I looked up and said, "I want to wait."

He nodded, and in an instant, the mood in the room lightened. He leant back into the couch again, taking me with him, nestling his face into my neck in a way that made me feel he was really nothing more than a very big version of Anton.

"Why do you love me?" I asked him.

"I don't know," he admitted. "It might have started because Anton is so besotted with you, and I like seeing him happy, but—also you have stirred me out of my cranky, self-centred existence. I needed that. And you're... interesting?"

"*Interesting!*"

"Interesting is better than pretty. I suspect life will never be dull with you around."

I shifted in his arms and traced my fingertip around his ear. "Can I ask you something?"

"Of course."

"Whatever did you do to get asked to take a year's leave?"

There was a long silence on his part which might have been damning had it been anyone else. But with Raymond, it was pure self-consciousness. He made a face and said, "I suppose your father must have found out about that?"

"He only wanted to determine what kind of man his daughter was getting entangled with."

He grinned sheepishly. "I know. It's all right. I suppose I should have told you before, anyway." He stroked my hand with his thumb, thinking how to answer, and finally said, "Superintendent Perkins told me I was going crackers."

"What did you *do*, though?"

"More than one thing. A string of things." He paused. "Initially, mostly me being grouchy to all my colleagues. By that, of course, I mean... *grouchier than usual.*"

I couldn't help smiling.

"And I'm mostly administrative, so it stayed safely inside the station for a while. But eventually it leaked into my interactions with the public I was supposed to be serving, and I started getting a bit too rough on some of the men we brought in for one reason or another. It was one thing to slam things around on my own desk, but completely another to threaten or lay hands on someone."

"You *hit* someone?" I asked, awed.

"Not quite. I caught myself just in time, but Perkins took me aside and told me that my anger was getting out of hand. Because I'd served faithfully for almost twenty years, he promised he would hold my job while I took a year off, bring in a temp to cover for me until I came back. And he told me to go get a psychiatric evaluation. I haven't done that. I find the idea appalling."

I nestled into him. "It's all right to let your weakness show sometimes," I reminded him. "Were you projecting your anger at Nazis onto them?"

"I suppose so. Also my guilt over that fight with Antonia, and rage at my neighbour for killing my cat."

Another silence. "You still haven't told me about your cat," I said.

"Sometime," he promised vaguely. "It's a long story." He sat up. "Wait here a minute—" He disappeared into the other room. I listened to drawers opening and closing for a minute until he poked his head back inside and said, "Something to sleep on. Catch!" And he tossed me a small box, which I reached for but did not catch, and he closed the door, leaving me alone.

I retrieved the box from the rug where it landed and stared at it. It was obviously a ring box; I'd seen enough of them to know. Finally I plucked up my courage and opened it.

Inside I saw a tiny piece of paper rolled inside an antique opal ring, probably not terribly expensive, but subtle and pretty. I sat down and read the note.

> *I really want to marry you.*
> *Not just for Anton. For you.*
> *All my love, Muffin.*
> *R.*

I took out the ring, tried it on, and held out my hand to examine how it looked. It was so different from the bulky loads of ice Mauritz used to give me to weigh down my lily-white hands. It looked *right*. I lay on my couch, closed my eyes, folded my hands over my chest as though laid out in state, and let my mind go.

I let myself relive the last several months, the changes I had undergone, the changes Raymond had undergone. He was an odd duck, like me, and I had become very fond of him indeed. I could have Anton too. I couldn't have one without the other, could I? And I would do almost anything to keep Anton.

Raymond

I WENT BACK TO my place beside Anton, but I couldn't sleep. I couldn't understand why I felt so attached and attracted to a woman for whom I'd originally held such disdain. Marrying her would be a risk in some respects. What if she said yes, only to tire of me or outgrow her need of me after she'd had time in the real world again? What if she said no, and I was back to where I'd been six months ago?

Only a few days before, her father had talked to me quite seriously and frankly about Leni. He said she simply couldn't be on her own, maybe not ever. He didn't want to infringe on her independence, but he wanted me to be aware that she had always been different, and from his observation, what she had gone through had only made her different-ness more pronounced.

"She's disconnected. Doesn't make friends easily. Gets made fun of. Frankly, Inspector Varela, considering what Leni has endured, I am amazed at how well she is doing right now, and I think that boy of yours has made a world of difference. And you as well. I think you understand her, perhaps even better than I do. You're very much like her. I don't think you'll try to 'fix' Leni."

"No, I won't," I said. "She's who she is. I wouldn't have her any other way."

I had decided I was willing to take the risk of having my heart broken by her in the future, but I wondered what she would answer and when. Antonia had taken a year and a half to finally say "I love you", let alone agree to marry me, and that was whilst engaged in a highly physical affair. As far as I could tell, Leni didn't even want sex at all. I could live without that. I'd lived without it most of my life, after all. But I also knew, if she once said she loved me, she would mean it, and having her love and friendship would be as good or better than sex.

Her poor body. It made me angry on her behalf, that she had been brutalised for so long. It didn't revolt me the way she seemed to think it should, but I understood that, for her, the visible scars were deeply graven into the invisible world of her psyche. Her shame came less out of vanity than from what they represented.

In the darkness I took the chain from beneath my shirt and rubbed Antonia's ring lovingly between my fingers. It had been my constant companion since the day I said my last goodbye to her. Perhaps it was time to say my last goodbye to it, too. Antonia was gone, and I was at peace with that. I had no more anger. Life moves on. I could move on too.

And with or without Madeleine Mayer, somehow it would be all right.

Leni

WE'D HAD DINNER WITH Daddy, and the four of us sat talking as I put all Raymond's photographs into albums, Raymond painstakingly and precisely labelling each one, until Anton and Daddy went to bed around ten, leaving Raymond and me alone together in my little room to finish. When he'd labelled the last photograph, Raymond switched the wireless on, the volume low, some sort of music, but neither of us paid attention to it. Raymond settled to lounging on my couch with some noises I could only describe as Bear Settling Down for Winter Nap, taking up its entire length and then some, reading the newspaper.

I felt jittery, and desperately sought something to keep my fidgety hands occupied, without much success, so I clasped them behind my back and paced in circles around the periphery of the room. The dress Raymond had insisted on buying me on this morning's foray into town was rustly and silky, silver with butterflies embroidered and beaded down one side: pure indulgence, but it did feel nice to know I looked respectable for a change. After my third circuit of the room I stopped to arrange and rearrange things on the mantel, and I nearly jumped out of my skin when Raymond came up behind me and laid light hands on my shoulders.

"Sorry," he said, when he saw how he had startled me. "You seem a bit—keyed up."

"I am." I turned around to see a warmth in his eyes that made my heart flutter.

He touched my cheek lightly. "You are incredibly lovely tonight."

I took hold of his arms and stammered out impulsively, "Teach me what it is to make love. Show me."

He looked surprised. "Are you sure?"

"Yes," I whispered. His hands came to rest at my waist and he stepped in closer, pressed his lips against my forehead, and took a deep breath.

"I haven't done this in a long time," he said, his voice not much above a whisper.

"I think you'll manage," I said, a bit squeakily. I stood on my toes, pressing into him, trying to get as close as I could.

His hand stroked my hair, tucking back stray wisps; brushed along my ear, my neck, following the V on the back of my dress. The light, sure touch tickled my exposed skin, and I shivered with pleasure. "I *did* rather envision something more conventional," he said. "There's no bed in here."

"Nothing about us is conventional," I pointed out.

"That's true." I could feel his fingers toying with the pull of my zip.

Take it off already, I wanted to say. But I didn't. Instead I said, "And we've been sleeping on the ground or in a wagon for months. The floor can't be much worse." I was chattering pointlessly now, to distract myself. "Will you burn me if I cry?"

"Never." He inched the zip down as if he had all the time in the world to get my frock off me. I tipped back my head. His lips brushed close to my throat, and he whispered, "I want you to close your eyes and let yourself *feel*. Don't do anything for me this time. This is for you."

I liked being pinned between him and the wall: firmly enough to feel safe, not so hard I felt trapped. The perfect, comforting amount of pressure. And he was so warm, his lips against my skin weakening my knees and setting small electric shocks popping in my brain like sparklers.

He worked off my dress eventually, pulled out my hairpins one by one. I don't remember undoing his shirt but I must have. I pressed myself into his chest, hard and muscled, and the heat of him filled me.

Even after he'd finally gotten my dress off, he took a long time about it all. He did things to me that no man had ever done before, lovely things I couldn't have imagined, and he was playful and pleasing about some of the things I was familiar with and had hated. I let him take the lead, allowed my body to relax into his, surrendering. Surrendering of my own free will. Every few minutes he would ask me if I liked what he was doing or if he should stop.

I *did* like what he was doing. He made me want it so much that, by the time we were on the floor getting to the part I'd always dreaded most, I had forgotten the fear that plagued me earlier—captivated by the novelty of this experience. I forgot to tense up, and I opened to let him in without even thinking. His hair tickled my chest as his head bent low over me. "Oh, *God*, Madeleine," he said, his voice thick and indistinct. He felt so good inside me, moving slowly, filling me. I gasped with the unexpected ease and delight of it. Instead of the usual terror-stricken clamping, I opened more and more until a pleasant ripple of shudders convulsed me. I gripped his shoulders until the shudders stopped and we both went limp.

"All right?" he asked me quietly, afterwards, pulling one of my blankets off the couch to cover us.

"What *was* that?" I asked. "Am I glowing? I feel like I'm glowing."

He folded me tightly in his arms, kissing the top of my head, but before he had time to answer me, I said, "It didn't hurt." I felt stunned by the glorious truth of this. "*It didn't hurt.*" I looked at him and I couldn't stop a couple of tears from escaping.

He kissed them away. "I love you," he said. "I'm so sorry you've gone through so much." He was crying too. He cared about me, really cared. I *had* known that, hadn't I?

I clung to him and pressed my cheek to his, letting our tears mingle. *I might be a lost cause, Raymond. I am completely lost in the idea of you and me.*

Raymond

THE MORNING LIGHT CREPT in over us where we lay together under the blanket on the thick carpet. For a moment I was disoriented, but then I felt Leni snuggled to my side, and I remembered.

For a moment I watched my companion sleep, her hair in a tangle, and felt again the rush of warmth and joy of last night. It had been so long, I had forgotten just what an intense and phenomenal thing it is to be with a woman. I wanted to shout my joy from the balcony, but more than that I wanted to take her in my arms and have her again.

Leni was, unsurprisingly, quite different from Antonia, chiefly because she'd made so little noise; a few breathy exhalations the only sound I got out of her. But her physical response made it clear she liked what we were doing. She clung close, arching her back to get me deeper into her. I had always complained like fury about Antonia's noise (whilst secretly adoring her for it), but it had also been nice to not have to constantly shush a noisy woman.

Mustn't let Anton find us like this, I thought, leaping up sharply to fetch my clothes from where I'd dropped them last night. I peeked into the other room. He was still sound asleep. Good.

Dressed, I went back to Leni, crouching down to kiss her cheek where the lacy edge of the blanket had left a deep impression. She stirred, and I whispered, "Better get your clothes on before Anton wakes up, muffin mine."

She gathered the blanket around herself and smiled with her eyes closed. I took her outstretched hand and helped her to her feet, held her close for a minute, and then she pulled away and began following the trail of her garments back to where I had draped her silver dress.

"What did you think?" I asked her, when she had zipped herself back into the dress and returned to the window with her hairbrush.

Her answer consisted of turning pink at the ears and biting her lip with a tiny smile.

I bent and kissed her, weaving my fingers lightly through her hair, drawing her close against my chest. Now that she had the dress back on, I had a sudden urge to take it right off again, Anton or no Anton, but I checked myself. "Last night was amazing, Leni," I murmured. "You are amazing. Thank you."

"Mmm," was all she said, as I was kissing her again, then, "I never, ever dreamed I would say this, but I could see myself coming to like sex very much if it is always like *that*."

We stood there and she made no sound, but something thrummed in the silence.

"Perhaps we can try it again sometime?" she said at last.

I could scarcely suppress a laugh at the solemn formality of her tone. "I would like that," I said, trying to be as serious as she.

"You weren't wearing the ring," she said, and seeing my blank look, clarified. "Antonia's."

"Oh." I felt oddly self-conscious and looked away. "I... took it off the other day."

"Why?" she asked.

I hesitated. "Well—I realised I can't let myself be mired down in memories and bitterness when I have a life to live *now*, and I want you as the centre of that life, without Antonia standing in the way. *Will* you marry me, Madeleine? Please?"

She fingered my tie as if contemplating taking it off. "I want to say yes, because it would be easy. I'd be taken care of and I'd be safe. But I may want to step out a bit on my own and figure out who I am and where I fit in a world that's so different from the one I left ten years ago."

"That's reasonable," I agreed. I wanted her to take off my tie. Among other things.

"I like the ring," she said. "It's beautiful and perfect. Can I keep it in here until I decide?"

"Of course." Was this smiling, blushing woman really the same strange hard character who had hidden in our truck six months before? I could scarcely believe it, even though I knew it was true. She stood on her toes and kissed me, and only the sound of Anton singing sleepily to Little Cat in the other room served to separate us.

Anton

PAPÁ AND TÍA LENI were in the other room when I got out of bed, standing in front of the window, looking at each other and talking quietly. She still had on her butterfly dress from last night, and she was brushing her hair, and he had his hands in his pockets. They both turned towards me as I came in. Tía Leni smiled and Papá scooped me, blanket, Little Cat, and all, and I snuggled into him and shut my eyes.

They were standing awfully close together. I've noticed they do that a lot lately. They remind me of those funny magnetic Scottie dogs Tía Lucinda brought me when she came back from her trip to America a few years ago. At first they were against each other, and trying to push them together only made them go further apart, but now it's like they want to stick to each other and only some unseen hand is keeping them apart.

And having a hard time of it too.

I'm so glad they are friends now.

Little Cat and I took a walk with Tía Leni and Papá, and Little Cat hopped along the metal fence around the park. He loves hopping. I saw a dog through the gate I wanted to pet, so I went over to the boy walking him. His name was Carmelo, and I set Little Cat on the grass for a minute while we played with his dog.

But Carmelo had to keep walking, and I turned to go back to Papá and Tía Leni, but someone in a black coat stood in my way.

"*Permiso, Señor.*" I tried to step to the side, but he stepped over too so he was still in front of me. Then I looked up.

The man was not so tall as Papá, but he was big anyway. He looked at me with eyes like ice chips straight off Glaciar Viedma and said to me that I needed to come with him, and if I made any fuss he would hurt Tía Leni or Papá or both of them. I started to ask him how he knew us when we didn't know him, but he told me to shut up. Something about the way he talked made me think I'd better do what he said, and cold fear filled me from my toes all the way to my head. What had Tía Leni said? *Don't look so starry-eyed, kid, capture is horrible?*

I hadn't ever thought about how horrible it really would be, and the worst part wasn't that I had no idea what this strange man intended to do with me.

It was that Papá and Tía Leni wouldn't have any idea where I had gone.

Raymond

ONE MINUTE ANTON WAS walking his cat along the railing, and the next minute he was nowhere in sight.

Leni noticed before I did. She stopped walking and clutched my hand. "Where's Anton?" she said, the sound of her voice terrible. Instantly I too was seized by dread, followed by helplessness.

"Anton!" I called, and I looked through the gate into the park, which loomed shadowy and dark. Leni ran forward and dropped to her knees, clapping her hand over her mouth to stifle a scream.

Little Cat lay abandoned on the grass. I knelt beside her, but I could not comfort her when I was so full of panic myself. How had we lost my son in less than a minute? It happened all the time, I knew... to *other* people.

Leni's hand shook as she reached for mine, but her fingertips managed to send me a message on my palm. *Erich.*

How do you know? I tapped back.

She took a long, shaking breath. *I'll get Anton. I know where he'll be. I have to go alone.*

I'm not turning you loose!

Stop. She jabbed her fingertips into my hand for emphasis. *Let go of your need to be a hero. Only I can do this. If you want Anton back, stay the hell out of it. Promise?*

I looked into her blanched face and saw wild, desperate determination. She would not, could not, let Anton down, even if it meant putting herself in danger, and I had to admit she was right. I did not know these men; she did, and she might be able to bargain with them.

I only hoped she would manage to escape with her life and come back to me.

Not once in my life have I felt so utterly *useless*. I watched Leni's retreating figure, stumbling more gracelessly than usual in her hurry. I thought of her and my son in the hands of Nazis, and the old rage bubbled inside me. I wanted their blood. I wanted them all dead, and I wanted to kill them myself. Erich, Mauritz, Mengele, the lot. I clenched my hand around Little Cat and turned and ran all the way back to the house we were staying in, taking the stairs three at a time until I'd reached Dr Mayer's door. I pounded on it, breathless from my run, and when he opened it and saw me, alarm flashed in his face. He pulled me inside and said, "What has happened?"

"They've taken Anton," I managed to get out at last, and I couldn't control myself any longer. I dropped to the nearest chair and started to cry.

"Who's taken him?"

"Sodding Nazis," I said.

His hands tensed. "Madeleine?"

"She's gone to find him. She says they may hurt him if I interfere." I clutched at my hair, despairing. "My *son*, Dr Mayer. My nine-year-old son. What are they going to do to him?"

The old man said nothing, only sank into his own chair, pale and trembling, and for an instant I was distracted from my own troubles, worrying he might suffer a stroke or cardiac arrest right in front of my eyes.

But neither calamity befell him; he was thinking.

"Do you know where she has gone, where they might have taken Anton?"

I shook my head. "She didn't say."

Anton

THE MAN PUSHED ME along the path of the park, every step further from Papá and Tía Leni, and then I remembered I didn't have Little Cat, and turned, thinking I'd go back and fetch him quick, but the man growled and yanked at me and I had to keep going forward.

He pushed me into the back seat of a gleaming black car and tied my hands and ankles. I kept looking at him. I was scared, but not so scared I wasn't curious. He was sulky-looking and handsome, sort of, I guess. He spoke to me in Spanish, but he had an accent that was definitely not English. I tried to picture in my head the way it sounds when Tía Leni speaks German with her father and I decided it must be a German accent. So this was probably a Nazi. And I had an idea. "Are you Mr Linzer?" I asked him.

He slapped me across my face with the back of his hand, and my eyes burned holding back tears. Papá—*no* one, actually—has ever done such a thing to me. Papá spanked me only once, when I was four, and then he was so upset at himself over it he never did it again. I *do* so dislike having people angry with me, or worse be disappointed in me. Especially when I don't know what it is I've done to deserve it, like now. The man growled again, "Shut up and you'll be all right."

I scrunched lower in my seat, more afraid than before. There wasn't anything I could do, tied tight like I was, and the man got in the front seat and drove away.

When the car stopped, he untied my feet so I could walk with him. We'd arrived at a lovely house with stone steps and a great wooden door with a brass knocker on, some terrifying creature. Like a lion, but also like a demon or something. He had his hand on my shoulder and he shoved me forward into the house, shutting the door behind him and throwing the heavy bolt. I forgot my fear for a moment, curious to see what the house looked like.

It was huge and shadowy and echo-ey, and there didn't seem to be anyone else anywhere inside. *That* made me feel a bit creepy. Tía Leni had called Mr Linzer a very cruel man, and if this was Mr Linzer (I was sure it must be), I did not want to be alone with him. So I kept quiet as he took me up a grand staircase and down a hall. He pointed me into a room, and I went in. He untied my hands and told me to stay here and not make any noise if I knew what was good for me, and the minute I tried any funny business he'd strap me with his belt. I looked at it, with its heavy silver buckle, and shuddered. I sat in the nearest chair and looked at him. "Yes, sir," I said.

He fixed me with a cold look and left the room, bolting the door from outside.

I was a prisoner, but I was far more scared of the man than of being locked in a room. As soon as he had gone, I slid off the chair and tiptoed to the window, rubbing my wrists where the rope had left rashy marks behind.

Below the window I saw a large veranda paved with flagstones, and the wall straight down, smooth, not a handhold in sight, even if I was good at rock climbing, which I'm not. And there didn't seem any way to open the window, either. No safe escape there. I climbed onto the sill and felt around for anything that would move to unlatch it. Nothing. I sighed and jumped back to the floor and decided to look around.

There was a bathroom attached to this bedroom. Everything in both rooms was colourless, grey, and dull. No pictures on the walls, no books on shelves, nothing to make it appear that anyone really used the room to live in. I began to think this might be Tía Leni's old room, since you couldn't leave unless someone unbolted the door to let you out.

With that in my head, I walked over to the wardrobe and peeked inside. It was full of furs and fine dresses, most of them grey or black, except for one fur that looked like red fox. I climbed in and drew my knees to my chest and sat with my eyes closed for a few minutes. Living in a room with no colour for such a long time would surely suck all the colour out of your soul too. Tía Leni was different now from how she was at first. Colour had come into her again—to her face and her eyes and inside too—and it made me shiver, thinking of her ever having to come back into this place. I wondered what I might try to do to a) get out of here myself and b) make sure Tía Leni did not get hurt. Papá would be able to take care of himself; I didn't worry about him. But Tía Leni might not be. She was still so fragile. Ever since we'd come back to Buenos Aires, she'd been jumpy and nervous and always, always, her eyes flitting everywhere, watching.

I fell asleep in the wardrobe. I know, because I dreamed I went to Narnia with Lucy Pevensie, and when I woke, darkness had crept into the room and I was hungry. But no Mr Tumnus came with any tea and toast. I got a drink out of the tap in the bathroom, and then, since none of the lights in the room seemed to work, I lay on the bed and fell asleep for the night.

Leni

I WALKED ALL THE way to Mauritz's house.

It took me a long time to find it. I knew the address; I'd seen it on the post, and addresses and telephone numbers are things my brain seldom forgets, but finding someone to ask directions was difficult. I was so scared, all my Spanish went straight out of my head.

When I finally arrived, twilight had begun to fall, and I found a place to secret myself among the trees until it was darker. The front door would be locked, but possibly the kitchen entrance would be open, and if not, I could force a window. Somehow. I'd never done such a thing before, but I'd find a way.

Waiting only intensified my fright and the leaden weight in the pit of my stomach. What would I find when I did get back into that house, where for so long I had been a prisoner, and would I ever come out again?

My eyes flitted about, alert, every muscle tense. Somehow, someone had known we were here in Buenos Aires, had known Anton was the perfect pawn, had watched us, waiting for the perfect moment to strike. My paranoia had not been unfounded, after all, and not only was the child I loved so fiercely now in danger, his father would fall apart if anything happened to him. I cared too deeply for these two now; I could not let that happen. Even now, I knew that back in our room, the policeman in Raymond would be cursing himself for not having noticed anything suspicious. Perhaps he would even be kicking himself for letting his blossoming love for me blind him to things he should have seen. Maybe he would be regretting my existence as a fatal distraction.

I shuddered and sucked in air, forced myself to breathe. In. Out. Deeply. I couldn't let myself panic, couldn't let myself cry.

Anton's life depended on me not losing my head. No matter how his father felt about me at the moment, I was here for Anton.

And at last, as dark thickened and a rainy mist floated out of the sky, I stepped out from the trees and looked one last time at the house to be sure nobody was watching. In the entire house, only one window had a light in it, and that was Erich's room. The curtains were drawn. Everything was eerily silent.

I made my way across the back garden towards the kitchen entrance, and hoped I could find a way inside.

If I perish, I perish.

Anton

WHEN I WOKE IN the morning, I saw the curtains at the windows were drawn shut. One little light burned on a table, and the man from yesterday sat in the chair smiling at me. I did not like the look of his smile. I thought about what Papá might want me to do in such a situation and I couldn't think of a thing. So I kept quiet and waited. He lit a cigarette and I felt tight inside from fear. *If I had a REALLY AWFUL COUGHING FIT here, without Papá...*

"You're Anton Varela." It didn't sound like a question, so I didn't answer him.

If I kept my mouth closed and tried not to inhale, maybe I could keep from coughing.

He shook out his match and tossed it aside, sucking in a leisurely drag. "How is it the bolt of this room is open from the outside?" he asked, puffing smoke like a dragon. His voice sounded like a knife. I had to answer.

"I was asleep," I said. "I didn't do it."

"Why are you making those faces?" he asked next.

"The smoke, sir," I said, through my teeth. It was so hard to not breathe.

He laughed and leant forward, exhaling another Great Mouthful of his smoke in my face.

I sat up on the bed and turned away, suppressing a cough, and failing. The man demanded again, "Who opened the bolt?"

"I don't know," I whispered, puzzled. Nothing seemed changed in the room that I could see, except—

Except the wardrobe door, which I knew I had left open, was now shut tight.

Someone else was in here. Or had been here.

The man got in my face, his cigarette smoking right under my nose again, one hand poised to take off his horrible belt. "Are you going to answer me, boy? Who unlocked the door, and where did they go?"

"I don't know," I repeated. I scooted backwards away from him and his smoke, tumbled onto the floor and began to cough myself silly.

And then the wardrobe door opened.

LENI

THE LOOK ON ERICH'S face when I emerged from the wardrobe might have made me laugh in other circumstances. It had not been the most comfortable night. I used to hide in there, finding tactile comfort in being surrounded by fur and silk, but not even these sensations could calm or strengthen me now. Anton's safety was all I cared about, and staying on the alert had begun to take its toll on me. I had thought as long as Anton remained asleep and alone, I wasn't going to make my presence known, but now—now as he lay on the floor in the throes of one of his coughing fits—maybe I'd been wrong. Maybe I should have sneaked him out under cover of darkness after all. Why was I so inept?

Erich had my arm in his iron grip almost before my feet hit the floor, and his cold eyes glittered snakelike out of the murk in the room. I glanced at Anton, who had his hand clamped tightly over his mouth, trying to get the coughing under control. He stared at me, blinking furiously. I gave him an apologetic, agonised glance. But then I saw he was not crying. He was blinking in a pattern. He was trying to tell me something.

Just one word. *Papá?*

I blinked back. *Safe.*

He made as though studying the ceiling and blinked another message. *Tell me what to do.* Then turned his gaze back to me.

Nothing yet. Wait.

He turned away and began to cough again.

All of that happened very quickly, and Erich didn't notice because his free hand was unfastening his evil belt. My brain went into overdrive. I needed to help Anton, but I didn't dare turn my back on Erich to go fetch him some water from the bathroom. I didn't know what monstrous deed Erich wished to perform, but

I did know if I begged him not to do anything in front of the boy, he *would* do it, just to be perverse. I needed to distract him long enough to give Anton a chance to do something, give me a chance to give the boy instructions for whatever that something was. If I let Erich hit me a few times, I could try using the blows to my advantage. If I could dodge across the room and get to the poker by the fireplace...

Erich's face was inches from mine now. "*This* will be a treat," he said, with diabolical enthusiasm, tossing his cigarette aside. "We'll show the boy what grown-ups do for fun."

He spoke in Spanish so Anton would understand. I glared at Erich, shaking my head, flinching away as he unbuttoned my blouse enough to grab my breast. I didn't stop him. Over his shoulder I fluttered my eyelids at Anton, begging, *Don't look.*

It is amazing how a few months away from abuse makes it seem ten times worse when you re-encounter it. I had been strapped with that belt so many times it had become routine. It wasn't that it ever stopped hurting or terrifying me, only I had grown *used* to it.

This instant, now? It made me angry, indignant. How dare this excuse of a man strike me? I lashed out and called him something insulting, almost forgetting my end goal of getting to the fireplace poker. I fought to get free. He struck again, on my legs this time, and I fell to the floor with a comedic sort of splat, arms and legs in all directions. I tried to scramble to my feet, but he felled me with another vicious whack. I was so stunned I couldn't move that time, and he sat on me, undoing his trousers. I looked helplessly towards the fireplace. I was so close to the poker. I had to think fast, and the idea that popped into my head made me shudder in horror. Could I manage something so repugnant?

Forgive me, Raymond, for what I am about to do. What we shared the other night made my life worth all the hell. And I will do anything, anything, *to get your son back to you alive and safe.*

"Erich," I said in an entirely different tone of voice. Meek, pleading.

"What, bitch?"

And I described to him an act I found particularly loathsome, that he had forever tried to bully me into with no success. "If you promise not to hurt the boy..." I said, hoping I looked doe-eyed and persuasive. He laughed again, so uproariously that he rolled off me. "That policeman of yours has changed your tastes, has he?" he asked. I glared, but I got to work at once, stuffing down my revulsion at putting things into my mouth which oughtn't be there, and tapping on the floor out of Erich's range of sight. *Get the poker, Anton.*

There wasn't any getting out of it, especially once Erich had my head in his iron grasp. He would never let me back out of this.

"Best way to fuck a barren woman," he taunted, in Spanish. "No point spilling seed anywhere else. Not as if it'll produce anything."

I flinched in spite of my resolve not to let his words hurt me. I had planned to time my strike at exactly the instant he was enjoying himself the most, but this was the last straw. For years, he'd reminded me at every possible opportunity how useless I was to the Reich without a womb. *Never again.*

So, prematurely, I bit him. I bit him so hard he howled and fell back., I spat blood as I snatched up his abandoned belt, leapt to my feet, and whacked him in the arm with it. I missed his head (no surprise), but at that point, I could have hit him anywhere and he'd hardly have noticed. He writhed in agony, cursing, and when Anton pressed the poker into my hand, I hissed into his ear, "Go downstairs and call your father. Hurry. Phone in the hallway." He scurried out, and I turned my full attention on Erich.

"Get up," I snarled at him. "Get up, you filthy man." I didn't say filthy man. I called him something else I don't know the English for.

He looked at me, his face contorted in such hatred, I quaked. I hoped it didn't show.

"Where's Mauritz?" I demanded, brandishing both my weapons as he whimpered, raging, at my feet. He shook his head. "Tell me!" I shouted, grazing his shoulder with the belt buckle.

"Piranha... food... by now," Erich managed, whinging.

Pathetic.

They must have dumped him in the river. One fewer Nazi in the world.

"Where's everybody else?"

Erich had staggered to his feet at last, purple with rage. I observed with detached satisfaction that the damage my teeth had done would keep him out of action for a while, even if I didn't manage to actually kill him. The blood oozed vibrant and wet between his fingers where he was clutching himself. I didn't want to look. I couldn't stop looking.

I shook myself out of my trance. I had to act now, before he got any closer.

My adrenaline gave me superhuman strength. If only it would give me grace and coordination, too. I dropped the belt, gripped the poker with both hands, raised it over my head, and swung.

It split his skull with a sickening, metallic crack, and instantly his face was obscured by blood. He fell to the floor, dragging me down with him. I gasped in horror at the realisation of what I had just done. I don't know how long I lay there, paralysed by my own panic and trapped under Erich's dead weight, before Anton reappeared. He scooted over and clung to me in the cold room, his little body trembling. I managed to drag myself away from Erich, whispering stutteringly to Anton, trying to calm and comfort him in spite of the numbness in my own heart, the thickness of my own tongue. I couldn't even cry.

"Oh God," I said, over and over again, dazed. "Oh God. Anton. I just killed him, I killed Erich. Oh God, what have I done?"

"Is he the one who hurt you, Tía Leni?" Anton asked. Our eyes were riveted on the hideous corpse beside us, the puddle of blood soaking into the carpet, spreading, staining.

"Yes," I breathed. "One of the many."

"Then I'm glad he's dead," Anton said. He had gone very pale, and the next thing I knew he was doubled over being sick onto the carpet. I didn't blame him. It was unspeakably gruesome.

When he'd finished heaving, he shuddered, wiped his mouth on his sleeve, and asked me weakly, "Why are you not sick, Tía

Leni? How can you not be sick to see that?"

"I've seen far worse," I said, slurring my words. "I—"

Anton

HER EYES ROLLED UP and she fainted dead away before she could finish her sentence.

There was so much blood everywhere. I hadn't ever thought about a real person dying. In the pictures, people get shot and it's always a little red paint trickling down someone's face, but this wasn't the cinema, it was real life, and Mr Linzer's blood had got all over Tía Leni's face, mostly from her biting his parts, but her hair and her blouse were soaked too, with the blood from his head. I wanted to scream or cry and I couldn't. Everything had happened so fast, and now she was unconscious.

I shook her, but she didn't stir, so I rolled her onto her back and dragged a footstool over to prop her feet on, since that's what Papá did the times she's fainted before. Well, he didn't use a *footstool*, but something high enough to get her feet higher than her head, and I went into the bathroom to try to find a cloth to wash her face with. I couldn't stand another minute seeing her with all that blood on her.

The cold wet cloth brought her round. I had to scrub a good bit, because the blood had started to dry and didn't want to wipe off, and she didn't do anything but lie there and breathe ragged breaths for several minutes. I rinsed out the cloth several times before I got her face cleaned up. It was still in her hair, but at least her face wasn't as scary now. I didn't want to think of what she'd done, or what he had been about to do to her. "What grownups do for fun," he'd said. I shuddered. It wasn't true, it couldn't be true. Papá wouldn't call it fun. I didn't think Tía Leni thought it fun. She'd told me not to look, and I tried not to. I really tried.

Leni

ANTON'S COLD WASHCLOTH SHOCKED me awake, but I couldn't move for several minutes. I just stared passively at the ceiling and let him wipe the gore from my skin. When he finished, he looked at me with wide, astonished eyes. His face was still ashen, and his lips quivered. "How did you get through it, Tía Leni?"

"Through what?"

"Living with people like him."

"I didn't have a choice," I said, hoarsely. I sucked in air, reached for the poker, and used it like a staff to raise myself to my feet. It was still wet with his blood. I leant hard on it a moment, and closed my eyes and said in German, "Curse all of you Nazis. Erich Linzer. Mauritz von Schlusser. Josef Mengele. Adolf Eichmann—" I recited a long litany of names. "God curse you for murdering six million Jews and one Jew in particular. God curse you for killing my child. May you all be as this man."

Tears welled in my eyes, and I couldn't speak another word. I staggered out of the room, overcome.

Anton trotted after me, most likely gladder even than I to leave that scene of death, and seized my hand as I made my way down the hall and opened the door to Mauritz's room, where I froze. Something kept me glued to the threshold. I had never been allowed in this room.

"What's the matter, Tía?" Anton whispered. I glanced at his frightened eyes and took a deep breath, trying to compose myself. The adrenaline rush that had given me the strength to whack Erich over the head had evaporated and I felt ice cold and wobbly. I leant heavily on the doorframe.

"It's his room," I said. "Mauritz's room."

Mauritz was dead, but he might well materialise before me as he so often had, and I'd have another Nazi to fight off. At least Mauritz was older and smaller than Erich and would be easier to overpower. My logical brain knew that if there were anyone else in the house, they would have heard Erich's howls of pain and come running long before now. I had seen nobody as I crept through the dark halls up to my old wardrobe last night. Yes, the house was empty now, save for Anton and me and Erich's corpse, but it did not change the fact that it was my former prison, and it had belonged to Mauritz, and so had I.

Anton

MAURITZ IS THE ONE she was supposedly married to. She stood there looking like she'd fall over any minute, her knuckles white as she clutched at the doorframe, her face white too. I worried maybe she would faint again.

"Come on," I said to her, tugging at her hand. "Nobody's here. It's all right to come in."

She looked at me like I wasn't even there, the scary look she'd had back when she was first with us, and she said something in German.

Leni

ANTON LOOKED UP AT me uncomprehendingly as I muttered aloud in German, but I could never explain to a nine-year-old boy the complexities of my relationship with Mauritz, so I just shook my head. I forced one foot onto the plushy blue carpet, then another. My eyes fixed on his polished teakwood desk. I had to make it that far. I had to keep moving my feet.

The room smelled so strongly of tobacco and cedarwood and Mauritz's favourite soap that I felt suffocated, as if he was still there, strangling away my breath for the crime of trespassing on his space. When I reached his desk, I leant heavily upon it. *I mustn't cry. I mustn't panic*, I told myself, and promptly burst into tears and panic.

"Anton," I managed to sob out, "we have to look in there for my papers. Help me!"

His little hands ran over the wood, trying to budge the cover. "It's locked," he said.

I snivelled there uselessly for five minutes, before I became furious at the entire situation and I waved him away whilst I went at the desk with my poker. It splintered and cracked and eventually the lock burst. Anton opened drawers and rifled through them, looking for anything passport-like. There wasn't anything in the first drawer, or the second, or the tenth, that was relevant. By then, I'd collected myself enough to help. We had to get out of here as quickly as we possibly could. So I hunted on one side and found a lock box shoved behind a stack of papers. The poker again came in useful, and I smashed it and Anton pried it open and rifled through its contents. He beamed at me and held up a blue-bound passport.

"It's yours, Tía Leni!" he said triumphantly.

It was mine. I recognised the little doodle I had made in ink in one corner of the cover, a heart with a smiling face. It had been my first personal passport; I'd just been listed under Daddy's name before, because we'd always all travelled together, and this time I'd be going alone to Austria to help Tante Madeleine. It was my passport, and the photograph was my photograph, but the name on it read Marlene von Schlusser. Someone had tampered with it. Again my eyes flooded, and only Anton's presence held me together. I had to get him out of here. I could fall apart later, when he wasn't depending on me.

My blouse was still half unbuttoned, and I tucked the precious bit of paper into my brassiere. I walked out of Mauritz's room, down the stairs, through the hall (my poker leaving a long trail of bloody scratches on the parquet behind me), out the front door, and into the sunshine. On the front steps Anton and I stood, hand in hand, frozen again at the sight of a car drawing up to the door.

Raymond

MY HEART NEARLY MELTED with relief at the sight of Leni and Anton on the doorstep as if they were waiting for us, and I fell into a crazed combination of laughter and tears as I tumbled out of the car and took the stairs in two bounds.

"Anton," I cried, and I picked him up and held him with one arm. "You're all right?"

He nodded. My other arm pulled Leni close, and I sobbed like a baby into her hair, kissing her filthy face and clinging to her. She sagged into me, clearly at the end of her strength, letting go.

"Is there anything you need from here?" I asked, holding her tightly. "Anything you want to take?"

"I will not take from a thread even to a shoelatchet," she said. "No, I don't want a damn thing from that bastard."

Then she stumbled out of my arms and down the stairs to the car and collapsed into the seat.

Anton

PAPÁ HAD GONE UTTERLY *MAD*.

    He leapt up the stairs, hugging Tía Leni as if he was never going to let go of her, and started kissing her face, crying and laughing all at once. Well, he did pick me up first, but it was clear he'd been as frantic about her as he was about me. Tía Leni still had that sort of crazy look in her eyes, and she didn't say anything, just kind of melted into him. She still had the poker in her hand, the tip dragging on the step as she slumped into Papá's arms. She looked so *right* there, and suddenly I had a thought that, until that instant, had NEVER ONCE OCCURRED TO ME.

    Papá... and Tía Leni... together? Like, really *together?* All those months, even though they had been friendly now a while, I never DREAMED maybe Papá might fall in love with her.

    And I wondered.

    I wondered too how he didn't notice she was covered in blood. When she came into the car, I felt cold again inside remembering what had happened in there, and I could still smell the heavy scent of it in her hair and clothes.

    It was a bench seat, and she sat in the middle, white as a sheet, and staring and staring. She was not crying now.

    Only staring.

Leni

WHEN RAYMOND GOT INTO the car beside me and started the engine again, I slumped against his shoulder, still holding the poker across my knees. Raymond was here; I could stop fighting now.

"It's not your fault," I murmured.

"What?" he asked.

"Not noticing," I said.

He turned the car around and sped away from the house before he asked, "Not noticing what?"

I sighed deeply. "Aren't you angry with me, for distracting you from noticing people watching us?"

"Don't be ridiculous," he said. "You weren't distracting me. I was watching all the time."

"You were?"

"Of course. But you were right, they have eyes everywhere. Invisible. Too good for me." Suddenly he began shaking with laughter.

"What could possibly be funny?" I asked, slurring again.

"You," he said. I heaved a deep sigh, not amused. "Standing out there like you were," he went on. "Feet apart, gripping that poker like you meant business. Warrior princess of the Amazons, clad in the blood of her enemies." His tone turned serious. "Leni, what happened in there? Why are you drenched in blood?"

What to tell him? *Every battle of the warrior is with confused noise, and garments rolled in blood; but this shall be with burning and fuel of fire...* Fire? That cigarette Erich had tossed aside. *Let it set fire to the place*, I prayed.

Anton, snuggled against my other shoulder, spoke up. "She was so brave, Papá. The man who tried to hurt her, he hit her with his belt. She blinked at me in Morse code to tell me what she wanted me to do, and whilst I got the poker for her she distracted him by—" Anton described in surprisingly frank detail what he'd seen me do, and my face flamed. I tried to hide behind the curtain of my bloody hair.

"Oh," Raymond breathed, the wind and humour all punched out of him. I do believe he even went a little green.

"I'm so sorry," I murmured. Even in my daze of shock, I felt some smug satisfaction in having done something to make even the unflappable Inspector Raymond Varela blanch. And I added more ferociously, "The damn fascist had it coming."

I hadn't meant it to be funny, but Raymond was, I believe, somewhat hysterical himself, and he went into silent laugh mode over my unwitting double-entendre.

"Oh, shut up and forget all that," I snapped, reaching into my brassiere and handing him my passport. "We're going home."

Anton

WHEN WE GOT BACK to the place we were staying, Tía Leni waited in the car until Papá fetched a coat and hat for her to put on. He didn't want anyone to see what a mess she was. He brought my coat too. He saw us safely into Dr Mayer's room and went to return the car to the person he borrowed it from, while Tía Leni and I took turns scrubbing up in the bath. Tía Leni started crying, and Dr Mayer held her tight until she'd gone to sleep. We piled blankets on top of her, the way she likes, and then Dr Mayer held out his arms to me and I climbed onto his lap.

"Are you all right?" he asked. I liked his voice, still accented even though he'd lived in England for almost fifty years. Comforting and warm like a soft blanket, but strong too.

I told him what I'd seen, and what Tía Leni had had to do, and I started to cry, and he was just as kind to me as he'd been to her. He assured me that what happened was *not* the way most grown-ups have fun, and I mustn't ever believe Tía Leni wanted to do what she did. That she'd never have done it to save herself.

She did it for *me*.

"Why?" I asked.

"Because she loves you," he said. "I believe she would have given her life itself, if it came to that, to get you safely back to your father. It's all right if you're scared by what happened, or upset, or whatever you feel. It's all right. Don't forget that."

For a long time we sat quietly, and I began to wonder what was taking Papá so long.

I'd never felt *really* afraid. But now I knew ugly terrible things existed out there that I hadn't ever seen before, or even imagined, and I thought, *From now on I am going to have anxiety churning inside me anytime I lose sight of Papá.*

Raymond

I EXPECTED THERE WOULD be a hearing, if not a trial, regarding the incident at the von Schlusser house. Leni scoffed at the idea. "They'll all go to ground like ants when you lift a rock," she said scornfully. "They don't dare press charges. I know too much, and I've got my own identity back and the protection of the British embassy. They wanted me to think they still had a hold on me, but I am too smart for them now."

Her tone might have been scornful, but her hands shook like aspen leaves, and I could see she was on the verge of losing her hold on herself again. She had woken several times in the night with panic attacks and nightmares, and Anton, who had never feared the dark or much of anything before in his life, was restless and jumpy too. He'd witnessed something which would haunt him for years, if not forever, and I hated that he'd lost a great deal of his precious innocence. But I didn't blame Leni for it. Clearly the boy had been in for a bad time on his own if she hadn't stepped in.

We needed to get out of there, and thanks to her passport, it would be easier. It had been tampered with, obvious if you looked at it closely, but not obvious to the casual glance of someone at a checkpoint or customs. Leni didn't worry about legal proceedings from her killing Erich, but she did warn me that all of us were now in danger from the Nazis, and if we didn't get out of Buenos Aires soon, we might never get out. They wouldn't draw attention to themselves by reporting Erich's death, but they might still kill us and dispose of us the way they did so many of their own.

Dr Mayer proved a tremendous help over those last few days. We'd agreed not to use sedatives to help ease Leni's sleeplessness and nightmares, because of her previous addictions, but somehow he managed to calm her without them. We had the embassy man come to us and made all our arrangements over the telephone for our passage out. We would be accompanied by several plainclothes men.

All this is of great novelty and excitement to my son. If only the rest of us could look at it that way. At least he finds distraction in it from the trauma he experienced. Leni's not really able to do that for herself.

SS Argentina

17 - 21 May 1952

LENI

WE BOARDED THE SHIP that would take us to New York. I hardly knew what to think; it felt dreamlike and unreal. The encounter with Erich had given me such a... *horrible* feeling. I did not regret he was dead, but the fact that I administered the death blow haunted me.

Raymond said I should remember I had acted in self-defence as well as in defence of Anton, and that had the case gone to court and the whole sordid story come to light, it would have been seen as such. Intellectually, I knew he was right; emotionally, I was not reconciled. Was it right to take a life in exchange for lives already lost? I wanted to see every Nazi brought to justice. But I didn't know how I'd prefer that justice meted out. I was too overwhelmed to give it much thought.

I spent the entire first day in the cabin I shared with Daddy, curled in a ball on my bunk, in all the blankets I could get. I didn't want to talk, even to Anton, let alone Raymond. And I slept some, so when night came and Daddy had long been asleep, I was wide awake, and I decided to go for a walk. I reached for my coat and opened the door.

The rhythm of the ship, quietly thrumming, gently rocking, was alien to me. I barely remember the voyage from Spain to Argentina. I suspect they kept me drugged a good deal of the time. This ship is different from being in Buenos Aires, and it is so far removed from being in the open air under the stars that Patagonia seems a distant memory to me, a dream. I stood in the door, disoriented.

Eleven years closely monitored by Nazis. Six months under the less suffocating but still vigilant watchcare of Raymond Varela. That night I stood alone on a ship, unwatched and free to decide my own movements. It was an intriguing notion, but also frightening. My warm bed, with its cocoon of blankets, meant safety; the wind outside would be cold.

But air. I needed air. *You're safe, Leni,* I reminded myself as I made the step from cabin to corridor. *It's all right to go out alone now. You're safe.* I closed the door, pocketed my cabin key, and tiptoed down the corridor and up the stairs until I got to the deck. I might not find my way back without help, but that didn't matter. Air was all I wanted.

The stars gleamed, vibrant. I found my way to the rail easily and leant into it, gazing into the bowl of sparkling space all around me, and I thought of Raymond and Anton, both of whom I had come to love so much.

The world is an immense place to navigate on my own, for anyone to navigate on their own, but especially me. I was not a fool. I knew that I couldn't live alone, that I would never be like ordinary people. Daddy had known it, and had tried to keep me from going to Austria because of it. I had learnt my lesson. I needed looking after. It didn't mean I couldn't still be an independent entity; it only meant recognising my limitations and moving forward as best I could.

In that moment I became certain of one thing. Whatever I did with my life in the future, I would be doing it with Raymond and Anton at my side. I was not going to go it alone.

I twisted Mauritz's ring around and around on my finger, until I'd worked it off. I'd never removed it since the day he'd put it on me, out of fear and submission rather than sentiment, and my finger had a deep groove in it. I took a deep breath, and I hurled the little band of gold as hard as I could into the wide open mouth of the Atlantic.

It vanished into the darkness
I did not hear it fall
I was free

Raymond

ANTON AND I DIDN'T get an answer when we knocked at the Mayers' cabin door this morning, so we went on to breakfast on our own.

"Maybe they're already there," Anton said, hopefully. He'd been very morose that Leni was not sharing our cabin and that she'd not even wanted to see him yesterday. "Do you think Tía Leni will be there already?" he asked me, his voice so plaintive that I squeezed his shoulder and said I hoped so.

She was there, sitting at a table with her father, but the minute she saw us she shot out of her seat like a rocket. She ran to me and threw her arms around me and kissed me with an intensity which completely took me aback. When she stepped away, her eyes shone with a mixture of wild determination and fondness, and she took a box I recognised out of her handbag.

"Have you asked Anton?" she said, holding it close to her chest.

Anton glanced from one to the other of us, bemused by yet one more bizarre example of Grown-ups Being Weird. "Asked me what?"

Leni reached for Anton's hand and held it tight, but she didn't take her eyes from my face. "Your father asked me to marry him. What should I answer, yes or no?"

Anton's face lit up and, with absolutely no hesitation, he burst out, "Yes, Tía Leni, YES!"

For a long moment she and I just looked at one another, barely noticing the excited bouncing of the boy beside us, and when she spoke again her voice was hushed. "In that case, I would like to marry you, Raymond Varela." And she held out her hand, minus the ring I'd never seen her without, and let me slip on the opal one I'd offered her weeks earlier.

Leni

WE HAD AN ANIMATED breakfast, during which far more talking than eating happened, at least on my part. I was far too nervous and excited to want food. Daddy beamed quietly, and Anton grinned and jumped up to hug me every two minutes.

"We can get married on the ship," Raymond said. "You can wear your silver dress."

I blushed, remembering what had happened the last time I'd worn that dress. I caught a glint in his eye that told me he remembered too.

"And I have my suit from London Gran," Anton said. "Papá made me bring it in case we had something special happen."

"I hope it still fits you," Raymond said. Anton just shrugged. He clearly didn't care if it fit or not.

"And I," said Daddy, "am glad my girl is going to be in good hands."

After breakfast, following Daddy and Anton, Raymond pulled me aside. "What did you do with your other ring?"

"The Atlantic ate it," I said.

He gave me a look with a great deal of smoulder in it and I shivered giddily as he swept me close and dipped me for a kiss. "You know what?" he said, his voice low. "I seem to have a habit of marrying slightly delinquent women whom I've already slept with, but I'm damned if I ever do it again. Thank you for saying yes, Muffin. I hope I'll never give you cause to regret it."

I felt my face flushing. He held me close, so very close. My brain was going addled. "Thank you for giving this slightly delinquent woman a fresh chance," I managed weakly.

Madeleine Varela

WE HAD AN UNCONVENTIONAL wedding to go with every other bizarre and unconventional thing which has represented our entire experience together. I wore the silver dress, and several ladies on the ship heard of the wedding and conspired to shower me with flowers and offers of all kinds of things to borrow. Some people even treated our party to champagne, of which I took none, and neither did Raymond. We'd made a pact that he'd never have alcohol in the house for my well-being, the same way he'd quit smoking for Anton. Nobody noticed; they were all too busy enjoying the party.

I hadn't had much opportunity to be alone with Raymond since our tryst weeks ago, and I thought I might relish a bit of snogging, and maybe even more than that. When we got into the cabin, I jumped onto the left-hand twin bed. "Left bed for Leni!" I called out cheerily. "Right for Raymond."

He laughed. "Good, because that's the one I've already been sleeping in." He hung his jacket on a hook, removed and rolled up his tie, and lay on his bed. For several moments we just stared at each other. It was the first time we'd ever been alone with no chance of Anton wandering in and interrupting anything. I hugged my knees, happily beaming at Raymond, full of butterflies—not the sick kind, the happy kind. I felt my face getting hot. We'd done this already, but I felt as shy and giddy as if we hadn't.

Raymond folded his glasses, placed them on the table, and rolled closer to the edge of his bed, hugging his pillow. He met my eyes across the yawning chasm separating those ridiculous twin beds, and his eyes said he had more imaginative plans than merely sleeping in them.

"I think," he said softly, "that you need to come over here, Mrs Varela."

I went.

Anton

THEY ARE *MARRIED*. I can't believe it.

I mean, I sort of suspected *something* might be going on because of the way Papá acted on the steps of Mauritz's house after she killed Erich, but I didn't think it would be THIS. Not in a million years. Not after me trying to find new mothers so many times and him always saying no! I never ever saw them kissing or going all soppy like people in the pictures do when they fall in love. I guess Papá is right when he tells me real life isn't anything like the pictures.

Tía Leni being my mother means I get another grandfather (I DO so like Dr Mayer!) AND a whole new herd of cousins. Oh, I do hope they'll like me! I hope we'll get to meet them all soon.

I'm in Dr Mayer's cabin now so Tía Leni could be with Papá for the rest of the trip. She looked so nice in her silver dress today. She's not pretty the same way a lot of other ladies are, but I like her just how she is, because I know she loves me. Maybe she married Papá because she can't imagine life without ME! I suppose I'm going to have to stop calling her Tía Leni now. I wonder what she'd like me to call her. I will ask her in the morning.

Thing I Will Miss About Argentina

1. Not having to have my hair cut for months

Things I Will Not Miss About Argentina

1. Camping in the wagon when it's damp
2. Campfire smoke A L L T H E T I M E
3. Never having my friends around to play with. I will be so glad to be around PEOPLE again.
4. Being kidnapped by Nazis

Things I Want to Do As Soon As We Get Home
1. Tell everyone I see that I have a mother again
2. Ask London Gran to make Tía Leni some pretty dresses that are not grey, silver, or black

Papá+Tía Leni=RADIANT. Neither of them can stop smiling. *And neither can I.*

Terezín
July 1983

Anton

TODAY I WENT TO Terezín.

I've meant to go for a long time, ever since Mamá wrote down for me all that happened to her there so I could be sure to tell my own children someday. At the time, fifteen years ago, she was at one of her low points, convinced she'd be dying any day, but she couldn't take her story to the grave. She needed it to get out somehow, and she couldn't do it all on her own. I was touched then, as I still am, that she willingly confided so many things to me which were so private and painful for her to think about.

Mamá has never *quite* gotten over all of it. She hid herself away in our house for the first two years or so after she married Papá. It didn't help that we got home in July, the worst month of the year for her. The month she was captured. The month she lost her baby. She couldn't face a brand-new town full of inquisitive strangers whilst drowning in painful memories, and as the months went by, it was easier for her to just stay safely out of sight, happy with her little radio, sending and receiving messages from all sorts of places. To this day she finds the predictability of its mechanics soothing, and her radio is as much a joy to her as butterflies are to Papá.

Her father died less than a year after she came home. He had not been in the best of health when he came to Buenos Aires, and knowing his daughter was safe seemed to enable him to let go.

The summer I was twelve, Mamá finally began to integrate herself into the life of the town. Papá or I went with her everywhere as much as we could, helping her get through it, introducing her to the people who mattered, fielding the nosy questions of the people who didn't. Some days nothing could phase her and she would go out and live life with all the confidence of any woman. Some days setting foot onto the front steps proved more than she could bear.

She never has quite stopped panicking about unexpected things. She still has times of intense depression when she reverts to starving herself and lying on the bed, paralysed and helpless. But Mamá is a fighter at heart. It is the only way she survived her ordeal with Mauritz von Schlusser, and it is the only way she managed to push her way back into ordinary life after she came home with us. She did not become a doctor; she was mentally and physically unable to tackle that sort of undertaking, but thanks to her, I did.

Not a medical doctor. I studied psychology. I wanted to know the human mind, not only for her benefit, but to help other people like her, who have been battered and abused, to find their way to peace.

And she loved me. Still loves me. She was there at the end of every school day, no matter what internal hell she was fighting through at any given time. Sometimes we chatted happily, and other times she looked through me as I had my tea and biscuits. But she was *there*.

They call it post-traumatic stress disorder, what Mamá suffers from. We know so much more about it now than back when I was a boy. I bring her every paper I find on the topic and she devours them all. She wants to understand it so she can beat it. She doesn't want it to ruin her life. I am proud of her for never giving up.

She would want me to add that the three grandchildren my lovely wife and I have given her have made a world of difference in her life. She never had a baby of her own, and I don't think that will ever not haunt her, but seeing the pure joy she had fussing over and loving on mine was the closest thing to heaven on earth I could have asked for.

I suggested, very gently, a year ago, that I would like her to come with me to Terezín, and her immediate reaction was to shut up like a clam and say ABSOLUTELY NOT.

But then she changed her mind.

I knew it would be hard for her, but I had not expected the heavy weight of the place to fall upon *me* just walking through the gate, the weight of the suffering of thousands of people that still lingers forty years after the ghetto shut down. I had to close my eyes and let the tears flow at the thought of all that had happened here. On either side of me, Mamá and Papá reached for my hands, and for a moment the three of us stood close, all holding one another, all our faces wet with tears.

Mamá has forgiven, but she will never forget. May the rest of us never forget either.

Author's Note

FIRST OF ALL, I must confess that I have never been to Patagonia myself, although I long to go. Thanks to lack of travel funds and then the pandemic, I wasn't able to make the trip, so instead I've done the best I can with the research options available to me online. I apologise for any errors I may have made in describing the locations mentioned in this book, or for any technical errors regarding the workings of radios. This *is* a work of fiction, after all, and I hope you will allow me a little creative licence!

This book began in 2018, with fleshing out the character that would become Raymond: a quirky, butterfly-loving, socially awkward fellow partly inspired by the character of Lowrie on Season 3 of the TV show *Shetland*. When I decided my character was also obsessed with Argentina, I thought, "I'll make this a post-WWII story and make the plot hinge on the Nazi presence in South America."

Raymond Varela's Super Secret Wartime Work was inspired by the actual existence of an airbase in Tangmere—an airbase with a secret called "The Cottage". Pilots of No. 161 Squadron (special operations pilots who flew to France on top-secret missions by the light of the full moon, collecting refugees and delivering spies and supplies) and Special Operations Executive agents lodged there. If you want to read more about what went on that Raymond couldn't write about because Official Secrets Act, see **Westland Lysander Owners' Workshop Manual** by Edward Wake-Walker, ©2014, pages 90-91; and **We Landed by Moonlight – Secret RAF Landings in France, 1940-1944** by Hugh Verity.

While Raymond was always a very straightforward character in my head, Leni underwent a good deal more evolution to become what she is in this final version of the book. Trying to decide a plausible way to get a British subject into the hands of Nazis took a good deal of thought. Her experience of prostitution under Mauritz is loosely inspired on the camp brothels at

Auschwitz and other concentration camps. Mauritz's obsession with recreating her in the image of his dead wife was inspired by the Alfred Hitchcock film *Vertigo*, which has lived rent-free in my brain since I first saw it at the age of 6. I also credit Hitchcock's *Notorious* and Irving Rapper's *Now, Voyager*.

Before you ask, I don't know what specifically Mauritz needed Leni for. All I know is what Leni and Raymond know. Knock yourself out, fanfiction writers!

The Germans' bombing of southern England in 1943 was called Operation Steinbock.

There are loads of conspiracy theories and misinformation out there about Nazis in South America, such as the idea that Hitler himself came to Argentina on a submarine, which is fun to speculate about, but not able to be substantiated. There's The Boys From Brazil, a thriller by Ira Levin, centering on a mad plot of a fictionalised Josef Mengele to raise an army of Hitler clones. But to get real, solid facts, I had to turn to biographies of Mengele and other Nazis, and the real-life story of the capture of Adolf Eichmann (the subject of the excellent 2018 film Operation Finale), to mention a few. Mengele is at the core of most of the (scanty) available novels set in South America post-WWII, and he is so evil I couldn't resist also incorporating him into mine.

I was also motivated by the increasing threats of fascist ideology in my own country. When Raymond calls the Nazis "a mindless collective, whose entire reason to exist was for the purpose of destruction, and whose pernicious ideology did not end with the war," and adds, "How can we ever hope to stamp it out, when it retreats to remote corners of the globe to grow and strengthen?" I was thinking of the way white supremacy and nationalism are a real and dangerous threat to the future of our national safety. The same communities that Hitler put into concentration camps are still targeted by hate groups today, and I hope that we can all fight with our votes to keep "white is right"/"America first" types out of our government, from the local to the national level. History cycles through repetitions and we can't afford to forget what happened in Germany before

WWII and the brainwashing of a nation by a deranged leader. Take out the trash, America!

And in case anyone wonders: yes, Raymond and Leni are both autistic. I couldn't call it by name within the story because, well, this was the 1950s. It was actually writing this book that led me to understanding that I myself am autistic, and I am super happy to contribute to the growing pool of Books By Autistics, About Autistics. Leni is a LOT like me (not exactly, by any means) but it was a fantastic journey of discovery and I am glad every day for having gone on it. Obviously their experiences with autism aren't going to exactly mirror any other autistic person's; while we have a lot in common, nobody is identical. I've pulled from others' experiences as well as my own to create the one-of-a-kind autism cocktails (or should they be mocktails?) that are Raymond and Leni.

Finally, the title of this novel, in keeping with Leni's penchant for dropping obscure, poetic Biblical allusions, is taken from Deuteronomy 2:7. You can find her other references in Daniel 4:33, Judges 14:3, Genesis 1:22, Isaiah 42:3, Esther 4:16, Genesis 14:23, and Isaiah 9:5 (King James Version).

Now for some thanks:

Thank you to the people on Twitter who voted in my poll about what to name Raymond's butterfly net WITHOUT KNOWING THEY WERE NAMING A BUTTERFLY NET. Nettie is the dad-jokiest possible name that could have come out on top, and I'm so proud of all of you.

Thank you to my first readers Elizabeth Gatland and Jennifer Waters, and to my beta readers Samantha Amenn, Wendy Cunningham, Marie Lavanier Gollias, Anne Margaret, and Karen Heenan, who collectively offered wonderful feedback, encouragement, ideas, screaming, and Accusations of Being a Horrible Person. I won't specify who did the last thing.

Thank you to Marie for the unintentional double-entendre. Had it coming, indeed.

Thank you to Lindsay and Jeannette for their help with the Castellano phrases used in this book. Argentine Spanish (Castellano) is different from the Spanish I am (marginally) more familiar with here in America, and I am incredibly grateful for their help!

And, of course, huge thanks to Karen Heenan, who edited the final version of this book.

Further reading which may interest you:

As If It Were Life: A WWII Diary From the Theresienstadt Ghetto, Philipp Manes, 2005

The Girls of Room 28: Friendship, Hope, and Survival in Theresienstadt, Hannelore Brenner, 2004

Hitler's Children: Sons and Daughters of Leaders of the Third Reich Talk About Their Fathers and Themselves, Gerald Posner, 1993

Hunting Eichmann: How a Band of Survivors and a Young Spy Agency Chased Down the World's Most Notorious Nazi, Neal Bascomb, 2009

...I Never Saw Another Butterfly..., Hana Volavková, 1959

In Patagonia, Bruce Chatwin, 1977

Mengele: The Complete Story, Gerald Posner and John Ware, 1980

The Nazi Doctors: Medical Killing and the Psychology of Genocide, Robert Jay Lifton, 1986

The Nazi Hunters: How a Team of Spies and Survivors Captured the World's Most Notorious Nazi, Neal Bascomb, 2013 (this is the YA adaptation of *Hunting Eichmann*)

Prague in Danger: The Years of German Occupation, 1939-45:

Memories and History, Terror and Resistance, Theater and Jazz, Film and Poetry, Politics and War, Peter Demetz, 2008

Prague Winter: A Personal Story of Remembrance and War, 1937-48, Madeleine K Albright and Bill Woodward, 2012

Women of Theresienstadt, Ruth Schwertferger, 1988

To get book recs, news, and the occasional cat photo, consider subscribing to Eva's email newsletter here: https://www.evaseyler.com/index.php/contact-eva-seyler/subscribe-to-newsletter/

About the Author

Eva was born in Jacksonville, Florida. She left that humidity pit at the age of three and spent the next twenty-one years in California, Idaho, Kentucky, and Washington before ending up in Oregon, where she now lives on a homestead in the western foothills with her husband and five children, two of whom are human.

Eva has previously published a WWI novel, *The War in Our Hearts* (available in paperback, ebook, and audiobook) along with a companion novella, *Ripples* (ebook only).

Twitter: @the_eva_seyler
Instagram: @theevaseyler
Facebook: /authorevaseyler

CPSIA information can be obtained
at www.ICGtesting.com
Printed in the USA
BVHW040750020522
635880BV00003B/13